Joachim B. Schmidt, born in 1981, emigrated from Switzerland to Iceland in 2007. He is the author of several novels and short stories and is also a journalist and columnist. Joachim, who is Swiss and Icelandic, lives in Reykjavík with his wife and their two children.

Foreign-language rights to *Kalmann* have been sold in nine countries so far.

KALMANN

Joachim B. Schmidt

Translated by
Jamie Lee Searle

BITTER LEMON PRESS
LONDON

BITTER LEMON PRESS

First published in the United Kingdom in 2022 by
Bitter Lemon Press, 47 Wilmington Square, London WC1X 0ET.

www.bitterlemonpress.com

First published in German as *Kalmann* by Diogenes Verlag AG Zurich, 2020.

The translation of this work was supported by the Swiss Arts Council Pro Helvetia.

A CIP record for this book is available from the British Library.

PB ISBN 978–1–913394–684
eB USC ISBN 978–1–913394–691
eB ROW ISBN 978-1-913394-707

Typeset by Tetragon, London
Printed and bound by CPI Group (UK) Ltd, Croydon CR0 4YY

swiss arts council
prohelvetia

For Kristín Elva

Langar nætur, ljósa kalda daga
hef ég leitað, það er mannsins saga.

Through my long nights,
through bleak days of worry,
I keep searching.
It's the human story.

JÓNAS FRIÐRIK GUÐNASON,
ljódskáld

1

SNOW

If only Grandfather had been with me. He always knew what to do. I stumbled across the endless Melrakkaslétta plain, hungry, exhausted and smeared in blood, and wondered what he would have done. Perhaps he would simply have filled his pipe and let the pool of blood disappear beneath the falling snow, watching calmly, to make sure no one else would find it.

Whenever a problem arose, he would fill his pipe, and as soon as our minds were woozy with the sweet smoke, things wouldn't seem so bad any more. Perhaps Grandfather would have decided not to tell anyone about it. He would have gone home and not given it another thought. Because snow is snow, and blood is blood. And if someone vanishes without a trace, it's first and foremost their problem. Next to the entrance to our little house, Grandfather would have tapped his pipe against the sole of his boot, the embers would have faded into the snow, and that would have been the end of that.

But I was completely alone up there, Grandfather was 131 kilometres away, and it was a long time since he'd been able to roam the snowy hinterland of the Melrakkaslétta. So there wasn't any pipe smoke either, and because it was snowing, and absolutely everything was white apart from the red pool of blood, and there wasn't a sound to be heard,

I felt as though I were the last person in the entire world. And when you're the last person in the entire world, being able to tell someone else about it makes you happy. So that's why I told after all, and that's how the problems started.

Grandfather was a hunter and a shark catcher. Not any more, though. Now he spent his days sitting in an armchair in the nursing home in Húsavík, staring out of the window – yet without seeing, because when I asked if he was looking at something in particular, he either didn't answer, or mumbled and gave me a strange look, as though I were interrupting him. His facial expression was usually morose nowadays, the corners of his mouth pointed downwards and his lips were pressed together, so that you couldn't even tell he was missing four teeth at the top, the front ones. He couldn't bite anyone now. Sometimes he asked me what I was doing here, and he asked in a curt way, and I would explain that my name was Kalmann, that I was his grandson and had come to visit him, like every week. So no reason to worry. But Grandfather gave me these distrustful looks and then stared back out of the window, completely sullen. He didn't believe me. Then I didn't say anything more, because Grandfather had the expression of someone who had just had their pipe confiscated, and for that reason it was better I said nothing.

A nurse had told me to be patient with Grandfather, as though he were a small, sulky child. I would have to explain things to him again and again, she said, that was completely normal and how life was, because those who are lucky enough to reach an advanced age become, in a certain sense, little children again, and need help with eating, getting dressed, doing up shoelaces and so on. Some even need nappies again! Everything starts to go backwards.

Like a boomerang. I know what that is. It's a weapon made of wood that you fling into the air, then it arcs around and flies back, cutting off your head if you don't pay damn good attention.

I wondered how things would be for me if I reached Grandfather's age. Because things with me had never really gone forwards. They suspected that the wheels in my head ran backwards. That happened sometimes. Or that I'd never progressed beyond the level of a six-year-old. I wasn't fussed. Or that my head contains nothing but fish soup, or that it's hollow, like a buoy. Or that my wires aren't connected properly. Or that I have the IQ of a sheep. And yet sheep can't do an IQ test. "Run, Forrest, run!" they used to shout during sports lessons, laughing themselves silly. That's from this movie where the hero is mentally disabled but can run fast and play ping-pong well.

I can't run fast, I can't play ping-pong, and back then I didn't even know what an IQ was. Grandfather knew, but he said it was just a number used to separate people into black and white, a unit of measurement like time or money, a capitalist invention, even though we're all equal, and then I lost track of what he was saying, and Grandfather explained that only Today counts, the Here, the Now. Me, here with him. Nothing more. I understood that. He asked what I would do if I was out at sea and storm clouds gathered. The answer was simple: Sail back to the harbour as quickly as possible. He asked what I would wear if it was raining. Easy: Rain clothes. What I would do if someone had fallen from a horse and wasn't moving. Child's play: Get help. Grandfather was satisfied with my answers and said I was clearly of firm mind.

I agreed.

But sometimes I didn't get what people meant. It happened. And on those occasions, I preferred to say nothing. There was little point. No one could explain things like Grandfather.

Luckily, I then got a computer with an internet connection, and all at once I knew a lot more than I used to. Because the internet knows everything. It knows when your birthday is and whether you've forgotten your mother's. It even knows when you last went to the toilet or rubbed one out. At least that's what Nói, my best friend, said when the thing with the Quota King happened. But exactly what it was that was wrong in my head – that, no one could explain to me. A medical bungle, my mother once said, back when she still lived in Raufarhöfn. It just slipped out, probably when I shot and dissected Elínborg's cat because I'd learned how from Grandfather and wanted to practise. My mother got very angry, because Elínborg complained to her and threatened to call the police, and when my mother got angry, she stopped speaking and *did* something instead, like taking out the rubbish. Open the lid of the outside container, heave in the bag and slam it shut – and open it again and slam it again. Bang!

But anyone who believes I had a difficult childhood because there's fish soup in my head is plain wrong. Grandfather took over the thinking for me. He looked out for me. But that was back then.

Now Grandfather looks at me with dull, watery eyes and remembers nothing. And maybe I'll disappear too, when Grandfather's no longer here, be buried with him, like a Viking chief's horse. That's what they used to do, the Vikings; bury the horse with the chief. They belonged together. So the Viking chief would be able to ride across the bridge of Bifröst to Valhalla. That's quite an entrance!

But the thought made me nervous. Being buried, I mean. Trapped beneath the coffin lid. You'd get claustrophobic, and then you'd be better off dead. That's why I usually didn't stay long in the care home. In Húsavík I could at least get something decent to eat. Sölvi's filling station cafe had the best burgers for 1,845 krona. I always had the right change, always, and Sölvi knew that too, he no longer even bothered to count the coins. But sometimes I didn't enjoy the burger because I was sad that Grandfather no longer knew who I was. And if *he* no longer knew, how on earth was *I* supposed to?

I had Grandfather to thank for everything. My life. If he hadn't been there, my mother would have stuck me in a home for the mentally disabled, where I would've been abused and raped. I would be living in Reykjavík now, lonely and neglected. In Reykjavík the traffic is chaotic, and the air is dirty, and the people are stressed. Ugh, yuck, that's not for me. I had Grandfather to thank that I was somebody, here, in Raufarhöfn. He had shown me everything, taught me everything a person needs to know to survive. He took me hunting and out to sea, even though I wasn't much help in the beginning. Out hunting in particular I was like the village idiot, stumbling and wheezing, and Grandfather told me I was tripping over my own feet, that I had to lift them up when the ground was uneven. So I started to do that, but only ever for a few paces, then I would forget again and stumble over the next grassy mound, and sometimes I fell flat on my face with such a loud crash – I was fat, after all – that the snow grouse flew away, startled, and the Arctic foxes took to their heels before we'd even caught sight of them. But anyone thinking this would anger Grandfather couldn't be more wrong. Because Grandfather didn't get angry. On the contrary. He merely laughed and helped me to my feet, brushed the dirt from my clothes and told me to be brave. "Don't lose heart, buddy!" he'd say. And I soon got used to the uneven terrain, and before long I wasn't so fat any more. I could stand upright on the small cutter, too, and not fall even when the boat swayed from side to side. I started to enjoy bracing my knees against the waves, and didn't even need to concentrate on it any more, but did it automatically, programming the motion into my knees, and out hunting I lifted my feet and no longer scared away prey, which meant we sometimes marched back to the village with two snow grouse or a mink dangling from one of our belts. Sometimes even an Arctic fox. I was so proud! And to make sure everyone saw, we would do a couple of laps through Raufarhöfn. Laps of honour. And the people would wave and shout out praise. You can get used to that kind of thing. Praise.

It's a drug, said Nói, my best friend, back when he was still my best friend. I should handle praise with caution and not get used to it, he told me. Nói was a computer genius, but his body gave him problems. He said he was my opposite, my counterpart, my opponent, and I had no idea what he meant by that. He said that if we were one person, we would be unbeatable. It was a shame he lived in Reykjavík.

And then the thing with Róbert McKenzie happened – he was the Quota King around here – and that was the beginning of the end, and no one likes it when things end. That's why people prefer to think back to the past, to when something has just begun and the ending is still far away.

The days with Grandfather out at sea and on the Melrakkaslétta were the best of my life. Sometimes I was allowed to shoot with Grandfather's shotgun, which now belongs to me. He taught me how to be a good marksman, how to aim, how to pull the trigger very gently, without shaking. When I aimed at a target during a practice run, he placed a tiny stone on top of the barrel, and I had to pull the trigger without the stone falling off. It's harder than you might think, because you have to *pull*, not press! Only once I could do that was I allowed to shoot for real. But under no circumstances was my mother to find out, that's what Grandfather and I had agreed, because my mother thought firearms were too dangerous for me. But she found out anyway when I shot Elínborg's cat right behind our house. That was stupid of me. Someone heard the gunshot and told my mother over at the cold-storage warehouse. She came straight home from work and was hopping mad, even though she'd been annoyed by the cat a few times in the past when it had shat in our potato beds. She got really, really angry, my mother, and maybe she felt offended too, because she said it was time to give it to me straight. And she did. I was different to other people, she shouted, tapping her finger against her temple. I was slower upstairs, and that's why she didn't want me running around Raufarhöfn with a gun, shooting animals, it would cause trouble in the village – and she was right about that, because Elínborg wasn't someone to be messed with; she immediately called the police.

But my mother shouldn't have said it like that. Because when someone yells at me, even if that someone is my own mother, I lose it. My mind switches off. And when I lose it, fists start to fly. My fists. Usually against myself. Which isn't so bad. But sometimes against others too, if they get in the way. That's worse, but I don't do it intentionally, and afterwards I can barely remember it. It's as though the needle on a record has skipped forwards. And that's why my mother tried to calm me down, assuring me that she trusted me completely to go around with a gun, that of course I was a good shot, which Grandfather could no doubt confirm. He merely shook his head at all the arguing and sent the police away again. He wasn't in the least bit angry that I had shot Elínborg's cat. He said my mother was exaggerating, that I wasn't that goddamn different, and in fact it was barely worth mentioning, because there were far greater idiots out there, it wasn't about school grades but how a person acts towards others, what kind of human being they are, and so on. And he gave an example, which he was good at, because it's important to give examples so everyone understands what you mean. He told us about this athlete who lived in America and who was good-looking and nice and even became an actor, but then he killed his wife because he was jealous. Just because of that. Jealousy. Bang! End of story. And that's why I was a better person than this famous athlete. But my mother said he could stick his athlete where the sun didn't shine, because Elínborg's cat probably didn't give a damn about that, but Elínborg did give a damn that I'd killed her cat, and so did the police and so did the school board. That's how it was, she said to Grandfather, certain behaviour, a certain level of achievement was expected, so he'd better hurry up and arrive in the twentieth century before it came to an end, and he had to stop taking sides, *she* was my mother, after all, and had the last word where my upbringing was concerned. But Grandfather put his foot down. Because he could get pretty angry too, when he wanted to, and he loudly reminded her that he was *her* father, that we were living in *his* house, under *his* roof, with *his* rules, and that he had the goddamn last word. And what's more, he spent more time with me than she did. When he said this my mother's words got stuck in her throat. She stormed out to do something. To take out the rubbish, maybe. And then I broke something, although I can't remember what it was. But something definitely broke. I have this clear picture in my mind, a scrap of memory: Grandfather, sitting astride me with a bright red face, pinning my arms to the floor, calling out desperately for my mother and yelling at me to calm the hell down.

I shot my first Arctic fox when I was eleven. Foxes are considered pests, even though they were here before the Vikings. You're allowed to shoot them, foxes. It actually happened very quickly, and I was so surprised I didn't even have time to get nervous. We were walking cross-country when one appeared in front of us, poking its head out from behind a grassy mound, spotting us but unable to find a hiding place in a hurry. Grandfather pushed the shotgun into my hand without saying a word. He just squinted at the fox, which stared back at him in shock, and I understood. I took aim, the fox made a run for it, but I kept it in my sights, the tip of my finger on the trigger, then pulled ever so gently until it went off. I didn't even notice the kickback from the butt. My heart beat faster. The fox keeled over, then did a somersault, and its legs twitched as though it still wanted to run away. But it no longer could.

I felt strange. Grandfather still didn't say a word, but he clapped me contentedly on the shoulder, and then we watched the animal die. It didn't take long before it stopped twitching and lay there, its fur soaked with the thick blood gushing out of its snout. To begin with its ribcage quickly rose and fell, but then its breathing became slower, jerkier, until eventually the fox lay there motionless. I felt sorry for it, but when I received the 5,000 krona at the community office, I suddenly knew what a vocation was. A vocation is when you come to something as though you've been called to it.

Grandfather didn't have much longer to live. Every time I said goodbye to him, I was perhaps seeing him for the last time. That's what one of the nurses had told me. And she had also said I would feel very sad when it happened, but that this was completely normal, as was crying, so there was no reason to worry. Nói once explained to me that my grandfather had taken on the role of father for me, something my mother would definitely have disputed. But Nói was right; my name was Kalmann Óðinsson, after all, after Grandfather, whose first name was Óðinn, and not after my actual father, who my mother sometimes referred to as the Sperm Donor.

Quentin Boatwright. That was his name, her sperm donor. And if I'd been given his name, I would have been called Kalmann Quentinsson. But that didn't work, because this name and the letter Q didn't exist in Iceland. Just like my father. He didn't exist here either. If I had lived in America, I would have been called Kalmann Boatwright. The names there are just plain wrong.

If I had children someday, I wanted to be there for them, like Grandfather was for me. I would tell them all the things Grandfather had told me. I would teach my children how to hunt, how to stalk Arctic foxes, spot snow grouse in the snow or catch Greenland shark. I would show them how to provide for themselves. Regardless of whether I had a girl or a boy. But if you want children, you need a woman. There's no other way. That's nature.

I was thirty-three years old already, with another few weeks to go until my thirty-fourth birthday. I urgently needed a wife. But I could forget that, because here in Raufarhöfn there weren't any women who would want someone like me. The range of women here was about as extensive as the vegetables on offer in the village store. Apart from carrots, potatoes, a couple of shrivelled bell peppers and some brown salad leaves, there was nothing. And the possibility that my future wife would stumble by chance into Raufarhöfn, 609 kilometres' drive from Reykjavík, was pretty slim.

My mother always said: "When you reach the end of the world, turn left!" I found that funny, but she never laughed. And she never made jokes; usually she was too tired from the long hours in the cold-storage warehouse. She told me I couldn't eat Cocoa Puffs every day, because I would get even fatter and have no chance of finding a wife. But my mother was no longer here, and nor was Grandfather, so I could eat Cocoa Puffs all day long if I wanted and no one would complain. But I only ate Cocoa Puffs for breakfast, and sometimes in the evening, while watching *The Bachelor*. Never for lunch. That was my rule.

People need rules in life, that's important, because otherwise there would be anarchy, and anarchy is when there are no police and no rules and everyone does whatever they want. Like setting fire to a house, for example. Just like that, for no reason. No one works, no one repairs faulty appliances like washing machines, or ships' engines, satellite dishes and microwaves. And then you end up sitting with an empty plate in front of a blank TV screen in a burned-down house, and people are killing each other over a chicken wing or Cocoa Puffs. But I could have survived something like that, because I could defend myself. I knew how to process Greenland shark so the meat was edible. And I could pluck a snow grouse. My grandfather's house was big enough, and perhaps then a woman would want to live with me, because here in Raufarhöfn anarchy wouldn't be so bad, simply because we would be far away from it. My wife would have to be younger than me, because we would need to have a lot of children to ensure mankind's survival. We would have sex practically every night. Perhaps even twice a day! And we wouldn't hear about the riots in Reykjavík, because the TV would no longer work. What's more, there hadn't been any police in Raufarhöfn since the financial crisis, and in that sense we already had anarchy. It was just that people hadn't realized it yet.

2

BLOOD

Grandfather made the best hákarl on the entire island. I make the second best. I know that because a number of people have told me, for example Magnús Magnússon, the sheep farmer from Hólmaendar, who gets his hákarl directly from me and is good at playing the accordion. He says it every time: "Kalmann minn," he says, "your grandfather made the best hákarl in all of Iceland. But yours is almost as good!" And that was of course logical, because I learned from the best.

If only Grandfather had been with me when the thing with Róbert McKenzie happened. Grandfather would have known what to do. And to be completely honest, I was a bit mad at him for having left me alone in this mess. I wished I hadn't even gone fox hunting that day. I wished Róbert had vanished like a ship on the horizon. Because there are no tracks on the ocean. The sea always looks as though it has never been touched by anyone, apart from the wind. Isn't it strange that only air can leave tracks on the water?

Why did it have to be me who passed by the spot near the Arctic Henge monument? I was only tracking an Arctic fox, who I had named Schwarzkopf, like the shampoo. He was a badly behaved fox, a young male, who had ventured right up to the houses looking for something to eat. Perhaps that was why I liked him. And if it had been up to me, I wouldn't have shot him. I had a secret pact with him. But Hafdís had asked me to teach the fox a lesson, and everyone knows what that means, and if the school principal – who is also on the town council – asks you for a favour, you don't just say no. In addition, Hafdís was a very beautiful woman, even though she wasn't young any more and had three grown-up children. Sometimes I wondered what Hafdís was even doing here in Raufarhöfn. Because she looked like a TV presenter. She told me that the little guy was lurking dangerously close to the town hall, and when people shooed him away, he sometimes headed off towards Vogar. I would be able to recognize him by his dark fur and even darker head, she told me.

So he had blue fur. That's what went through my mind, because at this point in time he would still have had white flecks in his winter coat if it had changed colour. Hafdís didn't know much about animals, even though she was the school principal. But I didn't say anything, because you're not supposed to lecture a school principal. She wouldn't allow it, anyway.

Schwarzkopf was an Arctic fox with blue fur, then. That's what you call it, even though the fur isn't blue at all. It's brown, grey or dark grey. The blue fox's fur doesn't change colour with the seasons, because it mostly stays close to the coast. It's the best camouflage among the black rocks, dulse and driftwood. White fur would stand out, because there's usually no snow on the beach, and that's why the Icelandic foxes don't need white fur like the foxes in Siberia or in Greenland, where everything is so beautifully white.

I could have explained all this to Hafdís, but I didn't. I just tapped my index finger on the rim of my cowboy hat – that's how people in America say "Okey-dokey", and my hat is from there – and picked up the trail behind the town hall, clambering up the slope and looking down over the whole village stretching out before me: the more recent wooden quarter with the school and sports hall to my right, the harbour and church to my left. The Kottjörn pond was still covered with a slushy layer of ice, but I wouldn't have dared venture out on it anyway. I walked along the edge of the slope until I was level with the school building, climbed back down, went past the school and the empty camping ground, then further on to the coast and along the shoreline to the Vogar bay. Apart from a few eiders, lesser black-backed gulls and kittiwakes that were sitting on the water doing nothing, I didn't see any animals. I imagined how I would scare the living daylights out of Schwarzkopf. Secretly, though, I hoped the fox would be trusting, so I could befriend him and keep him as a pet. That's a thing, you know. In Russia, for example. I reckon if I'd had a tamed fox as a pet, I would have had more luck with women.

Schwarzkopf could have done with a white winter coat that day, because it was snowing like mad; thick, heavy flakes that even settled on the pebbled beach. The water looked dull and grey, almost motionless; the weather was calm. Apart from the falling snow, it was so quiet that I couldn't help but sing a little song, because the snow swallowed the sound and no one could hear me.

I liked singing. No one knew that. Schwarzkopf did, perhaps; he must've heard me and hidden, because I didn't catch a glimpse of him that whole day, even though I spent hours on end tramping around out there, along the entire bay, into the Melrakkaslétta, up to the Glápavötn lakes and zigzagging over to the Arctic Henge, the half-finished stone circle which Róbert McKenzie had had built a few years previously. I wasn't even expecting to encounter any animals, because the weather was unsuitable, the visibility poor. I didn't even see any snow grouse. But it was no longer as cold as in winter, it was only around zero degrees. The March brightness was pleasant. And besides, I had promised Hafdís, and if you make a promise to the school principal, you keep it.

People always imagine hunting to be so thrilling, they imagine you reading the tracks, holding your nose to the wind, straining your senses, then ambushing the animals and chasing after them. That's nonsense. You spend most of the time sitting on the cold ground, hoping something will appear in front of the barrel of your gun. For that you need a good dose of patience, "a hunter's most important virtue", as my grandfather always said. He was like a mentor. A mentor is a teacher, but one who doesn't make you do exams.

On that day, though, I didn't feel like sitting on the cold ground, because I suspected Schwarzkopf was listening to my singing in his warm den and covering his ears. I wonder why I chose to go up to the henge that particular day. Why hadn't I just headed off home? That would have been better. Because up there, right by the monument, was where I stumbled across the blood. And there was a lot of it. It's actually astounding how much blood there is inside a human being.

The pool of blood glistened red and dark in the white snow. The snowflakes fell relentlessly, melting into it. I was hot and sweaty from walking, but because I had suddenly come to a halt and was staring motionless at the blood, I began to shake. Exhaustion spread within me. My limbs felt as heavy as lead, as though I had just done something strenuous. I thought of Grandfather as I watched the blood soak up the snowflakes, until the redness paled beneath the freshly fallen snow. I must have stood there for a long while, but eventually I returned to reality, stiff with cold, and awoke as though from a dream. I looked around and wasn't even sure where I was at first, until I recognized the stone blocks of the henge and remembered Schwarzkopf. Had he smelled the blood? Perhaps I could lie in wait for him here.

Naturally I took a closer look at the whole mess. I noticed some footprints, but they were very faint because of the fresh snow. The indentations led away from the pool of blood towards the village, down to the harbour, where they disappeared in the snow flurries. All of a sudden, I was no longer sure whether they were my footprints or somebody else's. Or were there two sets? More than one person? Which direction had I come from? Where had I been going? I looked around me in all directions. I was utterly alone. The snowflakes falling around me without pause were disorienting. When everything is white, white up above, white below and white all around, it confuses the senses. Perhaps the footprints weren't prints at all but merely indentations in the ground, between the mounds of grass, and I thought: it could even be a polar bear.

Polar bears are rarely encountered in Iceland, but are dangerous nonetheless. Very dangerous. If they come close, it means they're incredibly hungry. But I was too exhausted to worry. I'd had enough. I wanted to go home. I wanted to lie down on the couch, perhaps chat with Nói. The pool of blood was barely visible now. If it carried on snowing like this, it would soon be gone. That was good.

I trudged back towards the village, dropped in at the school to see Hafdís and told her I hadn't been able to track down Schwarzkopf.

"Schwarzkopf?" she asked, clapping her laptop shut. I blushed. I hadn't wanted her to find out the name. That was between me and the fox. So I said nothing and stared down at the floor. "Have you named him? Like the shampoo?" Hafdís smiled. She got up from her desk and stepped towards me, grabbed both my hands, lifted them a little and studied them. "Your hands are all red!" she exclaimed in shock. "Is that blood? Did you hurt yourself?"

I pulled my hands away, only now noticing that they were bloodied yet dry.

"Not mine," I said. I remembered I had put my hand into the blood. Had I fallen over?

"Not yours?"

"I found a pool of blood, up by the Arctic Henge," I blurted out, wondering whether Grandfather would have wanted me to talk about it. Perhaps I should have lied, but you're only allowed to lie if you want to protect someone, like a friend or a girlfriend.

"Blood?"

I shrugged. "Just blood. That's all. No reason to worry."

"Are you quite sure you haven't hurt yourself?"

"Completely sure," I said.

We both studied my hands more closely and didn't find any wounds, but they were a little swollen from the cold.

"Blood." Hafdís was deep in thought. "From an animal?"

"Possibly," I said, then added a "definitely".

Hafdís frowned, shook her head and muttered: "Some hunter you are!"

I grinned. I liked it when people called me a hunter.

Hafdís let me go, and I went home. After thoroughly washing my hands, I decided to spend the rest of the day watching TV. It was only three o'clock, but I liked watching

Dr Phil, because this shrink could genuinely read people's minds! When the people on there did a lie detector test, Dr Phil was never surprised by the results, because he knew precisely what games were being played. There were men who were in love with their sisters or who were older than me but still living with their mothers, and didn't want to move out, and the mothers then complained to Dr Phil. And there were women who had affairs and even had children with other men and didn't admit it, even though a DNA test proved the opposite. Once there was a white woman and a white man, and the woman had a black baby but denied having fucked a black man. And her husband even believed her, he said he trusted and loved her, that he'd go to the ends of the Earth with her. But Dr Phil saw through the woman's bullshit and swore at her until they were all crying and then the black baby had neither a black nor a white father. And then the audience clapped and cheered and Dr Phil's wife accompanied her husband out of the studio and praised him, even though you couldn't hear what she was saying. But she was always thrilled with his show. I'd have liked a wife just like that, but younger.

I heated up a frozen pizza in the microwave and spent the whole evening watching TV until I fell asleep on the couch. I was so tired that I even forgot to call Nói on Messenger.

The next morning, I looked out of the window and everything was white. The sea was deep blue, almost black, everything completely normal, so no reason to worry. The snow must have stopped during the night, because it didn't look as though more would be falling from the sky.

I wrapped up warm and went down to the harbour. There were lots of old warehouses and fish-processing halls down here, buildings that had been erected in the fifties and sixties and which were now crumbling: the British barracks and workers' quarters, the massive fish oil tanks. Everything was empty. I was allowed to use the Miami building for free, the part at the back at least, not that the rest of the building was being used by anyone else. The building was called that because its first owner Baldur had had a few palm trees painted on the facade, which you could no longer see, and the palms reminded people of Miami, where there are proper palm trees.

Inside the building it was dark and damp. A big building, sad at the absence of people. Melt- and rainwater dripped through numerous spots on the roof, and that was why I only used the part which stayed dry, right at the back.

Years ago, there was a herring boom in Raufarhöfn. People even came here from Reykjavík, because there was a lot of work for both men and women. But the space in the residential buildings wasn't enough, even though bunk beds were piled up to the ceilings. Before the hotel was a hotel, it was accommodation for workers. The shack diagonally opposite the old post house served as living quarters for the young female workers. The British barracks were accommodation too. Quite simply, a lot of hands were needed up here. Back then the village still had a cinema, a theatre club and dancing. The harbour master Sæmundur sometimes told me about it. At the events on weekends there were so many mariners and dockers that they wouldn't fit in the ballroom, which meant that no one could dance because the men and women were herded in there like sheep in a stall. In 1966, Hljómar even came to Raufarhöfn, and so that everyone got to see them, they played three concerts in one day!

But that was back then. Today, all the inhabitants of Raufarhöfn sometimes gather in the town hall, for example at the Þorrablót midwinter festival, and even then, the hall is only ever half-full.

The fishers fished all the herring that was to be found in Iceland's coastal waters, and once all the herring near the coast was gone, they tried to track down schools of fish by plane, really far out. The boats would often be out for a whole day to get to the schools of herring, and once those were gone too, the fish were simply gone, and the people moved back to Reykjavík and did something different. Then things calmed down in Raufarhöfn. There was enough room to dance again, admittedly, but those who had stayed behind only wanted to drink. That was when people realized they could catch and eat other fish too, not only herring, but also lumpfish, shellfish, pollock, ling, catfish and mackerel. And that's how the industry got going here in Raufarhöfn again, until the catch quota system was introduced by the politicians and the quota was almost entirely withdrawn from Raufarhöfn. Now the processing halls lay idle, and every third house stood empty. By now there was just one man who had a decent catch quota, though not a large one: Róbert McKenzie. Siggi caught cod for him from time to time with the manual winch, Einar with the longline vessel. And Júníús and Flóki as well, who were father and son and who everyone simply called Jú-Jú – that's short for Júníús and Junior – caught the fish with nets. They were the most hard-working out of everyone, and were usually out on the water and barely seen around the village. Sometimes they landed seven tonnes in one day! But I didn't care about that. I was the only one here who caught shark, so I was completely independent of the catch quotas. And that's why

29

I was allowed to use the empty Miami building, where the scraps from processing the herring, fish heads and things like that used to be rendered and made into fishmeal. You could still smell it. This was where I kept my vats and tubs in which I left the shark meat soaking in brine for a few days, assuming I didn't process them right away at the harbour. This was where I stored my bait, where I had my work desk, my corrugated iron refrigerator that hummed like mad when the wind blew, my knives, and the tools I needed for *Petra*. My boat. She was getting on a bit now. Grandfather had left all this to me – apart from the refrigerator; I'd got that from Magga.

I set to work on *Petra*. She needed an oil change. Sæmundur came over, watched me for a while, then climbed into the boat with me and helped, even though I could manage it alone. At one point he came so close that my face accidentally touched his hair. That tickled. Sæmundur had hair almost everywhere, not a proper beard exactly, but he was always unshaven and had messy hair on his head, untameable nose hair, bushy eyebrows, hairy forearms and hair on the backs of his hands too, and only a few white strands, even though he was very old already.

"Don't stare at me like that!" He laughed suddenly. "You're making me feel awkward!"

I laughed too. But when I put the funnel in the oil tank and Sæmundur carefully glugged oil into the tank, we were very focused. And perhaps that's why Sæmundur became all thoughtful, perhaps he simply wanted to get something off his chest, because he said:

"Róbert, Róbert. Just like that, poof, vanished. Our very own hotel owner. Our Quota King, ladies and gentlemen!"

Sæmundur put down the oil canister and shook his head. "There'll be a proper hoo-ha, you mark my words. No more peace and quiet!"

That was the first time I heard that Róbert McKenzie was missing. And the news shouldn't have surprised me, given that I'd found an enormous pool of blood right by the Arctic Henge the day before, and he was the one who'd had it built, after all. But somehow I was so thrown that I didn't tell Sæmundur about it. Sæmundur was still puzzling over where Róbert might be, for example in some brothel in Amsterdam or a rehab clinic in Florida. I didn't say a word, and once I was done with my work, I went straight home, because I felt as though I were hiding something, as though I had done something stupid, and that as soon as I told people about it, I really would be connected with Róbert's disappearance. But it was too late now anyway, Hafdís knew about the pool of blood, and that's how all the trouble started, and why I tried not to give it any more thought. If you're the person who finds a dead body or its remains, even if it's just a drop of blood, you're connected to it. You're part of the story then, you're written into the history books. And that's what I wanted to prevent, simply by saying nothing. But when a woman from the police called me on my phone and asked me to come down to the schoolhouse so she could have a chat with me, I got nervous, I felt guilty, even though I hadn't broken any laws and hadn't killed anyone. Regardless. I braced myself for trouble.

3

BIRNA

Barely an hour later, I was standing in front of the school-house. In full gear. That was the only way I felt complete. That was just my way. Cowboy hat, sheriff's badge and Mauser. Even if people sometimes laughed at me for it. The gear gave me protection. And I was in dire need of it if I wanted to go into the schoolhouse. I had to gather all my courage. The schoolhouse's grey facade, and the police car in front of it, even the playground and the three bicycles, scared me. Sigfús, who used to be the school principal, had once said at the start of the school year, in front of all the pupils, that knowledge was a backpack you carry around with you your entire life. Admittedly I hadn't learned much in school, but I was still lugging my school backpack around with me. It weighed down heavily, and became even heavier the closer I got to the schoolhouse. This building had swallowed me until I was fourteen years old. After that, luckily, I didn't have to go to school any more. There was no reason to worry, though. It could have been worse. I just didn't have any friends, which was a shame, because all the other children did. I always sat in the back row, alone, at a two-person desk. If someone was being noisy or hadn't done their homework, they had to sit next to me for a lesson. And it was only ever boys. They would hold their noses, because I usually had a few cubes of hákarl in a small plastic container in my trouser pocket. Grandfather's hákarl. My supplies. That was all well and good, but the lid sometimes fell off, and I would only notice once I put my fingers into my sticky trouser pocket, and then some people would notice the smell.

After that, Principal Sigfús said I was no longer allowed to take hákarl into school, but he left it at that; he didn't want to pick a fight with Grandfather, who was armed. And Grandfather knew very well that Sigfús couldn't forbid anyone from taking snacks into school, because Grandfather knew the law. And besides, the farmers' children smelled of sheep, he said, and the shipowners' children of money. That sounded plausible to me, but I could never smell either sheep or money in the schoolroom. Nor the hákarl either. Perhaps you get used to it and don't notice. So why all the fuss?

Once I stored a little jar of hákarl in my desk. And the next day it was gone. Someone had stolen it! I didn't dare tell the teacher, but I did tell Grandfather, and he only said that in future I shouldn't store any more hákarl in my desk. But I found that a little unfair. Because I had assumed Grandfather was on my side. I was angry and disappointed, and kept having all these thoughts, I really stewed over it, wondering who could have stolen the hákarl and how I would get my revenge if I tracked down the thief, so much so that I barely followed lessons for two whole days, all I did was sit there and try to solve the case. I imagined how I would corner the thief and clamp their head beneath the lid of the desk in order to force a confession.

I wasn't good at school anyway. I always got bad grades, even when Romeo sat next to me. Romeo was my only – and therefore best – friend during my school days. He moved here from Seyðisfjörður, his father was from Italy and worked as a cook in the canteen of the fish-processing plant, that's why Romeo had a foreign name and brown skin. He was only in Raufarhöfn for about three months though, because the cooks in the canteen were always changing, and that's why Romeo didn't have any other friends either. He was allocated the seat next to me, which I was pleased about, and I shook his hand right away, because I wanted him to feel welcome, and so we sealed our friendship with a handshake. He was the only one who was truly nice to me. Before he moved away, he even dropped by to see me, and gave me a drawing of Batman swinging from a skyscraper, holding on only by his gun, a rope and hook tied to it. That's a kind of magic weapon that Batman has. Romeo was very good at drawing muscles, even though he didn't yet have any himself, and he shook my hand like I had his on the very first day, and then I never saw him again and don't even know where he is today and whether he's even still alive, and as we said goodbye, I was sadder than I'd ever been in my entire life.

I always got the worst grades, and that's in the whole of Raufarhöfn, in the entire history of school grades, and I'm not exaggerating, because a substitute teacher once told me that in his entire career he'd never seen such a bad report card. And he must have known, given that he'd been a teacher all across the country. And I wasn't mad at all, but somehow pleasantly surprised. My classmates always looked forward to my report, because thanks to me they weren't the worst. Each time, they laughed in relief. I laughed along with them, because it's better to laugh along than to be the only one who's not laughing. Otherwise you're alone.

The letters in my school notebooks were always tumbling messily over one another. Arithmetic was impossible. I was good at geography, at least, perhaps even the best in all of Raufarhöfn. I knew the names of all the fjords and mountains, the passes and villages, whether three thousand people lived there or only twelve. I had a big map of Iceland on my bedroom wall, and I sometimes did tours around all of it on a single afternoon. Deciphered all the names. Because reading was something I could do. Books were too long for me, comic books too chaotic, but maps were just right. In the other subjects I always had the worst grades. No one complained. No one shouted at me.

"No reason to worry," Grandfather remarked. There were more important things in life than numbers and letters, he said.

My mother wasn't happy about my performance at school, but she blamed the teachers. That's why she wanted to send me to a special school in Reykjavík, where I would fit in, as she put it, but Grandfather protested, saying I was more reliant on family than better teachers, and I was totally with Grandfather on that, because family is the most important thing in the whole world. What's more, I belonged to Raufarhöfn like the Eiffel Tower does to Paris. I had grown up here, wanted to spend my life here. And I wanted to die here too. Eventually, my mother accepted this. Even ten horses couldn't drag me to the city. The filth of two hundred thousand people gets washed unfiltered into the ocean there. You find used sanitary pads, baby wipes and condoms on the beach. No thank you! Not me! I'd much rather eat another raw fish.

I once ate a raw fish. It wasn't anything special really, kind of like sushi, I imagine, but back then we didn't have sushi in Iceland yet, and the people didn't eat raw fish. Only the Inuit over in Greenland and the Japanese in Japan did that. It was a stupid dare, and I did it, that's all, no reason to worry. We were by the lighthouse at Hraunhafnartangi, the northernmost point in Iceland; me, Palli, Arnór, Kiddi, Steini and Gulli, who was sixteen already and used to borrow his father's car, for example when his father was out at sea and his mother was taking a nap. Hraunhafnartangi is above the Arctic Circle. After that it's not much further to the North Pole, and if you stand on the last rock and look out across the water, there's just water between you and the North Pole. All kinds of things get washed up on this spit, driftwood, ropes, nets, buoys, actually mainly fishing debris, but sometimes things that don't belong in the sea and that are mostly made of plastic. Kiddi was searching the washed-up containers for a message in a bottle, and Arnór found a deckchair, opened it up and sat on it as though he were sunbathing on a beach in Spain. In his hand he held a broken buoy, into which he had stuck a rye stalk, making it look as though he were sipping on some exotic cocktail. It was hilarious, and I laughed so much I almost fell over, and Gulli said that I laughed as idiotically as a handicapped donkey. Steini, meanwhile, had poked around the tumbledown fishing huts and found a completely rusted-over frying pan.

"Children, dinner's ready!" he called.

"I've got something too!" cried Gulli, who had found a dead fish in the water among the rocks, left there by the tide. The fish looked pretty fresh, just dead, and stared at us in horror – they always do that, fish, even when they're still alive. Gulli said I had to eat a fish eye, that it was a dare and they'd all done it already, all of them except me. Luckily, I had my jackknife on me, I always had it on me. And once everyone had taken a look at my knife, I cut the fish's eye out of the socket, as Grandfather had once demonstrated. Child's play. I also knew how to eat a fish eye. You swallow it down in one go, without thinking about it – that's the trick.

My friends screamed, especially Kiddi and Palli, because their voices hadn't broken yet, but I didn't even pull a face, I acted as though there were nothing easier in this world than eating a fish eye. I also cut the second eye out of its socket and offered it to the boys, but they almost fell over in disgust. Then Gulli said that the dare would only be completed once I had eaten the entire fish, apart from the head and the fins and so on. Because they had all completed this dare already, and if I wanted to be one of them, I had to prove myself.

"Child's play," I said, filleting the fish and removing the parasites with the tip of the knife, following the usual process, as I had learned from Grandfather – and then bit into its flesh.

The flesh was tougher than I'd expected. And soapy. I had to really chew before I was finally able to swallow down the first bite. And then the commotion began. Palli, Arnór, Kiddi, Steini and Gulli hopped around and yelled and held their stomachs, doubling over in disgust. I took a few more bites, until they were all curled up on the floor, practically throwing up and assuring me that I'd completed the dare! I was insanely proud, even though the fish tasted weird and left a strange taste in my gums. It was kind of disgusting actually, not like hákarl. Completely different. And we didn't have anything with us to drink to wash down the foul taste.

So as I stepped into the schoolhouse to meet the police-woman, I couldn't help but think of my schoolmates, of

Palli and Kiddi, Arnór, Steini and Gulli, who had only been friends with me because the grown-ups told them to be, but they never let me properly belong, and all of a sudden I could taste the fish in my mouth again and smell it in my nose.

On the journey back to Raufarhöfn, the raw fish made itself felt in my stomach, gurgling and rumbling. But you couldn't hear it, because we were driving along a potholed gravel road. So I did a good job in not letting it show. But Gulli stepped hard on the pedal and sped along the bumpy road as though we had the police chasing us. And suddenly I began to feel dizzy. Everything went hazy and blurry, I almost couldn't see a thing, my head got really heavy and swayed back and forward, my neck was like rubber, and at first I thought Gulli had crashed, that perhaps we'd come off the road, because everyone in the car started to scream at the top of their lungs. Gulli was sitting at the wheel, Steini next to him, Palli, Arnór, Kiddi and I were sat in the back, crammed in like sardines, and I only realized that the fish had come back up when I suddenly had loads more room. It was strange; as though I was watching myself as I threw up. I had no control over myself. I vomited not only the fish, but my breakfast and lunch too, in reverse order, first the fish, then lunch and finally the Cocoa Puffs, and I turned around in all directions, because I didn't want to just throw up forwards, to where Gulli was sitting, wrenching the steering wheel and bringing the car to a standstill at the side of the road. I thought that was really nice of him. But by the time the car was finally still and everyone had thrown themselves out into the open air, I was pretty much done. So Gulli might as well have kept driving, because we had to go back to the village to wash ourselves and the car anyway. We couldn't do it where we were. The sea was far too cold, and you're not supposed to clean car upholstery with seawater, everyone knows that, so I stuck my head out of the car and said:

"I'm done, we can carry on."

"Hi there, cowboy!"

I was so startled that I swore loudly: "Fuck, shit!"

And that's why the woman who had addressed me was startled too, and even jumped backwards. I was standing in the entrance to the school and had no idea how long I'd been there. After a few moments, the woman ventured towards me again.

"Did I startle you?" she asked carefully.

I stood there, stiff as a lighthouse, my cheeks glowing beacons. She really had startled me. And I told her so. She laughed, and I gradually relaxed, because she actually was nice, but I was still a little flustered. My heart was pounding, my palms were moist, and I was afraid that I smelled of shark. They didn't want this smell in the schoolhouse.

"So you're Kalmann the shark catcher, right?"

Suddenly feeling self-conscious, I nodded and looked down at the floor. I like it when people call me a shark catcher. People usually call me something else. I looked around surreptitiously, but there was no one who could have heard, here in the school where I'd been called so many names. No witnesses. It was a shame.

The woman was around the same age and height as my mother, although a little fatter, but not actually fat, just fuller. She had heavy breasts and a large stomach, but not a fat behind, almost no behind at all actually, and rather thin legs. She had a round face and short, curly hair. Dyed, for sure. All women of this age dye their hair. Nói told me that.

I've learned much more from him than from the teachers. The woman studied me and stretched out her hand.

"I'm Birna," she said. "We spoke on the phone. I'm from the police."

I left her hand hanging in the air, even though she gave me an encouraging smile. I stowed my hands in my trouser pockets. So Birna was from the police, even though she didn't wear a uniform. Was she working undercover? Or was she a superintendent and therefore didn't have to wear uniform any more? Eventually she lowered her arm, studied my outfit and pointed at the sheriff's badge affixed to my chest.

"Is that real?" she asked.

"Yes," I said, rotating the star a little between my fingers to straighten it. "It's from the United States of America."

"From America?"

"Correctamundo."

Birna smiled. "Have you been to America?"

"No. My father left it to me, but the sheriff's badge doesn't mean anything here. Only in Los Angeles County. That's written on it. Look, here. Los Angeles County. And here, that's the symbol they have there."

I showed her everything. Birna came right up to me and took a close look at the sheriff's badge. She smelled of women's perfume, and her eyebrows were filled in with black pencil.

"You're the Sheriff of Raufarhöfn!"

It was a strange thing to say. I mean, she knew very well that I wasn't a proper sheriff. After all, she was from the police.

"And the gun?" She pointed at my Mauser, which was in its holster.

"That's real too," I said, no longer feeling self-conscious. I had an advantage over her, see, because the police in Iceland don't carry any weapons besides pepper spray. They're not allowed, it's the law. Only the special unit carry guns. In an emergency. And there was no emergency here in Raufarhöfn. Not in the slightest.

Birna stiffened a little but held my gaze until I looked away.

"May I?"

I was about to hand her the gun when the door of one of the classrooms swung open. Hafdís stepped out into the corridor, spotted us and made a beeline for us, swinging her arms vigorously as though she were in a really good mood.

"I see you've found one another!" she declared, pleased. She shook Birna's hand and exchanged a few friendly words with her, which made me feel uneasy. Hafdís was a full head taller than the policewoman, probably due to her heeled shoes, and so she stared down at Birna. And I had always thought police officers were taller!

"We've just been chatting," said Birna. "I'm guessing you know there's a shortage of police officers in north-eastern Iceland, but was it really necessary to appoint an armed sheriff?" Hafdís laughed loudly, patted my back and said that I was a good guy, that I helped her to keep the Arctic foxes at bay, and that this old antique – she pointed at my gun in the holster – wasn't loaded.

"That's right, isn't it, Kalmann?" Hafdís said.

I shrugged. "I inherited it from my American grandfather," I said. "My father is in the army too. And my grandfather was even in the war."

"Which war?"

"The Korean War."

Birna looked at me again, studying me from head to toe, but this time more seriously, and after Hafdís had said her goodbyes, Birna said: "So, follow me, Sheriff of Raufarhöfn!"

She led me into one of the empty classrooms, which I can't have been inside for a good two hundred years. There might not have been any drawings or charts hanging on the walls, nor any half-finished craft and group projects on the back tables, but the room still felt familiar. When the schoolhouse was built, over one hundred children went in and out of here each day, and back when I was at school, there were still around seventy schoolchildren. Now there were just nine or ten, depending on whether Óli was staying here in Raufarhöfn with his father or in Egilsstaðir with his mother. Only two of the classrooms were needed now, most stood empty, and apart from Hafdís, Marteinn the sports teacher and the caretaker, Halldór, there was only one teacher: Dagbjört. I'd known her forever. She'd gone to school here with me. Actually, she should have been here too, but her red Kia Picanto wasn't outside. Perhaps she had taken the day off because of her father's disappearance. And that's probably why Hafdís was in school, to teach the children.

The classroom still smelled the same. Down to a tee. And the view outside was the same too. I knew these buildings well; the same low, wooden houses, which were admittedly no longer freshly painted, but at least still inhabited. I had often spent my hours in school gazing out of the window, daydreaming. I can't help it. I look somewhere, and my thoughts fly away like wild geese in autumn, like an Apollo rocket at supersonic speed, I leave Raufarhöfn behind me, one window is enough, and I'm away. Sometimes it can be less than a window, just something my brain can get caught on. It doesn't even need to interest me, it can be the cover of a magazine, a parking car, a gull flying past the window or a screw in the desk. But Principal Sigfús had sometimes strolled through the rows of desks and paused in front of me without my realizing, slammed his palm down on the desk or slapped me on the back of the head, not hard, but because I was so far away in my thoughts, I jumped out of my skin and almost fell off the chair, and so did my classmates, although admittedly with laughter, and I sat on the floor and laughed along like always. And yet I felt really bad, and on the way home I beat someone up, and at home I broke things, smashing them to the floor: the sewing box, dirty dishes, one of the owl figurines my mother collected because she believed owls protected us. She also had some made of plastic, but they weren't as easy to break as the porcelain ones. I boxed myself around the ears or pressed the tip of my pencil into the back of my hand until it bled, until the lead broke off and got stuck. The dark spot on the back of my hand is still there today. Sometimes my mother tried to stop me, and then I threw her to the floor like one of her owl figurines, because I was already twelve or thirteen and stronger than my mother, stronger than all my classmates, who were three or four years younger and a whole head shorter than me, because I'd been kept back three or four times, and that's why I could have thrashed the lot of them if I'd wanted to, but Grandfather said not to abuse my strength, otherwise they'd send me to Reykjavík, and he was right. That's the only thing he and my mother agreed on: I wasn't allowed to thrash anyone. My mother usually managed to prevent the worst, even though from time to time she came away with a few scratches or a black eye, but she knew I didn't mean it and would feel sorry later, and when it came down to it, she was stronger than me, because she had to be. I believe that mothers are sometimes stronger than men. She held onto me, sat astride my chest, knelt on my arms and pressed my head against the floor. Sometimes she managed to put a cushion under my head, but not always. My feet kicked out around me. That usually helped. It tired me out. My mother waited, red in the face, until I was no longer thrashing around, until I had calmed down, and then she fell down next to me on the floor, so that the two of us were staring at the ceiling, and I heard her wheezing and gasping for air, then she pulled herself upright, wiped the tears from her face and said that everything was okay, no reason to worry, then she would simply leave me there on the floor, because she didn't have time to lie next to me, she still had to do housework, cook the evening meal, she'd only just got back from the cold-storage warehouse after all, and soon Grandfather would be home too, and then we would all be hungry.

"Hello! Kalmann! Please take a seat, okay?"

I was still standing in the doorway to the classroom. Birna, already sitting at the teacher's desk, glanced at her watch and pointed me towards a chair standing opposite the desk. In front of her were files, documents, landscape photographs and her phone. A half-empty bottle of cola stood on a yellow Post-it, making the writing on it impossible to read.

I took a deep breath in and out, concentrating hard like I had learned, closing my eyes too, but only briefly. That's meditation, and it's actually a kind of contemplation, even though you're not supposed to be thinking about anything. Birna gave me a concerned look, which only made me more nervous, because I didn't want her to think I was a freak.

She didn't know me at all, so she didn't know there was no need to be afraid of me. And so I obediently sat down on the chair.

"Now then, Kalmann," she said. "I'm from the criminal police department of the city of Reykjavík. So I'm a police officer, even though I'm not wearing uniform —"

"Like in *CSI: Miami*," I interrupted.

"Yes, you could say that," said Birna. "I'm dealing with the missing person case of Róbert McKenzie."

"I'm Kalmann Óðinsson," I said. "Shark-hunting is my profession, and I'm almost thirty-four years old. I will be on the twenty-fourth of May, to be precise. That's in around two months and a few days, so very soon indeed."

"Thank you for the information," said Birna and smiled. "Listen, there's no need to be nervous, okay? Hafdís told me you were fox hunting yesterday and discovered a pool of blood in the snow up by the Arctic Henge, and I'd like you to tell me about it. That's all. It won't take long."

I felt caught out. So Hafdís really had snitched to the police. I wouldn't have expected that of her. I didn't say anything, but I must have been staring at the cola bottle, because Birna asked if she could offer me something to drink, a cup of coffee or a glass of water perhaps? It seemed cola wasn't on offer, so I shrugged. But she read my thoughts and said:

"Cola, perhaps?" I was astonished. "Wait a moment." She smiled wearily and left the room.

For the first time in my life, I was completely alone in one of these classrooms. It had always been the other way round: the teacher and children in the classroom, and me alone out in the corridor. Sometimes we were called to the front during the lesson to write a word on the blackboard or to solve a mathematical problem – everyone but me. I couldn't remember ever having held a piece of chalk.

So I stood up, went over to the board and did a drawing. The chalk felt strange in my fingers. As I brushed it across the board, white chalk dust drizzled down to the floor. Almost like snow, but much finer, so not like snow.

I drew the whole of Iceland. I moved down the outline of the coast, drew the Ost- and Westfjords, the deep Eyjafjörður, the south coast, the peninsulas of Reykjavík and Snæfellnes – everything was there. And I did a really good job of it. Right at the top, in the north-east, I made a dot where Raufarhöfn was. Then I drew the five biggest glaciers and coloured them white, holding the chalk lengthways. The stub of chalk eventually became so small that my fingertips touched the board and smeared the chalk. As I looked around for a new piece of chalk, I noticed Birna standing in the doorway. She looked impressed.

"Wow!" she said, coming over to take a closer look at the drawing. "Wow!" she said again. "You're really talented."

I nodded. "I know. I have a map of Iceland at home," I said.

"It shows," said Birna. "Not many people can do something like this."

We stood there for another few seconds, admiring my work, then sat back down at the teacher's desk. Birna pushed a bottle of cola towards me. I was thirsty and downed the whole bottle.

I love cola. Along with malt drink and fizzy orange Appelsín, which people only have at Christmas, it's my favourite drink. I put the empty bottle in front of me on the table and struggled not to burp, blowing the rising air sideways out of my mouth. Birna didn't notice.

"Is it okay if I record the conversation?" Birna didn't wait for an answer, opened the recording app on her phone and pressed the red record button. "It's 15.36, the twentieth of March, Raufarhöfn, missing person case Róbert McKenzie, and I have sitting opposite me the only eyewitness to date, Kalmann, Kalmann, er …" She flicked through her files, because she had forgotten my name once again, but then she suddenly remembered. "… Óðinsson! Kalmann Óðinsson." Then she turned to me. "Kalmann," she said. "Tell me where, how and when you found the location with the blood."

That was a lot of questions. What should I start with? Where? She knew where, though. She'd said it herself. At the Arctic Henge. How? Well, how does a person find something? By keeping their eyes open! It seemed to me that Birna wasn't the best police officer in the world. And why was she alone? Why was she recording this conversation as though I were a suspect? Was I a suspect? And why had she given me a cola, even though she'd only offered me coffee or water? Was she trying to wrap me around her little finger? I thought Birna was very nice, sure, perhaps a little too matronly for my taste, but all the same I was getting hot under the collar.

"Why are you alone?" I asked.

Birna seemed surprised, opened her mouth, but said nothing. Then she leaned back on the chair with a sigh. "That's a good question, Kalmann," she eventually admitted, which made me feel relieved, because I'd become aware that I hadn't answered any of her numerous questions, which perhaps made me look suspicious or was against the law. I decided not to ask any more questions.

"Okay then," she said. "We'll do this at your speed. After all, no one's going to get away from us up here. It's complete chaos in Reykjavík, because of the important state visit. Like it was with Reagan and Gorbachev. And that's why we need all the officers there. Or rather, almost all of them, because someone has to deal with matters in rural areas." Birna clicked her tongue, as though she were angry. "But I'm not completely alone. A few colleagues are in Húsavík, and could be here in ninety minutes if I called them, one is still in Þórshöfn, and almost seventy men and women from the rescue service are on their way here."

"What, right now?"

"You bet! Right now."

"And the coastguard?"

"Of course, the same goes for the coastguard. Boats, divers. Already on their way. All it takes is one call, and the helicopter will fly over too. A press of the button, so to speak. At least, that's if everything goes smoothly in Reykjavík. The state visit takes priority, of course." I was impressed. This woman was powerful. "And I have you," she said, and now I was floored. "But yes, really," she emphasized. "You know this place like the back of your hand, you've got a cartographic memory, you've just proved that." She pointed her thumb over her shoulder at the blackboard. "You know where the location with the blood is, and I'm sure you can answer a few very important questions for me, right?"

I looked down at my hands. I didn't want her to see my proud grin. I reached for the empty cola bottle and rotated it in my fingers until it fell out of my hands, danced around on the floor for a while and eventually disappeared beneath the desk. I bent down, crawled under the desk and found the bottle between Birna's feet. Birna was wearing black ladies' shoes, which were somehow too small and looked uncomfortable. I picked up the bottle, moved a little too

48

quickly and banged the back of my head on the underneath of the tabletop. It must have made it really shake above. I crawled out from beneath the table, rubbed my head and put the bottle back in its place.

Birna was sorting through her files, looking downwards, which meant I couldn't see whether she was angry at me.

"So, Kalmann," she said after a few seconds. Was she smiling? "What were you doing up there, anyway, when you found the pool of blood?"

My head throbbed. I touched my skull and inspected my fingers, fearful that I would see blood. But there wasn't any blood. I just had a bump on my head.

"I was hunting," I said. Men don't let on that they're in pain. "I'm also a hunter."

"I know. So what were you hunting up there?"

"Schwarzkopf."

"Who is Schwarzkopf?"

"Dammit!" I blurted out.

"It's okay," said Birna in a courteous tone. "There are no wrong answers here. Every detail counts. So, who is Schwarzkopf? I presume you weren't looking for a bottle of shampoo."

"No! An Arctic fox."

"An Arctic fox. Aha. One with a black head?"

I nodded.

"And blue fur?"

I looked at her in surprise. This woman wasn't so dumb after all.

"Correctamundo!"

"And were you successful?"

Because I shook my head, Birna said I had to say yes or no, because a nod or shake of the head couldn't be heard on the audio recording. So I nodded immediately, but said:

"Yes! I mean, no! I didn't see him, the fox, I mean." I looked down at my hands in embarrassment. "You don't always come back with a kill when you go hunting."

"You need patience, right?"

"Lots of it," I confirmed.

"And you go hunting with your pistol?"

"No way," I said. "I have a shotgun for hunting, but I only had my pistol on me. Actually, I wasn't even planning —"

I fidgeted around on my chair and looked at the school desk behind me, counted the screws.

"So you hunt Arctic foxes with your pistol?"

"No. You can't hunt with the pistol. I was just given it. And I'm not allowed to … with the gun, so that's why —" I felt angry. Was she trying to make me look silly?

"Kalmann, you're doing really well." Birna tried to catch my gaze. But I looked away. "Now tell me how you found the spot with the blood in the snow."

I sighed in resignation. This was going to take forever!

"I walked through the snow for ages, and then I found this dark red spot up by the Arctic Henge, and it looked as though someone had poured out an entire bucket of blood, and because I wanted to know whether it was really blood and whether it was fresh, I put my hand in it. I guess that's why I had blood-smeared hands."

"Very good, Kalmann, that's really helpful. And? Was the blood fresh?"

I shrugged. "It wasn't warm, but it wasn't properly cold either. The snowflakes melted into the blood."

Birna made a note.

"How big was the pool of blood?"

"About this big," I said, stretching my arms out wide and showing her the estimated size of the pool of blood.

"So about as big as this school desk behind you?"

I nodded.

"You're nodding," said Birna and chuckled.

"Yes!" I said and found myself laughing too. Clearly I did some things right.

"Did you notice anything else, up there?"

I shrugged.

"Did you run into anyone, or see a car, or were there any tracks in the snow?"

"Footprints," I said quickly.

"Footprints!" Birna was pleased with me. "And did you take a closer look at the footprints?"

I shrugged again. "I'm not completely sure they were footprints. It had snowed so much. Perhaps they weren't even footprints, but indentations beneath the snow."

"So the footprints were pretty much snowed over already, right?"

I nodded.

"Say yes or no."

"Yes!"

"How long did you stay up there?"

I peered up at the ceiling, cocking my head slightly, and thought back. Only every second bulb was working. But that wasn't so bad, because it was light outside, and the classroom wasn't being used nowadays anyway. "No idea," I said, and I meant it honestly.

"A few minutes?"

"No, longer."

"Half an hour?"

"Perhaps."

"An hour?"

"Mmm."

"Two hours?"

"No, not that long."

"So what did you do that whole time?"

"No idea. I just stood around and wasn't sure where to go."

"I see," said Birna. "That's all wonderful. But let's come back to the footprints, if they were in fact footprints. Where did they lead?"

"Down to the village."

"To the southern or northern part?"

"To the harbour."

"To the harbour?"

I nodded.

"I think so."

"Did you follow them?"

"No."

"And if they were footprints, were they from one person or more than one?"

"More than one," I said. "Maybe."

"I see," said Birna, making notes again.

"Perhaps —" I said, but hesitated.

Birna looked up from her notes. "Perhaps what?" she asked.

"Oh."

"Go on," Birna persisted. "There are no wrong answers here."

I took a deep breath. "Perhaps the prints were from a polar bear."

"A polar bear?" All of a sudden, Birna's voice no longer sounded friendly.

"Yes, a polar bear. It has four legs. So that would look like the footprints of two people."

"A polar bear!"

"It's possible. Sometimes polar bears come from Greenland to Iceland. They can swim across distances of three hundred kilometres, if not more... supposedly."

"You're right about that," said Birna, shaking her head back and forth. "But do you remember what happened in the summer? Two Frenchmen spotted a polar bear, up at the Hraunhafnar river, where they were angling, and they ran back to their car as quickly as their legs could carry them. Four kilometres! They called 112: Polar bear! And then we searched deep into the night, with the coastguard's helicopter and volunteers from the rescue service and everything. Nothing. Do you know what the Frenchman probably saw?" I didn't reply. "A sheep," Birna revealed, even though I knew the story.

"There aren't any sheep now," I mumbled.

"But you didn't see *anything*! Not even a sheep."

"But there did used to be polar bears in this region."

Birna laid the pen down on her notepad and sighed deeply. "So you really suspect that the footprints in the snow could have come from a polar bear."

I nodded.

"You're nodding!"

I looked at her, startled.

"It's like this," said Birna, leaning forward slightly. "If there's any suspicion that a polar bear is roaming around the Melrakkaslétta, we've got a problem, do you understand? I can't just send dozens of volunteers off to hunt for it."

I understood and looked down at my hands, feeling worried. "I'm sorry," I said.

"No!" said Birna, suddenly becoming friendlier again. "It's just… we simply have to be sure that there's no suspicion of that, do you understand?"

I nodded.

"How sure are you that it could have been a polar bear roaming around here, that it could even have eaten Róbert?"

"I'm not that sure," I admitted. "Not at all, actually."

Birna sighed and let a few seconds pass by. Her phone buzzed, dragging us out of the moment.

"Yes?… Five o'clock?… By seven o'clock it'll be dark… Okay… See you then." She tapped around on the phone for a while, probably sending an important message, then laid it back down in front of me on the desk and said: "Is there anything else you'd like to tell me?" I shook my head. Birna picked the phone back up, looked at the time and said: "At five o'clock my colleagues from Húsavík and Akureyri and some men and women from the rescue service are coming. Could you show us the location then?"

I nodded.

"Good. We'll come and pick you up. And if there's time, you can show me your gun collection too."

4
NADJA

Outside, I drank in the fresh air and let out a whoop of relief. It felt like I had spent two years in the classroom with Birna.

It had begun to snow again. The fresh snow reached my shins, and now there certainly wouldn't be anything left to see up at the Arctic Henge. Janitor Halldór had attached the snowplough to his pickup and was clearing the streets. All over Raufarhöfn, at that. It was his job to clear the snow. When necessary, he also drove the ambulance, and he was responsible for the schoolhouse and the town hall when something broke and so on. I imagined it being quite fun: clearing snow. But I wasn't allowed. Because to do that you need a driver's licence, even in Raufarhöfn. That's just the law.

Halldór never bothered with the pavements, so I walked along the middle of the road, which you're allowed to do in Raufarhöfn, because there's barely any traffic here. Only Kata, who's been doing the horse-breeding alone since the divorce, puttered past me slowly in her old Mitsubishi. She was taking her little dog out for a ride, as she so often did; he was sitting on her lap and staring happily over the steering wheel. It had been a long time since Kata had looked upon the world as contentedly as her lapdog, who was called Al Capone and didn't like being stroked, only cuddled.

Then I passed the poet's house. It stands between two vacant houses and is just as run-down, but stuffed full of junk and about a thousand books. It's the only house in the whole of Raufarhöfn with a small fir tree next to it. The house's occupant, Bragi, runs the village library, but lives off social support. The library is only open on Wednesdays, from four until five. That's been the case ever since I was a kid. Bragi used to write poems, though I've never read one of them in my life. As I walked past his house, I noticed him, Bragi, the poet, but he didn't notice me. He was standing at the window, holding a coffee cup in his hand and thinking. Meditating, perhaps. Or making a poem in his head. Today his fingernails were painted red. Only when I waved did he look up, and raise his coffee cup as though he were toasting me, but then he turned around and disappeared behind a pile of books, although I couldn't see that clearly, because there wasn't a single light on in his house, so the living room window reflected the snowy street. And me. I glanced at my reflection briefly, pulled my gun holster higher and my belly in, and walked on.

At the filling station there were two off-road super jeeps from the rescue service, a nineteen-seater minibus and some private cars which certainly didn't belong to Raufarhöfn. Had Jens opened the store to mark the occasion? The filling station building, after all, had remained closed since Jens retired. The pump had stayed in operation, though, because you could fill up even without Jens: all you needed was a bank card and an empty tank. Screenwash, engine oil, lottery cards, soft-serve ice cream and dried fish – those you had to procure elsewhere. But today someone seemed to have opened the filling station and fired up the hot dog grill, because the building was full to the rafters with hot dog-munching and coffee-slurping rescue workers, and I would have liked to pop my head in, but there were too many strangers for me and Jens was nowhere to be seen. The people must have only just arrived; they were chatting eagerly, and now and again someone laughed. When they saw me standing outside, they stopped talking and gave me questioning looks. I walked on.

At the Hotel Arctica, Nadja was in front of the side entrance, smoking a cigarette. With one trembling arm pressed against her stomach, she hopped from one leg to the other. For sure she didn't want to stay outside long, just long enough for a smoke, because she was wearing neither a winter coat nor a woollen hat nor gloves. She was wearing her work gear: black leggings and a black T-shirt with the silhouette and name of the hotel. Smokers aren't usually properly dressed when they smoke. That must be how things are. But I'm not sure. I've never smoked.

Nadja was a beautiful woman. I would even go so far as to say she was the most beautiful woman in all of Raufarhöfn. But she wasn't Icelandic, and therefore the most beautiful Icelandic woman in Raufarhöfn was maybe Hafdís, even though she was almost old now. Ever since I had bumped into Nadja out at sea, she'd always been nice to me. Before that she had barely paid attention to me. Now it was different, and that's why she waved me over.

"Kalmann!" she cried. "So much snow! Why? Where is spring?" She laughed, shivered and took a drag of her cigarette.

I laughed too. "That's Iceland," I said.

"Come here!" she called, blowing the smoke sideways into the air. I obeyed. If a beautiful woman calls you over, you don't just walk on. You go over. "How's things?" she asked.

"Great!" I said. Women like men who are cheerful. Nói told me that.

"It's chaos here," said Nadja. "Work, work, always cleaning, always cooking. And where is boss? Just disappeared? Fallen drunk into sea, for sure." Nadja looked at me and took another drag on her cigarette. "You not cold?"

"No way," I replied. "But you cold!"

"Yes, I outside only few minutes. In Iceland, can't smoke in building. Or police come."

"Watch out, the police are here in the village!" I said, but I was able to immediately reassure her: "Don't worry, Birna has more important work to do." I tried to choose simple words so she could understand me.

"You spoken with police?" she asked me.

I nodded and pointed at the schoolhouse. "There. A policewoman from Reykjavík is in school. Because Róbert disappeared."

"Did you tell about blood in snow?"

I was stunned. How did Nadja know about the blood? Well, I guess I had told Hafdís, after all, and Hafdís had told Birna, but perhaps not only her, and that's why now everyone in Raufarhöfn knew about it.

"Yes," I said, as though I wasn't at all surprised. "I'm helping the police with the missing person case."

"You sheriff or something?" Nadja laughed at me, and I blushed, because she was so beautiful. "Did you see footprints near blood?"

"Correctamundo," I confirmed. "From people or from a polar bear."

"Polar bear? You crazy? You trying to scare me?" She wasn't laughing any more.

"I'm not crazy," I said.

"Is polar bear here?" Nadja looked around fearfully.

I laughed, because I wasn't afraid of polar bears. "You can never be too careful!" I looked at her mischievously but then burst out laughing.

"You pulling my leg!" she said, slapping her palm against my chest. She laughed too. The world was okay. Nadja had never touched me before. Perhaps this whole thing wasn't so bad after all. Nadja took one last drag on her cigarette, threw the butt into the snow and stubbed it out with the tip of her foot.

"Bad, what happens," she said, shivering all over her body now. "Róbert perhaps eaten by polar bear. Perhaps fallen drunk into sea." She was trembling all over. If she had been my wife, I would have hugged her and pulled her close to me.

"You have to go into the warm," I said, "otherwise you'll become a snowman! Or a beautiful snowwoman!"

She laughed. "You are funny, Kalmann." And before she went into the hotel, she said: "You tell me if something new in the case about blood, yes?"

I nodded, even though I hadn't completely understood what she meant. But I didn't want to unnerve her, perhaps she had just got her words mixed up, it happens. At least she had a better command of our language than the other three Lithuanians who lived in Raufarhöfn. Unfortunately, one of these Lithuanians was her boyfriend, and he had an unbelievably well-toned body, so he wasn't to be messed with. He worked with her in the hotel, and so did the other two Lithuanians, who were also a couple. But Nadja was the only one I knew well, because she was the only one you could talk to. If she had been my wife, I would have done all I could to learn Lithuanian. And perhaps I would even have visited her homeland. With her, of course. She would have known exactly which flight and which bus you had to take. She would have taken me home with her and introduced me to her parents. She would have grown up on one of those typical Eastern European farms, with chickens and pigs that run around freely, that's how I imagined it. And her wrinkly grandmother would have spent the whole day sitting on a crooked bench in front of the house. And her father would have asked me to help him. Because to mark the occasion – the occasion being me – a goat would have to be slaughtered, and Nadja's father would probably have wanted to see whether I was a proper man. And I would have been, because I was good at that kind of thing, even though I had never slaughtered a goat before, but I had slaughtered many other animals, so no reason to worry. Essentially, we all consist of flesh, bones, innards and lots of blood. I can look at blood and I know my way around a knife, and that's why I would surely have been welcome in Lithuania.

I continued on my way. The snowplough came back, so I crossed over to the other side of the street. Halldór gave me an almost imperceptible wave, lifting only his index finger. He looked moody, as usual, as though the snow was annoying him. He was somebody who got annoyed about everything, he always found fault with everyone, and in such a way that you ended up getting annoyed too.

I waved back.

My neighbour Elínborg was shovelling snow from her driveway. Her car engine hummed away, little clouds of exhaust puffed out, and yet the car was still covered with a thick layer of snow. Elínborg noticed me – she noticed everyone who passed by her house – and paused. I wondered where she was going in this weather; the road to Kópasker or across the Melrakkaslétta was sure to be almost impassable.

"Do you have to go somewhere?" I asked.

"For the love of God," answered Elínborg, wheezing. "In this weather? That would be foolish."

"But why is the engine on?"

"Don't you see? I'm clearing the snow off the car, and it's easier when the car's warm."

I didn't have a car. I didn't know these tricks, but I made a mental note in case I ever got a car. It would be a Volkswagen. You can rely on the Germans. But certainly not an electric car. That's what Nói says too. He says that between the Germans, the Japanese, the French and the Americans, the Germans come off best. At least where cars are concerned. With women, it's different. On balance, Asian women are supposed to be the best lovers. But I knew as little about women as Elínborg did about cars. Because under the thick layer of snow was a Nissan Pixo, and Nói said this car was a bad joke.

"Where have you been?" asked Elínborg. She used to work at the Íslandsbanki, until the branch closed, and she took early retirement when her husband got sick with cancer.

"I was at the schoolhouse," I answered truthfully.

"With the police?"

I nodded. "I'm helping Birna with the missing person case."

"Birna is the detective's name? You don't say. Have you already showed her the pool of blood?"

I said no.

"Did you notice anything else up there? Perhaps a knife or an item of clothing? Bullet casings?"

"The snow covered everything," I said.

"What a stroke of luck for the murderer," said Elínborg.

"I don't think Róbert was murdered up there," I said.

"Oh no? And why not?"

"The blood might be from an animal."

"And what animal might that be, Kalli minn?"

I shrugged. "Perhaps someone shot a reindeer."

"Nonsense! It would be the first time a reindeer had come up here."

"Perhaps a sheep. Or a polar bear."

"A polar bear? Are you serious? Are you suggesting Róbert was eaten by a polar bear?"

I shrugged, and Elínborg stared into the snow for a while. Perhaps she was imagining Róbert being torn to pieces by a polar bear. Was she smiling? Eventually she said: "It would be nature's justice." She went back to shovelling the snow, then paused again and, with a shake of her head, said: "And yet a polar bear would be the last thing that crook needed to be afraid of."

I said nothing. I wanted to get home, because soon the search team would be picking me up. I wanted something to eat, and I had to go to the bathroom. Rather urgently, in fact.

"One thing's for sure," said Elínborg, looking at me. "Something's not right. I mean, how has Róbert been able to keep the hotel going for so long? It was making a loss from day one. Hardly any tourists come up here! And four employees, to boot?"

"Five," I said. "The Lithuanians and Óttar."

"Óttar the Pressure Cooker! Of course. I almost forgot about him. He can't keep the business going on his catch quota alone. At least Óttar isn't drinking his bar dry any more. But then he already ran out of money with the Arctic Henge. And we all contributed to the project!"

"I didn't," I said.

"I did!" said Elínborg. "Twenty thousand krona, if you please!"

My eyes widened. "That's a lot of money," I said.

Elínborg waved her arm dismissively. "No, it's not a lot of money. A project like that costs a hundred or thousand times that."

"But it's still a lot of money."

"Well, if you just dump it up there in the dirt, then yes!" Elínborg loaded snow onto the shovel. She was really strong. "I don't even want to know how much money others lost. And the pile of stones still isn't ready. And then his blood gets found close by. There has to be some kind of —"

"Hey, Elínborg," I interrupted her. "I have to go to the bathroom."

"Oh!" cried Elínborg.

"Bless, bless," I said, and ran off. There was a lot of space between our two houses, because one of the British barracks used to be located here.

"How's your grandfather doing?" Elínborg called after me, but I didn't turn around, I hid myself away in my little house, closed the door and listened. Elínborg didn't follow me. I hung my jacket, my cowboy hat and my gun belt on the coat hooks. A lot of snow fell from the brim of my hat onto the floor. I squashed the snow together and threw it into the toilet bowl. Grandfather didn't want the entranceway to get wet and the floorboards to be ruined.

It was almost April already, but up here we were still in the depths of winter. That didn't bother me. I like snow, and even winter storms. Ever since I was able to think, I've felt comfortable in the snow. I never get cold. I'm hot-blooded. I never got cold as a kid either. Quite the opposite. I was always too warm. Much to the adults' outrage, I usually ran around in a T-shirt. They didn't want me to get sick, but I didn't care. I always wondered what was so bad about being sick, because you didn't have to go to school, you could spend the whole day watching TV and then get looked after by your mum in the evening. Sometimes I even forgot it was cold outside, for example when we had snowball fights – that is, until I could no longer feel my hands. I was really good at snowball fights. I had strong arms. I could throw powerfully and far, and it didn't bother me when the snow dripped down my neck onto my back. It only made me wilder, more hot-blooded, and I roared like a Viking and felt like one too, which is why sometimes I wasn't allowed to join in any more, because we no longer live in Viking times. I wasn't allowed to beat up my schoolmates, the teachers said. So then I would simply stand on the sidelines and throw the snowballs as high and straight into the air as I could, so that they fell back down on my face as I gazed up at the sky. I cheered so loudly that my classmates got scared. Those cowards. Apart from Dagbjört, none of them live in Raufarhöfn any more. I wish I'd had a teacher like Dagbjört. She was sure to be much better at it than the teachers who taught me. And if there had been fewer pupils back then too, I might have had friends, because when there are only a few kids, like now, everyone's allowed to join in.

I peed on the snow in the toilet bowl and thought about snowball fights. Then, in the kitchen, I made myself a few Nutella sandwiches. My house is a small, old house, painted white, with a red corrugated sheet roof, over a century old, one of the oldest houses in Raufarhöfn even; it has a small, low entranceway with a tiny kitchen alongside, a living room with a supporting column in the middle that's decorated with carvings, a tiny bathroom, and a steep flight of stairs leading into the attic, where there are two bedrooms. My grandmother died when I was in my mother's stomach and living with her in Keflavík, she died in front of the TV, in the middle of an evening programme. She just stayed sitting there, even though she was no longer watching. It took a while for Grandfather to realize, because when someone's sitting in front of the TV, it's kind of hard to say whether they're alive or dead. So I had never met my grandmother, but I've heard that she liked to work and only ever cooked the same three dishes: broiled fish with potatoes, fish balls with potatoes, or lamb soup with carrots, turnips and potatoes. But perhaps that's why we moved to the north to live with Grandfather, so that he wouldn't be so alone and so that my mother wouldn't be so alone and so that I wouldn't be so alone with my mother. I shared the larger attic bedroom with her until I was fourteen. She worked in the cold-store warehouse until it closed down because of the quota distribution, but by then I was old enough already, and so my mother moved to Akureyri and studied, became a nurse and didn't have to work in the fishing industry any more. Then I lived here alone with Grandfather for quite a while, until he was put in a care home in Húsavík, where people like him have to go, even though he didn't know why he had to go there, and so didn't want to go at all, and even got kind of loud when he was picked up, he swore and spat, and even tried to bite the men, until they realized I was up in my room beating my face black and blue. Not that it changed anything. They took Grandfather away with them. Since then, I've lived here pretty much alone. And I want to die here too.

I usually fell asleep in front of the TV. If you have no one, there's no one to get bothered by it. But if I had a wife, we would have watched movies together, brushed our teeth together and gone to sleep in the bedroom upstairs together. That's how couples do it.

Whenever someone moved around in the attic room, the house creaked. Sometimes I woke up because of it, for example if I turned over in my sleep. Before, when there were still three of us, it often creaked, but now that I was completely alone, every creak gave me a fright. Perhaps that's why I preferred to fall asleep on the couch. I would lay down across it, put my head on the Pamela Anderson cushion, spread my grandmother's crocheted blanket over me and watch my favourite shows: *The Biggest Loser* and *The Bachelor*. Sometimes I imagined that I was the bachelor and able to choose the most beautiful of the twenty-five candidates. I would always give her the rose first, in every single ceremony, and I would also immediately know which woman I'd like best, because I always know immediately. (But in my imagination she looked just as pretty as Nadja.) Right at the end of the show, during the interviews, I would say that I'd known from the beginning that she was the only one for me and that we could have made the show much shorter, and everyone would laugh for sure, and after we'd got married and were finally here in the little house, I would suggest that we watch the entire series, and it would be proof that I'd only made out with her and messed about in the hot tub with her, in other words, the most beautiful proof of love that a man can offer a woman. Our relationship would last, because it would be based upon the foundation of the series. All the other *Bachelor* couples split up sooner or later, because the bachelor messed around with everyone at the same time. And who wants someone like that! Not me. If I had a wife that wonderful, who wanted me too, I wouldn't treat her like that. And we would have a good life, here in the little house, and we would watch the *Tonight Show* with the famous Hollywood actors, or repeats of *CSI: Miami* and *CSI: Vegas* and would then perhaps even fall asleep on the couch. That's romance.

Sometimes I woke up again after midnight because I had to pee, and then I would turn off the TV and go up to bed in the attic room. And the bed was always cold.

5

ARNÓR

I waited for a knock at the door, waited by the window, looked down towards the harbour, where Siggi was mooring his cutter. I watched as he conversed with harbour master Sæmundur, but I didn't know what they were talking about. Then I cleared away a few pizza boxes, flattened some cola cans and put them in a plastic bag. For cans and PET bottles, I could get cash back if I returned them to the store. I then mostly used it to buy myself something sweet. Then I had earned it. I folded the blanket on the couch, brushed crumbs off it, straightened the cushions, really got into it. My mother would have been pleased with me.

Then I took a break. Siggi was unloading his cutter. Two whole bulk containers full of lumpfish. These fish can only be caught in spring, from the twentieth of March, and only for two months. It's easy then, because the lumpfish come to spawn in the coastal water of the fjords and bays. You have to stretch the nets across the seabed, because the fish swim along the bottom. Siggi was sure to be happy now, even if he didn't let it show. He salted the lumpfish caviar himself, filled little glasses with it and called it Viking Caviar. He sold it all to China, and got a lot of money for it. I didn't know how much. But it was sure to be a lot.

I sat down at my laptop and called Nói on Messenger. He answered right away, because he spent the days mostly at home on his computer because of his health issues. The nights, too. He was actually kind of strange. He didn't want to be seen. It's really true: I had never seen his face! I didn't know what he looked like. The camera was always pointed at his sweater, and it was usually the same brown Gandalf sweater with the same quote: *You Shall Not Pass!* His profile picture was of this cheerful horse's head, wearing sunglasses and smoking a cigarette. On Facebook, he was a young Arnold Schwarzenegger. There were no photos of him. Nói was a computer genius and a pro gamer. He said he earned more money than his parents but blew it all on whiskey, women and cars. I suspected he didn't always tell the truth, though, because he was always at home, and he'd never visited me either, even though he allegedly owned numerous cars. I mean, he could have easily driven up to the north. He said he could do the six hundred and nine kilometres to Raufarhöfn in under seven hours, but that the roads up here were bad, and he didn't want to inflict that on any car. Nói was only nineteen years old, fourteen years younger than me, but he was much smarter, he knew all kinds of things, and if there was something he didn't know, he asked the internet. It even knows what your kids would look like if you had them with Lady Gaga or Elsa from *Frozen*. Nói said that when artificial intelligence gets plugged into the internet, that'll be it for humanity. We'll no longer be needed. He said that in a few years' time, men won't be needed any more. We'll be replaced by machines, and the women will impregnate themselves, or maybe using sex machines.

Nói never said hello. His *You Shall Not Pass* sweater simply appeared on my screen, and then he was there. He was usually immersed in a computer game, and sometimes paused mid-conversation because he had to gun someone down, but he always had time for me. He was my best friend.

"Mr N!" I said, as I always did.

"The sheriff is back in town!" he replied.

"You motherfucker!" I said.

"And? Who was it?"

"Who was what?" I asked.

"Did you catch the murderer?"

"The murderer?"

"Tell me who bumped off the hotel owner!"

"How do you know —"

"The internet, baby! Are there any suspects?"

"What?"

Nói was probably pulling my leg! But he continued to fire questions at me. He wouldn't let up.

"Do you lot have a gardener there in Raufarhöfn?"

"Here? I don't know, perhaps in summer…"

"It's always the gardener."

"Oh, right. I don't think we have a gardener. I mean, nothing grows here."

"Do you have a janitor?"

"For the schoolhouse, yes."

"Suspect number one."

"Halldór? But —"

"Is there a cook?"

I paused. "Óttar," I said. "He's the hotel cook, but because he used to be a ship's cook and beat up a few people on board, everyone calls him Óttar the Pressure Cooker."

"Now we're getting somewhere!"

"What?"

"You'll have to follow him."

"Why me?"

"This is your chance, boy! You're always complaining that there aren't any chicks in Raufarhöfn. If you solve the case, you're the hero! A national treasure. Women will throw themselves at your feet!"

"You think so?"

"I know so!"

My heart beat faster. Almost a little too fast, because the thought of national fame and women throwing themselves at my feet was too much. I mean, *one* woman would've been enough for me.

"Don't worry. I can help you. I can google the possible suspects if you like. But unfortunately, I can't get any information through illegal means. The Dark Web is off limits, my friend! If they catch me hacking again, I'm done for. They'll pull the plug."

"Oh, right."

"Lights out, see?"

"No."

"Right. Give me his full name."

"The Pressure Cooker? All I know is that he's called Óttar and he's almost two metres tall."

"No problem. Where does he live?"

"Mýrarbraut."

"House number?"

"Hm. I'm not completely sure. Seven or eleven."

"What colour's the roof?"

"Blue."

"Óttar Ólason. Mýrarbraut number four."

"That's right!" I was flabbergasted. Nói was a genius.

"So why didn't you say so to start with?"

"I don't know, I… I just didn't —"

Nói sighed loudly. "What else do you know about him?"

"You mean, what he looks like?"

"Correctamundo."

I thought for a moment. "He's tall, and kind of stocky, but not fat. He used to be an alcoholic, but now he just drinks too much coffee. And he doesn't get so angry at people any more. But he still smokes. And you can hear that when he talks."

"Very good. Perhaps we'll find cigarette butts at the crime scene."

"Cigarette butts?"

"Keep going."

I thought some more. This felt pretty damn exciting! "He has a girlfriend from Thailand, and she only just comes up to his chest."

"I bet she's good at blow jobs."

"I don't know. Maybe they're married."

"Believe me, Kalli. They're married."

"Why?"

"Because otherwise the doll wouldn't be allowed to stay in Iceland!"

"Oh, right."

"How old is he?"

"About fifty."

"Does he drive a car?"

"Yes, a Toyota Land Cruiser. And he has a tiny cutter that he sometimes goes fishing in, and then he processes the catch in the hotel, even though you're not actually allowed to do that."

"So he knows how to break the law and how to cut throats," commented Nói. "He could be our man. Any kids?"

"No."

"Impotent."

"What?"

"He can't make babies."

"Or his wife can't," I suggested.

"I don't believe that. If that were the case, he would've had babies with some other bitch ages ago. Sailors fuck non-stop when they're on dry land. And now he's got himself an Asian sex slave. But he's shooting blanks, mister!"

"She's actually really nice. Her name is Ling."

"This Pressure Cooker is a manipulative pig."

"What? I think Ling's pretty happy in Raufarhöfn, she works in the kindergarten and makes lunch for the kids. Sometimes Thai food, it's really delicious. And she speaks good Icelandic too."

"Kalmann! Slow down! How do you know her food is delicious?"

"They sometimes let me eat at the school."

"Okay. Weird, but okay. What else do you know?"

I wondered whether it was smart to reveal any further details. After all, I saw no reason to blacken the Pressure Cooker's name. Why would he have wanted to do away with his employer?

"Hey, Nói," I said carefully. "I don't think Óttar is the murderer."

"Belief has nothing to do with police work. We're constructing a profile here, that's what it's called. We're *sketching* a profile, coming up with a theory, trying to find out where the Pressure Cooker was around the time the hotel owner disappeared. And if he actually could be guilty, we try to prove his innocence, and if we can't, the Pressure Cooker is definitely guilty."

That sounded sensible, but exhausting, and even though I wasn't completely following Nói, I said:

"I understand."

"But we won't only do it with him, we'll do it with everyone that comes under suspicion, everyone who wanted to see the hotel owner dead."

"That'll be a lot of work," I sighed. I remembered Elínborg's words: a polar bear was the last thing Róbert needed to be afraid of.

There was a knock at the door. "I have to go!" I cried, clapping Nói shut.

I listened intently, looked at the clock. Quarter past five. I knew exactly who was knocking on my door. Birna, probably. Or the rescue service. Or perhaps other police officers. So I didn't know after all, and that's why I got nervous.

Another knock. I groaned so loudly that it could be heard outside for sure. Then I trudged over to the door and opened it, a sulky expression on my face. It wasn't Birna who'd knocked on the door; it was Arnór, who was wearing red and blue rescue service overalls and had lifted his hand to knock again but now lowered it. We knew each other from our school days, but he now lived in Húsavík and had a pretty wife and three little children. The perfect life. I had run into him and his family in Húsavík on the last national holiday. He'd said hello, and I had stared at his wife, because she was really beautiful. The lucky devil. He had a well-groomed red beard, and he took tourists out to sea, whale watching.

"Hello, Kalmann, how are you? Long time no see! Aren't you coming?"

I sighed. "I am," I said. "But first I have to go to the bathroom." I didn't have to, though. I left Arnór standing in the entrance but could hear him talking to someone on the phone: Yes, I was at home, I heard him say, and then he explained where my house was located. I got even more nervous and had to pee a little after all.

Arnór was still standing outside the door as I came out of the bathroom doing up my fly. He watched me as I got ready, commentating. When I put on the cowboy hat, for example, he said that a woollen hat would be more appropriate, because it was damn cold up there. I ignored him and put on my holster, and Arnór said we were going on a missing person search, not a manhunt, but I pretended I hadn't heard him. I pulled on my jacket, the sheriff's badge still affixed to the chest. Arnór looked at me as though he somehow wasn't sure whether he should take me along, but eventually he nodded, passed me a yellow high-visibility vest and said: "Put this on! We don't want to lose you."

Outside, a hell of a jeep with tyres as big as a small child roared up and swung to a halt alongside us. The snowflakes were melting on the windows, so it was nice and warm inside the jeep, too warm in fact, as I established once I climbed into the back seat, happy I hadn't put on a woollen hat. One always has to listen to one's inner voice. And not to Arnór.

Sitting at the wheel was a man I didn't know. As a rule, I don't tend to like people I don't know. Apart from women. But that's different. Because you have to like them, that's nature. Continuation of the species. The stranger glanced at me as I belted myself in on the back seat.

I have a superpower. I notice when people glance at one another, and I can read those glances. When I meet someone I've never met before, these kinds of glances always get exchanged. But I've learned to ignore them. Sometimes people look at me, stare at me in this completely backward way, and then I can't help but grin, even though I don't want to grin, but I do, and sometimes someone or other says: "Why is he grinning like that?" And then someone else says that it's just how I am, or someone defends me, says that I'm okay, and it's always the people from Raufarhöfn who defend me, because people know me here, here I'm somebody.

"The shooter isn't loaded," Arnór mumbled into his red beard, and the stranger pulled a face, shook his head and said, in this tone, as though he were talking to himself: "Welcome to Raufarhöfn!" And yet he wasn't even from Raufarhöfn. People can't welcome themselves somewhere, that doesn't work. That's how things are.

The stranger had huge muscles and a broad neck. He was what people call a muscle mountain. The opposite of Nói, my best friend. For sure the muscle mountain could have lifted the jeep and balanced it over his head, but now he was struggling to get it into four-wheel drive. He cursed. But eventually he managed it, and the jeep jolted a little and the four-wheel drive was engaged, and only then did the muscle mountain turn around to me and stretch out his hand, without saying his name. He had a tattoo on his forearm, but I only saw it up to the sleeve.

I didn't react, just stared at his hand and tattoo.

"Leave it," said Arnór.

The muscle mountain made a thumbs-up sign and asked, very casually:

"So, you found the pool of blood?"

I nodded and looked out of the window.

"What a coincidence! Can you take us there?"

"Child's play," I said. "It's not that far."

"Very good. Where to then, Captain?"

"It's just up the hill here, but first you have to go down to the village and turn left by the sign."

The muscle mountain nodded, engaged first gear and drove off, following the direction of my finger. Perhaps he wasn't as arrogant as I'd first thought. I almost wished the location was further away, not just a kilometre but ten, so we could have driven for longer and I could have guided the whole rescue service across the high plain. It wasn't long before we arrived, not even five minutes actually, and there were lots of people already there, standing around in the snow and looking at the stone structure, some from the rescue service, some in police uniform, and I almost got a bit dizzy, because I hardly knew anyone, but when I spotted Birna among the people I was relieved, firstly because I knew her, and secondly because she was a woman.

But the people had clearly found the pool of blood without me, and had even cordoned off the location with yellow plastic tape. It fluttered in the wind, holding defiantly on to the tiny posts. Two people in white suits were squatting down, poking around in the snow, taking samples or something. Alongside them stood a windowless white delivery van.

"Hello, everyone!" called Arnór, at which practically everyone gathered around him. "Come here!" he said, pulling me alongside him.

The wind was blowing really cold, and I held on tightly to my cowboy hat.

"May I introduce: Kalmann. The Sheriff of Raufarhöfn." He clapped me firmly on the shoulder. Arnór was bigger than me. And he was better looking. For sure everyone liked him. If you look like Arnór does, everyone likes you. "No one knows this terrain like our Kalmann. He grew up here. He knows every fox den and every mound of grass. Perhaps some of you still remember his grandfather,

Óðinn." Some nodded. "Kalmann is a hunter and shark catcher, like Óðinn was back in the day. Anyone in need of a good piece of hákarl should ask Kalmann. Isn't that right, Kalmann?" Arnór looked at me and waited for an answer, but I stood there as though I'd turned to stone. Was I supposed to provide them all with hákarl? I would have to set up more longlines! My blood was rushing so loudly in my ears that before long I couldn't even hear what Arnór was saying about me, and so I positioned myself behind him, moving discreetly as though I were trying to get a little shelter from the wind, and there really was shelter from the wind, so I didn't have to hold onto my hat any more. But people laughed, and Arnór wouldn't let it go, he turned around to me and said: "There's no need to be shy, they won't bite, even if they look like they will!" He put his arm around my shoulders and pulled me back alongside him. His touch was unpleasant. Like an anaconda. He wasn't even talking about me any more but instead about how we would organize the search, and Birna took over, coming to stand on the other side of me, so that I was completely hemmed in and probably grinning like the village idiot. Birna said something about circles, a radius, a grid, the Arctic Henge monument, a section of coast, until darkness, snowfall and so on. But then Arnór turned to me unexpectedly and asked loudly, so that everyone could hear, if I had any other suggestions, but I didn't have any other suggestions, and at that moment I wasn't even sure what had been suggested so far, but Arnór said I should take my time thinking about it, so I felt like I had to say something in order to free myself from the stranglehold, and suddenly I knew what I had to say.

"Watch out for polar bears," I mumbled.

"What?" asked Arnór.

"Watch out for polar bears!" I said.

"Shit!" said Birna with a grimace.

Everyone apart from her laughed, even though I hadn't made a joke. But I was used to that. Sometimes people laughed even though I hadn't said anything funny. I laughed too, but then a man I didn't know asked:

"Have polar bears been here before?"

"You bet!" I cried.

The laughter stopped dead. Everyone was listening now.

"Really?" asked Arnór, looking at me with a frown. "When was that?"

"I can't remember," I said, and then someone laughed again, and I tried to remember the last time a polar bear had roamed the Melrakkaslétta.

"It was last summer," said the muscle mountain. He was laughing so much that his neck was becoming even thicker. "When those two Frenchmen saw a sheep for the first time!"

Everyone laughed. And loudly too, even Birna. But I was still thinking hard, because I was almost completely sure that polar bears had once been sighted on the Melrakkaslétta.

"Kalmann," said Arnór, "you were joking, weren't you?"

I looked at him, then at Birna, then back at Arnór again, and eventually I shrugged. "No reason to worry," I mumbled.

Birna came to my aid. "I think the possibility that there's a polar bear roaming around up here is a million to one, so…" She clapped her hands together. But Arnór was still curious.

"What made you even think of it?"

I shrugged again. "The tracks I saw could have been from a polar bear. And Róbert has disappeared, so that's why."

"We don't even yet know for sure whether the blood in the snow is Róbert's," Birna interjected, sounding really impatient now.

It was as though everyone was holding their breath.

"Complete hogwash," blurted out the muscle mountain, and he stomped back to his jeep. Birna and Arnór exchanged glances. Arnór was stroking his beard, because he was thinking.

"It's your decision."

"We'll start the search!" said Birna, and Arnór nodded and called out: "Right then, let's go!"

The search party kicked into motion; everyone knew what was to be done. I heard someone say that we would end up wishing my toy gun was loaded.

Birna got into the passenger seat of the jeep, and I watched her until it disappeared into the snowdrifts. Meanwhile, Arnór was still standing next to me, and it gradually went quiet.

"Kalmann, this might sound like a strange question, but where would you hide a corpse up here?"

I didn't think it was a strange question. It was very logical, in fact. You had to put yourself into the mind of a murderer to track them down.

"Fish food," I answered, pointing out to sea.

Arnór nodded, as though I had answered his question correctly. "Fish food," he echoed.

We trudged down the direct path to the sea, past the harbour and church, making our way along the coast of the peninsula from the cemetery to the lighthouse, and every few metres we looked over the cliff, which jutted further and further out of the sea the closer we came to the lighthouse. Beneath us, the waves foamed against the black rocks. If

Róbert had fallen over the cliff, the waves of the incoming tide would have washed him away from the rocks and carried him out to sea. The fulmars flew along the cliffs in a kind of bored manner, using the upwind, letting themselves be carried effortlessly, circling again and again. They could have told us whether they'd seen Róbert. How simple life would be if we could converse with animals. Although perhaps then life would be even more complicated, because the animals would complain about us humans.

We looked around by the lighthouse too, peered over to the islet which protruded out of the foaming sea spray, and saw no Róbert there either.

"Beautiful, the cormorants," said Arnór, but I just nodded. I mean, they're always there.

We went further along the cliff, but I was kind of tired now and no longer looking properly, instead just walking behind Arnór, and when he asked whether we should take a look around the cemetery, I simply shrugged. We did end up taking quite a close look at the cemetery, but everything seemed untouched, and now I understood why Arnór had wanted to look at the cemetery, because someone could have buried Róbert, and if so, it might have been evident. It was a pretty good idea, one I wouldn't have thought of; burying a murder victim in the cemetery. I mean, it's the least conspicuous place for a corpse to be. But at this time of year it would have been a difficult undertaking, because the ground was still frozen, and you would have needed a little digger. So, not such a good idea after all.

By the time we arrived in the harbour, I was exhausted already. But luckily we didn't have to search the harbour, because a good dozen women and men from the rescue service were there looking under every jetty and in every old fish-processing hall. Hafdís and Sæmundur were there too, attempting to locate the owners of the buildings and open the locked doors. Sæmundur was battling with a bunch of keys. My hall was never locked, because I needed it, and it was empty apart from my stuff. Now the wind changed and a stiff breeze blew off the sea directly into the harbour, so that I had to grip onto my cowboy hat again and my ears got really cold. The wind whirled the snow about between the rusty halls, piling up drifts, the snowflakes dancing in all directions.

"I'm cold," I said to Arnór. He looked at me for a while, then said he wanted to walk along the sea to the school with me.

When we finally got there, he made a few phone calls, and because it was almost dark, he finally called off the search mission. "Touch base soon!" he called after me, but I had already turned round.

Sometimes I watched crime shows. The murderer is usually the person you'd least suspect. Someone like Arnór. Perhaps I would ask Nói to find out a bit more about him.

Right where Halldór had piled up a mound of snow, the children were still playing, even though it was now completely dark. They slid down on their behinds from top to bottom and dug little caves in the mound. Halldór was standing nearby with his pickup truck, shaking snow off his shovel.

"Children!" he shouted grumpily. "Don't push all the snow back into the street!"

"We won't!" the children cried back, saluting and laughing. Then they pounded me with snowballs. An ambush! Everyone against me, me against everyone. I didn't need to be asked twice. I certainly had enough strength to inflict a torrent of snowballs on the kids, and they retreated into their caves, screaming. Halldór shook his head, but didn't say anything. The children ventured another counter-attack, although it wasn't to be taken seriously, because they had run out of steam. But I stayed another few minutes and let them – from the oldest to the youngest – hold my Mauser. I told them that there might be a polar bear roaming around up there, that we couldn't rule it out, and the children got really excited and not at all scared. Óli said that he would shoot the polar bear in the head, like that, pow, but before he could press the trigger, I took the gun out of his hand and showed him how to hold it properly, not with both hands like American policemen in the movies, but in one hand, arm outstretched, feet shoulder-width apart. Like that. And I explained that you don't aim at the head, but at the heart, because you'd have to shoot very precisely to hit the head, the risk of missing is too great, you would only hurt the animal, shoot away its jaw or something. Then the animal would run away and live until it died of hunger or thirst. Because without a jaw you can't eat. That's just the way it is. And that would be animal torture.

The children listened to me open-mouthed. I aimed at Arnór, who was now standing by Halldór's pickup, talking to him with his back to us, and I said: "Bang."

6
RÓBERT MCKENZIE

I wondered who was sad about Róbert's disappearance – besides his daughter, Dagbjört. She was sure to be really sad; Róbert was her father after all, and she his only daughter, and when someone in your family dies, you're sad, that's just how it is. That's kinship. If my father were to die in America, I would feel it, and perhaps even be sad, without knowing about his death. As I hadn't seen Dagbjört at the schoolhouse, I presumed she had gone home, cried, stuffed herself with chocolate cake and watched romantic movies. If she had been in the schoolhouse, she would have said hello for sure, because she was always pleased to see me. Always.

I was thinking about Róbert a lot, but I didn't really know that much about him. Only that he had a few siblings, who didn't live in Raufarhöfn. His ex-wife had moved away too, but I didn't know where to, or why they had divorced. Nor did I know whether Róbert had a new wife or what his favourite TV programme and favourite food was. Perhaps there would soon be a memorial or burial service, and then all the people who had known Róbert would turn up, and you would see who was sad and who wasn't. This was actually a good trick for getting wise to a murderer. So I hoped that Birna would also think to come to the memorial.

I wasn't. Sad, I mean. Sometimes I was sad because Grandfather was so old that he could die at any moment.

And sometimes because my mother was no longer here, or because I didn't have a wife. But I wasn't sad about Róbert's disappearance. No, not a bit. Not even in the slightest.

Even though Róbert McKenzie had an extraordinary reputation and called the shots, he was a small man, one you could easily overlook. He was smaller than Grandfather, smaller than Sæmundur and smaller than Hafdís, even. Perhaps he had Celtic forefathers. The Celts were smaller than the Vikings. He was kind of wiry and not in the least bit fat. He always made such quick movements, was always clean-shaven, with well-groomed hair, and wore glasses with UV-reactive lenses; if the sun suddenly peeked out from between the clouds, he didn't have to put on sunglasses. A brilliant idea, really. Nobody else in Raufarhöfn wore glasses like that. Róbert was always in a hurry, always on the go, always on the ball, and I didn't like him. And I don't think he liked me either. No matter where Róbert McKenzie went, he was always the boss. If he wanted, he could shut down Raufarhöfn with a simple snap of his fingers. He was the king of Raufarhöfn. That's what Grandfather used to say, back when he still got worked up about Róbert. But Róbert didn't just call the shots, he also had money. And if he wanted something, he paid for it: the Arctic Henge, Hotel Arctica. The golf course in Hólsvík, the football field, the sauna, the delicacies for the Þorrablót festival: sheep's head and fermented whale blubber, blood sausage and dried fish, ram testicles and my hákarl. He saw to it that the entire village was decorated for the national holiday, and for New Year's Eve his fireworks were the biggest to soar into the sky. A few years ago, he wanted to sell half of the harbour to the Chinese government. But the deal never came about, and perhaps it was only ever a rumour I had overheard from a conversation between Jú-Jú and Siggi down at the harbour. Our king had almost sold us to the Chinese!

It occurred to me that I had never spoken to Róbert. I didn't have anything to say to him. Perhaps Róbert didn't like me because I had pushed his daughter Dagbjört down the stairs when I was about twelve and she nine. Some people really bear a grudge. They never forget a thing. Róbert was still married to his wife back then, and there were still things going on in Raufarhöfn. I can't even remember why I pushed Dagbjört down the stairs, and it wasn't even that many steps, only around seven, but they were enough to inflict damage. I was probably trying to be funny, because I did have kind of a crush on her, back then, not any more, no thank you, you should think yourself lucky you didn't shackle yourself to a woman too early, because you never know what they'll look like later. Nói says that too, by the way. But Dagbjört still looked good. She had a beautiful face, almost the same as it used to be. As though she were somehow still a child. If you looked at an old photo of our school class, you could recognize her immediately: her brown, smooth hair, her broad smile, her little upturned nose. She was still quite short, she only came up to my shoulders, even though I'm hardly a giant. I wanted to marry her, back when I was little. I didn't want that any more, though. Because Dagbjört had become significantly broader around the hips. And she waddled a little as she walked, like an eider duck, but I still would have snuggled up with her in the feathery nest. Although it was really stupid of me to push her down the stairs, when you're that young, like I was at twelve, you do stupid things. More than you can count. And I don't think Dagbjört had provoked me in any way, she was probably standing there so invitingly at the top of the stairs that I had to do something, and I gave her a shove, like children do, nothing more; in any case, she tumbled down the stairs and then sat there at the bottom, not saying a word, just looking at her arm bone, which was poking out through her skin. I saw it too. The bone was white. The wound didn't bleed anywhere near as badly as you might think. Then I hurried away, and I'm still ashamed about it today, for the whole stupid thing. I regretted it as soon as I saw Dagbjört sitting there at the bottom so confused, and that's why I ran off, hoping that no one had noticed. But someone had been watching and immediately called out my name, so everyone heard, and then I came to a standstill like an imbecile, standing motionless a few metres from the scene of the crime, and I couldn't even see Dagbjört any more, I was a bit further down the corridor, and stayed there the whole time; when our schoolmates crowded around Dagbjört and looked at the white bone, when the teachers came rushing over and called out instructions, and when Halldór hurried over with his first aid box and led Dagbjört out into the ambulance, slamming the door shut and speeding off with the blue light flashing. Even then I remained standing there. Þóra, who was my teacher back then, gave me a smack on the back of the head, said I was an idiot, and sent me off to the principal, Sigfús.

And when I remembered it now, it was as though I was still standing on the same spot, feeling the slap on the back of my head and the humiliation of being sent to the principal's office, even though Dagbjört had probably long since forgiven me. Because she was always incredibly sweet to me, which meant I sometimes almost got the wrong idea, but she had a husband and two children, the sweetest

little kindergarteners, a girl and a boy, and sometimes I
wondered whether they could have been my children,
had I not pushed Dagbjört down the stairs. But that was
almost impossible, because they would have been different
children, not exactly the same ones, because *I* would have
been the father. I didn't even dare ask the internet what
our children would have looked like, because I feared they
wouldn't have been as pretty. After all, I'm not the pretti-
est. Whenever I see myself in a photograph, I really don't
like how I look. Dagbjört's husband wasn't from around
here and wasn't even in the village during the week, only
at weekends, but he was always very well dressed and good-
looking too. I think he was a businessman or a sales rep
or something. He always smelled good too, and that's why
you could smell him even from a distance. Now, though, I
remembered when Róbert had been unkind to me, namely
when I was in the office of Principal Sigfús, who didn't know
what to do with me – until the door opened and Róbert
stormed in, because then Sigfús too was suddenly furious
with me. I can't remember every word, but I do remember
that Róbert was wearing a black leather jacket and his tinted
glasses. The palm of his hand came close to my face, he
could barely control himself. Sigfús only just managed to
calm him down, even though he was on his side. Oh yeah!
Now I remember what Róbert said! He said that people
used to make shark bait out of people like me! And when
I was finally sent home, I asked Grandfather whether that
was true, and he got angry and said that someone should
give Róbert McKenzie a good thrashing. Good and proper!
Then he made himself a pipe and told me there was no
point in time when children were used to make shark bait,
not before and not now, neither disabled, nor naughty, nor

red-haired children, and in fact no children at all, and if one really wanted to turn an idiot into shark bait, then they should use Robert, that schmuck! And I was relieved, and almost a bit mad at Dagbjört for having fallen so clumsily down the stairs that she broke her arm, but the shock must've gone deep, because my heart still pounds today thinking about it.

Her father ignored me after that, but he sometimes stared at me as though he were wishing I didn't live in his village. I say *his village*, even though he was never president. That office was held by others. But he was the richest man in the village, he owned the last catch quota for capelin and cod, the Hotel Arctica and a lot of land. He drove the most expensive jeep, played golf and sometimes invited rich people to stay, who travelled up here by plane to play golf with him. He called it "Arctic Golf". With him, everything was "Arctic" something or other. In Raufarhöfn, you're way up by the Arctic Circle. At the end of June, the sun doesn't even set. Unfortunately, it's usually cloudy, and then you don't see the sun the entire day. But it stays light, and now and then tourists drive their rented cars all the way up here, and you even see huge cruise ships on the horizon, carrying ten times as many people as there are in Raufarhöfn, and all these people want to experience what it's like when it's always light; in other words, always light.

Grandfather had once explained to me that Róbert might be the richest man in the village, but that he had the least money, which I didn't understand, and Grandfather said that Róbert was piling up a mountain of debt and burying the whole of Raufarhöfn beneath it. You have to imagine it literally! Then it's not so complicated.

*

It was already eight o'clock and pitch black when I went to the Hotel Arctica to eat. I always did that on Thursdays, but this particular day I was late and so I hurried along. Then I was suddenly unsure whether the hotel would even be open; after all, its owner was no longer there. But the hotel was open, of course, and busier than ever! All the tables were occupied by people from the rescue service and four young tourists, who were looking around them in confusion. I was lucky, though, because my seat at the bar was free. It was my regular seat. I always sat there. It had a good view of the TV, because football games were sometimes shown here. If there was anything unusual on the evening news, Óttar the Pressure Cooker or someone else would turn up the volume.

Óttar was sweating. I could see him through the bull's-eye window in the swinging door that led to the kitchen. Once he came out, grabbed Nadja by the arm and said:

"The chicken is finished, no more chicken orders!" and she nodded but didn't even look at him, even pulled up her shoulders a little, because she was busy typing a few numbers into the till.

"It's insanely busy here!" I said, so that someone would notice me.

Nadja smiled at me briefly, then immediately turned away and marched over with the card machine to the tourists.

"All good, Sheriff?" Óttar asked me, and I wondered how old he actually was.

"All good." I placed my cowboy hat on the counter.

"I kept the seat free for you. Hamburger with fries?"

"Correctamundo!"

Óttar pulled a cigarette out of the pack, placed it between his lips, looked at me, returned the cigarette to the pack, clicked his tongue and disappeared into the kitchen.

It was warm and loud in the restaurant. Almost unbearable! I looked around. I had never seen most of the people before, but I knew that they'd been up there in the snow with me, because some of them returned my gaze and even nodded, smiled or grimaced. One called out:

"Have you found something, Sheriff? Polar bear tracks, perhaps?"

"No way," I muttered and turned around. On the TV, they were showing the heads of state who were due to meet tomorrow or the day after in Reykjavík. I realized that people were talking about me behind my back, but I couldn't hear what they were saying, so I couldn't prove it. Sometimes I just sense these things. It's something in me. Call it supersense.

I had to wait a long time for my hamburger, so I was all the happier when Nadja came out of the kitchen and served it to me.

"There you go," she said and smiled. She was wearing leggings and a short black skirt. She had the most beautiful behind in all of Raufarhöfn. Anyone with eyes in their head knew that.

Once I'd cleaned the plate, the situation in the hotel restaurant calmed down, everyone had had something to eat and Óttar could take a break, but Nadja and her Lithuanian colleague were still busy bringing people drinks or desserts. Their Lithuanian men were in the kitchen, where together with Óttar they prepared the desserts and dealt with the dirty crockery. Óttar came out of the kitchen, bathed in sweat, and made himself a gin and tonic as though I wasn't even there. But then he raised the glass in my direction, said "To the Devil" and drank down half the contents in one go. Then he took my glass, refilled it with cola without asking me, and placed it in front of me. I knew I didn't have to pay for it. It was "on the house", as people say when something is free.

"It's goddamn tragic," said Óttar. His eyes were red. "Business has never been this busy! Someone has to die for life to come into the joint."

"Could you fill this?" Fisherman Siggi appeared alongside me, waving his empty beer glass. He was probably cheerful on account of his lumpfish catch. A good start to the season.

"If Róbert could see this, he'd be happy," said Siggi, looking at me through glassy eyes. I grinned and watched Óttar as he deftly filled the beer glass. It wasn't the first time he'd done it.

"Who knows, perhaps he will see it," said Óttar thoughtfully.

"Yes, he'll be looking down on us! Like always."

"They haven't found him yet."

"Don't build up any false hopes, okay?" Siggi was indignant.

"Hope? In Raufarhöfn? There hasn't been any of that around here for years." Óttar placed the full beer glass on the counter in front of Siggi, who immediately grasped it with his sailor's paw but without bringing it to his lips. He was in the mood for conversation.

"Well," he said, "the moment will come when Raufarhöfn dies out. One after the other. Will the last person please turn out the lights!"

"Don't listen to him!" said Óttar, glancing at me. Perhaps I had looked shocked, I don't know, but I now realized Siggi had probably been joking, meaning that I had to laugh. He'd really had me going there!

"To Róbert McKenzie!" said Siggi. He lifted his glass and drank. Then he put it back down, let out a small burp and said: "I've always wondered where he got his name from. McKenzie. That's just not the kind of name people have!"

"He chose it himself," mumbled Óttar, as though he didn't really want to say it.

"Did he?" Siggi looked surprised and burped again. "Are you sure?"

"As sure as I am that he has a Swiss bank account!"

"Why didn't *I* know that? So what's his real name?"

"No idea. But he would have been named after his father, of course."

"Some people don't want anything to do with their fathers, isn't that right?" Siggi looked at me. "How's your grandfather doing, by the way? Is the old bruiser still alive?"

I nodded. "Yes, in Húsavík."

"I know he's in Húsavík!" said Siggi, indignantly. "And he can stay there too, the damn commie."

"Siggi," said Óttar, but nothing more.

"No, with all honesty, and I have absolutely nothing against you, Kalmann, you're a great guy, really decent. But if Óðinn were still here in Raufarhöfn, I'd report him to the police myself, because there's nobody else who would have wanted to kill Róbert."

"Óðinn hasn't hurt a fly his entire life," Óttar said, defending my grandfather, and I was grateful to him for it.

"That's a bit of an exaggeration!"

"Well, he didn't kill anyone, anyway."

"What's a commie?" I asked. If you don't understand something, you have to ask.

Siggi laughed. "A commie is someone who's pro-Russian, someone who doesn't want there to be any rich people, you see? A goddamn socialist!"

"A commie is a communist," said Óttar, making himself a second gin and tonic.

Nadja darted past us into the kitchen, opening the swing door with her back, balancing a tray full of dirty dishes and glancing at me as she passed, but she didn't smile. She was definitely very busy. I was proud that she'd looked over. After all, I was having a grown-up conversation with grown-up men.

Siggi wasn't yet done: "Commies want everyone to be having a hard time, don't they, Óttar?"

"That's true," he said. "The opposite of capitalism."

"Everything nicely distributed. Everyone equally poor. Those who have worked damn hard to make their fortune get —" Siggi looked at me, poked his tongue out of the corner of his mouth and mimicked cutting his throat with his thumb. I now knew exactly what a commie was.

"Like Robin Hood!" I said. Siggi stared at me, and Óttar burst out laughing.

"You've got it!" he said, praising me.

It had stopped snowing, and the stars above Raufarhöfn were twinkling. It was insanely cold. Perhaps the ice on the pond would become so thick again that you could throw stones on it and they would bounce off and skid away; something I really enjoyed doing. If Róbert were still out there somewhere, he wouldn't have survived the night. On my way home, I wondered whether I was also a commie, like Grandfather. Probably. And yet I didn't look anything like a commie in my cowboy hat. More like an American, and they're capitalists. In America, the strongest wins. The weaker ones simply aren't strong enough and have to join the back of the queue, but they stay at the back. Sometimes I get laughed at because of my cowboy hat, my sheriff's badge and my old Mauser. "Lucky Luke!" they cry in English, or they make a pistol shape with their hands and say "Hands up!" Once I was even stopped by tourists in a minibus with about six or seven women and just one man in it. The man, who was at the steering wheel, wound down the window and asked whether it was carnival time, to which I answered no, because I didn't know what a carnival was.

Back at home I chatted with Nói, who liked communists even less than Siggi did. He was a capitalist, as he said, and earned his bitcoin honestly with computer games, slaved away for it day and night, and so no one should get the idea into their head of taking his dough away from him, he had earned the sports cars and the women fair and square, and anyone wanting to get their hands on his wealth would be swiftly acquainted with his samurai sword, which I of course already knew about because he'd shown it to me when he bought it, he'd rolled on his chair out of the picture, which meant I was able to study his bedroom wall for a while, until he rolled back into view with a samurai sword in his hands. The sword didn't even fit into the frame, because he was sat too close, so I asked him to roll away from the screen a little, which he did, and then for the first time I saw a little of his face, but only his chin. And ever since then, I've known that Nói has a strange scar on his chin and very few whiskers, not even enough to grow a beard. I don't know how many hairs it takes to grow a beard, though. I don't have one myself either.

7

HÁKARL

The Greenland shark is a miracle of nature, even though it wouldn't win any beauty contest. It has a marvellous sense of smell, probably better than that of a dog. Dogs can track a scent or sniff out drugs by keeping their snouts close to the floor. I'm not sure whether you could employ sharks in that way. I don't think so, but presumably we'll never know for sure, because there are some things we'll never know. We do know, however, that sharks have a good sense of smell, because it's been proven, and if you want to catch sharks, you need to know that.

The most important thing about a good shark catcher is their bait. The Greenland shark is far down on the seabed, two hundred metres deep or two thousand metres deep, it doesn't matter to the shark. It's dark everywhere down there. It feels at home in the dark, where it's always the black of night, even in broad daylight. It sees hardly anything, its eyes are full of parasites, but its sense of smell is really good, and that's why it's important that the bait smells strong. It's complete nonsense that red-headed children used to be used as bait – even though you could use them if you really wanted. Because the sharks wouldn't care, they would bite anyway. They're hungry and that's all there is to it. They don't have a guilty conscience, and so they're not picky.

I usually use smoked horsemeat. A lot of shark catchers use horsemeat. But there are others who swear by rotten seal meat. The Greenland shark likes that too. Or salted mutton. Essentially, he'll eat anything that ends up between his choppers; bait that sinks down to the seabed, and not only bait, because entire seals, polar bear paws and whale flukes, tin cans, broken buoys, stones and rubber boots have been found in sharks' stomachs. The fearsome Greenland shark isn't as scary as many people believe, though, because there are movies in which sharks eat people. You're far more likely to be bitten by a seal than a shark if you go swimming here. But no one goes swimming here, nor does anyone know what goes on two thousand metres deep. Only the monsters who live there know that. It's much too dark for us down there, darker than in space. That's why we know more about space than we do about the ocean. We know almost nothing about the Greenland shark either. They might as well be extraterrestrials; perhaps they are, it wouldn't make any difference. We don't know how many of them there are or what they think. We know very little. And I find that incredibly reassuring, because I don't know a great deal about the world either, and anyone who acts as though they have all the answers isn't quite right in the head. But whenever something gets discovered about the Greenland shark, I want to know about it. After all, shark-hunting is my job. For example, it was recently discovered that they can reach the age of 512. That's actually true! Nói sent me a link, and he asked me whether it made me feel guilty to kill 512-year-old creatures, given that nowadays everything that's 512 years old is protected, for example houses, books or trees. And to be completely honest that made me think, because you're not supposed to cut down 512-year-old trees, and 512-year-old books don't belong in the recycling bin. But I defended myself regardless, said that in these parts we've always hunted Greenland shark, that's how it is, and eventually Nói agreed, because some things are just how they are, you don't even have to explain them. After that, though, I couldn't get it out of my head. I visited my grandfather in the care home and told him, but he didn't want to hear it, he got really grumpy and swept my words away curtly with his hand, meaning that I couldn't even finish what I was saying, so I don't know what he would have thought of the whole thing. But I tried to imagine what his answer might have been, because I had spent many hours, perhaps even years, out at sea with him, and I of all people should know what his opinion was. He would probably have said that he'd always suspected as much, that you could tell by looking at the critters that they had reached a ripe old age, and so he wasn't surprised that, when it came to appearances, sharks weren't exactly the crown of creation. And that's true. Their blue-grey skin is covered with fissures and scars, their eyes are colourless and expressionless. God was probably having a bad day, Grandfather would have continued, which I would have found funny, and I laughed a little even at the thought. But he would have added for sure that we should still show the sharks respect, because not every creature wants to live down there on the ocean floor. And for 512 years at that! But at the end of the day, we human beings had to eat, like every other living being, and humans are at the very top of the food chain, and you shouldn't get down about that, that's just how it is, that's nature, so no reason to worry.

What Grandfather might've said made sense to me. He was always good at getting right to the heart of things.

Sharks had to eat too, and for a whole 512 years. Now that was something to think about!

The thing that interested me most, though, as a shark catcher, was what sharks best like eating, because that was the only way I could catch them. In a sense, I was the cook, and the sharks were my clientele. My menu was horsemeat. I got it from Magnús Magnússon, who had a sheep farm and also around thirty horses in pasture. But horsemeat alone wasn't enough. Greenland shark are gourmands. You have to pickle all the meat, and in a marinade whose contents are strictly secret. Every shark catcher has a secret recipe. I had taken over my grandfather's recipe, and that's why it was a family secret, one no one else was allowed to know: Cognac. Or rum. Captain Morgan, for example. You can smell it from a long way away. It didn't have to be expensive rum. I always bought the cheapest. I poured around a bottle into a sixty-litre barrel which was already filled with brine. Then vinegar. Apple cider vinegar. Two litres. Then I left the pieces of bait lying in the barrel for a few days, just long enough that they soaked up the aromas but not so long that they went bad. I then went out to sea with a few select pieces of bait, pulled the longline out of the water with the electric winch and skewered the bait on the hook. The hooks were fastened at around ten-metre intervals on the longline, which was stretched between two anchored buoys. The buoys were marked so that everyone knew who they belonged to; me, in other words, even though I was the only shark catcher left in Raufarhöfn. The baited hooks sank down into the depths with the weighted buoy anchors, around a hundred and seventy metres deep, and down below the sharks smelled the bait and sometimes bit. And once one had bitten, he would be stuck hanging there, awaiting his fate. A few days later, I would come chugging up, check the hooks, and whoever was hanging on the hook was unlucky. Bang!

In Greenland, they don't do it like that. There, the Inuits make a hole in the ice, lower the hook down on a chain hanging from an 800-metre rope, and once a shark has bitten, they put the rope over their shoulders and march off, pulling the rope up until they're 800 metres away from the hole. So they can't do it alone, like I do. Because if they were to go back to the hole, the shark would sink back down into the sea.

The next day, I tended to my bait. It was snowing again, so the rescue service and the police postponed their search. Their plan: wait until the snow let up. The village was full to bursting, the hotel was full to bursting, the town hall, gym and showers were needed too, the number of inhabitants had probably half doubled. People were standing in front of the filling station and smoking cigarettes, standing in front of the municipal building and hopping from one leg to the other, standing in front of the hotel and drinking coffee out of paper cups. In the places where one might have expected to find Róbert Mackenzie, namely in the village, the harbour or near the Arctic Henge, nothing had been found. So there was no need to search any further in those places. There were a few rescue service vehicles down by the harbour, too, but what caught my attention was a car from the national TV network. I recognized the logo, underneath which it said *Daily News*. I had never seen a car from the daily news in Raufarhöfn, and I'd been living here my whole life! Usually nothing happened that would interest the media. This was "a pretty big deal", as Nói had said.

The presence of national TV therefore made the Róbert Mackenzie case a matter of national importance.

I'm curious by nature. That's why I wanted to get a closer look at the car, without having noticed, from a distance, that two people were sitting inside it. I had assumed they were probably somewhere else, smoking cigarettes or drinking coffee. But when they saw me striding directly towards them they jumped out of the car and ran towards me. Or at least one of them did; the other remained composed.

"You're the Sheriff of Raufarhöfn!" cried the one who'd dashed over, as though I didn't know that. I recognized him immediately too, from his face and shiny bald head, because he often appeared on the seven o'clock news whenever something happened in the north of Iceland. That was his territory. I recognized him by his bow tie and trendy glasses with thick black frames. They were his trademark. He was always elegantly dressed, because he sometimes interviewed politicians, and once even the president. He never wore any kind of hat, regardless of whether it was snowing or if the sun was blazing down on his bald head. Today his bow tie was as red as his ears. The man who had climbed leisurely out of the car and had a camera on his shoulder was the cameraman. He was younger and at least a head taller than the reporter and me, and unlike his colleague he had a fur cap on, which made him appear even taller. It's definitely an advantage to be tall if you're a cameraman. You can get a good view of things then.

I couldn't help but grin. Sometimes I have to grin even though I don't mean to. The reporter knew exactly who I was, and had recognized me immediately. That kind of thing only happens to famous people, and that's why I grinned, because I was confused and proud at the same time, and I kind of wanted to run away, but I didn't.

The reporter introduced himself, said that he was from the daily news, and told me his name too, which I immediately forgot, but now every time I see him on the TV in his glasses and his red bow tie, I cry out: "He once interviewed me!"

And that's precisely what he wanted from me; an interview, because he'd heard that *I* had found the pool of blood, and he wanted to ask me a few questions about it. I immediately told him where I'd found the pool of blood, namely up by the Arctic Henge, because it was now a matter of national importance, and you want to be helpful with that kind of thing, that's just how it is. But the reporter interrupted and said not to tell him everything right away, that the cameraman wasn't ready yet. And then he discussed some filming technicalities with him, that's normal, that's always the case with TV interviews. They asked me to position myself near the old rendering hall, which had gone to rack and ruin – rusty doors, smashed-in windows, a lopsided conveyor belt that was hanging on for dear life to the rusty framework – which I found odd, because the McKenzie cold-storage warehouse next door had been freshly painted two years ago and belonged to the missing person, after all, so it would have been a better backdrop, but you don't tell a reporter from national TV how to do his job.

The cameraman unfolded a tripod, attached a lamp to it, put in the battery and flicked it on. The white light blinded me, but as long as I didn't stare directly into the lamp it wasn't so bad. The reporter, at the cameraman's command, pushed me a little to the left and then a bit more, yes, right here, perfect, and then the reporter asked whether he was already recording, and the cameraman, who still hadn't introduced himself, said from his great height that he'd already been recording for ages, upon which the reporter looked at me for a while, as though he were thinking up a question. And then, taking me by surprise, he asked:

"Róbert McKenzie has been missing since the day before yesterday. You found a pool of blood in the snow. Do you think there's a connection?"

"Yes," I said.

The reporter looked at me expectantly. I avoided his gaze, looked into the glare of the lamp, and for a few seconds couldn't see anything at all.

"Do you believe Róbert McKenzie was murdered up there?"

"No," I said.

The reporter lowered the microphone and said that I was welcome to say more, not just yes or no, I was welcome to say whatever came to mind, there was no need to be nervous, and that I should take a breath from time to time too.

As soon as he'd said that, I had difficulty breathing. Until that moment I hadn't had time to be nervous, even though I genuinely had forgotten to breathe. I had somehow been preoccupied with watching the two TV people at work. I was wondering, for example, how much the camera weighed, because I imagined it was heavy, and whether, after the interview, they might let me put the camera on my shoulder, to try it out, and I would have liked to see how I looked on camera. Would I get sent the *Daily News* clip? These were the things going through my head. But as soon as the reporter said there was no need to be nervous, I became really nervous. My pulse skyrocketed! And I thought back to the interrogation with Birna and how she'd been pleased with all my answers, whether they'd been yes or no so long as I didn't just nod or shake my head. But the reporter had very different wishes, and so I now had to adapt completely, and that made me nervous after all.

"How about you tell us how you came to find the pool of blood?"

I took a deep breath and a small step backwards. The reporter and cameraman exchanged glances and followed me. I took another step backwards, until eventually I was standing with my back to the rusty wall. The cameraman repositioned the lamp. So there was only one way out: I had to answer the question.

"I was up there the entire day, looking for an Arctic fox. I'm a hunter, like Grandfather was, but he's old now, very old, he lives in Húsavík now, he's still alive but no one knows how long he'll live, they say he could die at any moment and that then I'll be sad. But I go to visit him once a week. Magga drives me, because she needs to go to Húsavík anyway, to go shopping and to the hairdresser. And that's why I was alone up there in the snow, and then I told Hafdís that —"

"Kalmann," the reporter interrupted. "Try not to stare directly into the camera, okay? And just tell us about the pool of blood."

I nodded. I hadn't even realized I'd been staring into the camera, but now that the reporter had pointed it out, I noticed that I was staring into the camera again, and so I directed my gaze at the ground.

"So, start from the beginning again. But without going off-topic. Just briefly and precisely, and relax. Tell me about the fox hunt."

I took a breath.

"Schwar—, I mean, the fox, sometimes roams around the schoolhouse, and Hafdís asked me to teach him a lesson, and that's why the day before yesterday I was tracking him, but it was snowing, like it is now, well, perhaps a little more, and I knew right away that I wouldn't find the fox, but patience is a hunter's most important virtue, that's what Grandfather always said, even though he doesn't say it any more because he's old and in Húsavík, and that's why after I set out from the schoolhouse I went —"

"Tell me about the pool of blood."

My heart was beating kind of irregularly. It distracted me. And a TV interview was turning out to be much harder than a police interrogation.

"Up at the Arctic Henge monument, I mean, really close to it, I found blood in the snow."

"Very good. Can you say that one more time without looking into the camera?"

I nodded, concentrating, stared at the reporter and said: "At the Arctic Henge. Blood everywhere. In the snow."

"Was the blood fresh?"

"Fresh?"

"Warm perhaps?"

"No… But it wasn't frozen yet either."

I noticed that, while I'd been talking, a few snowflakes had landed and melted on the reporter's bald head. The drops of water on his head looked like pearls.

"Do you think it was Róbert McKenzie's blood?"

"Yes… I think so."

"Why do you think that?"

Did the reporter not know that people were searching for Róbert? I mean, who else's blood would it have been?

"Well, because he's gone missing!"

"Do you think he was murdered?"

"No."

"You don't think so?"

"No."

"And why not?"

I shrugged. This interview was turning out to be like an interrogation after all. And that was something I was familiar with. "Perhaps a polar bear ate him," I said.

"He looked into the camera again," murmured the cameraman.

"Doesn't matter," said the reporter in irritation, wiping the pearls from his head with his free hand and studying his wet palm. "Can you tell me one more time why you believe that Róbert McKenzie is missing?"

"Okay."

"… then tell me!"

"A polar bear."

"No, in more detail."

"But I don't really know," I mumbled. I wished I'd never mentioned the polar bear.

"No, you do. Again. Like before! But without looking into the camera. Why do you think there's no sign of Róbert McKenzie?"

I had to just get through it. I defended myself: "Sometimes polar bears come from Greenland to Iceland."

"He did it again," said the cameraman gloomily.

I groaned and looked around, searching for help. How much longer was this going to take?

"That doesn't matter now!" hissed the reporter, pushing his glasses to the bridge of his nose. "Kalmann. Did it look as though someone had been eaten by a polar bear up there?"

"No," I said.

"No?"

"No way."

"So then why do you believe a polar bear —"

"I don't know!" I yelled, making the two TV men stiffen.

Next to me against the wall stood a rusty oil drum with holes at the top and which was completely full of rainwater. I kicked it, clunk, clunk, twice, making water squirt out of the holes, and my cowboy hat almost fell off my head. It was really funny. So I kicked the drum again, but harder this time, which hurt quite a lot. I genuinely wondered whether I had broken one or several toes. So I limped away, and neither the reporter nor the cameraman said a word. They simply let me go, staring after me open-mouthed. I don't know whether the cameraman was still filming me.

The damn media. They always cause so much stress! I hid myself away in my hall and walked up and down until the pain in my foot had subsided. The snow on the roof was melting, it was dripping everywhere. Luckily my toes weren't broken, but when I slipped my boot back on, it had somehow shrunk.

I cut up a few pieces of meat and immersed them in my rum-brine-vinegar marinade, and doing that helped me calm myself down a bit. It felt kind of good to chop up the pieces of meat, to ram my sharp knife into the soft flesh, so hard that the tip of the knife got stuck in the tabletop.

When I was finished and completely calm, I knocked on Sæmundur's container door, simply to tell him I didn't want to go out today.

"That's definitely a good decision," said Sæmundur, throwing his pen down on the papers that were spread out in front of him and running his fingers through his windswept hair a few times. "You wouldn't be able to fish anything besides Róbert out of the sea anyway."

I must have given him a funny look, because he laughed and said not to look at him so strangely, that surely making a joke was still allowed, and that's why I laughed too. And once I'd recovered, I told him that I'd given a TV interview.

"You'll be famous yet!" remarked Sæmundur, and I got really embarrassed and excited at the thought of becoming famous.

I then spent the entire day waiting for the evening to come, and I also instructed Nói to watch the daily news, saying that there was going to be a surprise. I would be on it!

And the Róbert McKenzie case was the top story on the daily news, right at the beginning, even though the preparations for the state summit were running at full speed and, by the sounds of it, not that smoothly. There weren't enough beds for all the journalists, and something to do with the security wasn't okay, that's what they said on the news. So it wasn't long before the houses of Raufarhöfn appeared on the TV. First, it was announced that the blood found at the Arctic Henge in Raufarhöfn really was Róbert McKenzie's. The DNA test had proven that. No one was that surprised about it. Then an interview with Birna was broadcast, and Birna said that a violent crime was now suspected and that the search would be intensified as soon as the snowfall abated. The weather forecast was promising. I glanced out of the window and noticed that it was no longer snowing outside. It was almost dark already, and the light from some houses and street lamps was struggling to illuminate Raufarhöfn. It only gets that dark when rain clouds gather, but I hadn't even noticed, because I'd spent the whole afternoon watching TV and chatting to Nói. And suddenly

I appeared on the TV screen, and really close up too, you could see only my cowboy hat, my face and my chest with the sheriff's badge, and I looked somehow completely different to how I did in real life, and I wasn't at all happy about it. I looked dumb, as though I had a warm fried egg under my hat, and you could tell I was uneasy, on edge and suspicious. And then they broadcast the end of the interview in its entirety, where I expressed my suspicion that Róbert may have been eaten by a polar bear. And because I was looking into the camera, it sounded as though I was warning the entire TV nation about polar bears. And because of this I hit myself around the head a few times and pounded my fists on the coffee table. Luckily, they didn't show me kicking the oil barrel about, and I was relieved about that. But now Birna was being connected live by telephone with the TV studio, and she assured everyone that they didn't believe there was a polar bear roaming around up on the Melrakkaslétta. There was no indication of it at least, she said, and if someone had been eaten by a polar bear, more than just blood would be found, like tattered clothing or gnawed bones. That sounded logical to me. And now I felt even more stupid, like the village idiot, and was convinced the whole of Iceland was laughing at me. Then I wanted to smash the TV, but suddenly some more Raufarhöfn residents appeared on the screen, because the reporter and his cameraman must've positioned himself in front of the store to ambush people. Elínborg, for example, said that it couldn't be a coincidence that Róbert had been killed up by his Arctic Henge. "Perhaps a ritual?" she suggested, but she didn't want to expand upon her suggestion, even when the reporter asked her to. "It's just a thought," said Elínborg, looking into the camera.

Halldór was stopped too. He had wound down the window of his pickup and said that this incident was really bad for Raufarhöfn, because this negative news report could have devastating consequences, on tourism for example, and we were fighting to survive up here as it was, that after the introduction of the quota system we had been left in the lurch by the government.

"Written off, just like that," he said then, and nothing more, and he held the reporter's gaze without looking into the camera.

No sooner was the report finished than Nói called me on Messenger and laughed himself silly, and because he was laughing, I found the whole thing kind of funny after all, and that's precisely why Nói was my best friend, and so I didn't smash the TV. Friends are there to make one another laugh, and anyone who thinks Nói isn't a good friend is plain wrong.

Nói delved around the internet a bit more to find out how people were reacting to the polar bear thing, and I could tell he didn't read me everything, but a few people thought my suspicion was completely justified, that nothing could be ruled out, all possibilities had to be taken into consideration, and so in the end I felt like I was being taken seriously after all, and that was a nice feeling. But I still decided not to mention the suspicion about the polar bear any more, because somehow it didn't make any sense, and Nói agreed.

8

MAGGA

Then Saturday came. That meant I visited my grandfather
in Húsavík. That was understood, and had been ever since
Grandfather was taken to the care home in Húsavík, after
I had found him lying in his own piss on the kitchen floor.
At nine o'clock every Saturday morning, there was a beep
outside my house, and I would put on my nice coat. I left the
cowboy hat, sheriff's badge and Mauser at home, because
in Húsavík not everyone knew who I was.

By now, the search for Róbert was in full swing again. I'd
been hearing the noise of the jeeps and quads since early
that morning, but I guess I wasn't needed any more. No one
had asked for me. I went outside and climbed into Magga's
little Skoda tin can, which was always a little lopsided when
Magga was behind the wheel.

"Good morning, young TV star!" she said, and I couldn't
help but laugh. So that's what being famous was like. Then
Magga didn't say anything for a few minutes, because she
was getting the car going and had to concentrate. Three
vehicles from the rescue service were approaching from the
opposite direction, and Magga said: "Look at all this traffic!"

I wondered, as I did every time, how she was able to
squeeze her fat body behind the steering wheel. Driving
wasn't her strong point. Only once Raufarhöfn was behind
us and the road just a line through the landscape did she

relax and begin to talk until my head was filled with her chatter. It was like she'd been waiting all week to air her thoughts. She repeated what the TV news had said and everything she'd observed from her window that morning. "The rescue service's meddling," as she put it. She always had something to talk about, there was always something on her mind. And I didn't even need to answer her. That was okay. Sometimes I said nothing the entire way and sat there listening to her – or not, sometimes I would stare out of the window, thinking about my grandfather or perhaps seeing animals that could have been hunted or observed. A hunter has an eye for these things. On the Melrakkaslétta, there were Arctic foxes and wild geese, falcons and snow grouse. Once, and only once, I saw a snowy owl.

"Don't you agree?" asked Magga, pulling me from my thoughts. "I mean, you're a hunter, and you know what you're talking about. A suspicion like that should be looked into! If there really is a polar bear running around, it's dangerous, and not out of the question, don't you agree?" I shrugged and said nothing. "You really did an excellent job, yesterday on the daily news." Magga swerved slightly, and I gripped the edge of my seat. "Did you notice anything up there? Did you find tracks in the snow?"

"Perhaps," I said. "Polar bears have often come to Iceland in the past. Once to the Westfjords, north of Hornstrandir. Fishermen saw the polar bear swimming and hung it from the bow by a rope. Just hoisted it up a bit. Like this." I mimicked the action.

"Poor animal," sighed Magga.

"They shot a polar bear in Fljótum at Skagafjörður, one on Grímsey Island, and one recently in Hvalnes on the Skaga peninsula."

"I remember that."

"They swim."

"Yes, on drift ice."

"No," I contradicted. "They sometimes swim the whole way from Greenland. Because there's always drift ice."

"Surely that's too far."

"No way! They can swim three hundred kilometres or more! And from Greenland to the Westfjords it's three hundred kilometres. To here it's around a hundred kilometres more. So —"

"Now you're over-exaggerating, Kalmann minn. Four hundred kilometres? Swimming?"

"It's possible, if they take a break in the Westfjords for example." I was used to people not believing me. No reason to worry.

"Well," said Magga, "if there is a polar bear roaming around up here, then he's definitely hungry, whether he swam, drifted across on an ice floe or flew here with easyJet."

I found that funny and laughed. Magga could sometimes be very funny. She laughed too, looking over at me and letting the car drift onto the other side of the road. So I stopped laughing, Magga looked back at the road, wrenched the steering wheel round, and then she didn't say anything for a while. I stared fixedly out of the window, as though I were trying to spot a polar bear.

"Do you think," Magga asked me, "that a polar bear like that could eat a human, skin, hair and all, until there's nothing left of them?"

"Hmm," I mumbled, even though I knew the answer to that.

"Let's change the subject," suggested Magga, but then she stayed silent.

A car was coming towards us, so Magga slowed down massively until we'd passed the car, even though the road was wide enough for two cars.

"Dagbjört," exclaimed Magga in astonishment.

I turned around in surprise and stared after the car. Magga was right. It was a red Kia Picanto, but Dagbjört was going so damn fast that it wasn't long before she disappeared over the horizon.

"Poor Dagbjört. First her mother and now her father. And if we lose the quota for Raufarhöfn, the last few jobs will be lost, and then there'll be too few children here, the school will shut, and Dagbjört will have lost everything. Her job too." Magga paused, thinking. "But perhaps Róbert's still alive. Perhaps he just injured himself and – no. That would be unrealistic, given the blood – they say no one can survive that kind of blood loss. But perhaps it's a misunderstanding. That happens sometimes. Like last summer, when the rescue service was looking for that missing tourist, remember? Where was that?"

"In the Eldgjá ravine."

"Exactly, Kalmann. You always remember precisely where things were!"

I nodded. Magga laughed, leaning over a little as though she were trying to hug the steering wheel.

"They searched and searched. And the tourist herself was taking part in the search, a woman of course, it had to have been! And she had no idea they were searching for her, that's why I think it's not good to bring all these tourists to Iceland, because we get stuck with all the work, and tourists are so stupid, they're constantly putting their lives in danger, and when we have to save them, we're in danger too, aren't we? But the government in Reykjavík doesn't have to come here and deal with the consequences, so they keep luring more and more people to Iceland, not just tourists, but migrants too, you see it on TV, even though we're not much better off than them. I mean, we don't even have enough money to save the fishing villages from bankruptcy! No, they just let us wither away up here, they think we can live off the good air and the beautiful views. I mean, what in heaven's name are we supposed to live off if they take the quotas away from us?"

She looked at me as though she were expecting an answer. But she just wanted me to nod. So I nodded, even though most of what she was saying wasn't actually true.

"I don't think Róbert has joined his own search party," I said.

"Of course not!" cried Magga. "But perhaps it's a misunderstanding. Perhaps he injured himself, and a tourist took him to Akureyri, and he hasn't even realized that... No. That can't be it either." Magga accelerated, only to immediately take her foot off the pedal again. She drove like that the whole way. Accelerate, foot off the pedal, accelerate. "Róbert isn't around any more," she said. "Either a polar bear ate him, or someone turned him into fish food."

I nodded. "Fish food," I said, and Magga sighed.

On the way to Húsavík we made just two short stops. One on the Melrakkaslétta, in the middle of nowhere. Because I was desperate for a pee, Magga stopped her Skoda at the side of the road. And because there wasn't another car to be seen for far and wide, Magga got out too, squatted down at the edge of the road and peed into the crowberry bushes. I was done before her, though, and Magga laughed:

"Don't look!"

I didn't look.

The second stop was in Kópasker, where I was allowed to buy a cola and Magga chatted for a while with Gummi, who always like to chat.

In Húsavík, Magga dropped me off by the filling station. She wanted to drive me to the care home, but she had to fill up, and I suggested I head over to the care home on foot. After all, I wasn't a little kid any more. Magga agreed only reluctantly, but promised to pick me up at two o'clock that afternoon.

I crept around the filling station building and waited by the rubbish containers until Magga was done. That took quite a while, because she was tapping around for ages on the self-service machines – evidently the machine wasn't accepting her card – and then she fumbled for a while with the filler cap.

Women and cars! Why are *they* allowed to drive and yet *I'm* not? I'd like someone to explain that to me! The theory test was completely over the top. We didn't even have traffic lights up here, nor motorways, nor roundabouts; just roads, some of them tarmacked, with a top speed of ninety kilometres per hour, others not tarmacked, with a top speed of eighty, and I'd known that for ages, that was the law, in the villages you weren't allowed to go any faster than fifty. And sometimes thirty. It depended on whether there were any children or a school nearby. The speed limit was always written somewhere, after all, and I knew how to read. So you didn't even have to know it off by heart. But the fact that you had to put on your seat belt and turn on your headlamps, that you did have to know, that's the law, and Magga did neither of those things. But I wasn't allowed. Even though I'd already driven a car, when I was eighteen, and everyone involved had survived the journey. There was a dance in

Kópasker, and I had to go because my cousin Draupnir was visiting from Reykir and wouldn't take no for an answer. Soon, though, everybody apart from me was too drunk to even stand up straight. So I had no choice but to drive my cousin and a few other bachelors home, so that I could get home myself. They didn't even need to persuade me, I'd been wanting to go home for hours anyway, because I was secretly in love with a girl who was making out with one of the Húsavíkings. The boys assured me that I didn't need to be scared, because it wasn't like I had a driver's licence that someone could take away from me. That sounded logical, and by that point I didn't really care anyway.

I didn't like going to parties as a rule, because I didn't drink alcohol or dance, but most people did drink and dance, and after a while they lost all control. They enjoyed talking to me then, even if it was all nonsense, but they were nice to me in any case, and then it was fun for me too. They were happy to have someone like me in Raufarhöfn, they said, someone who looked after the village a bit and gave the old dump some character. They said everyone was welcome up here, obviously including me, everyone apart from Muslims, because religions shouldn't be mixed. That was human nature. And that made sense to me, but most of the ones who held this opinion didn't even go to church or anything, and so I wondered whether they even had a religion. They were just drunk and talking nonsense and didn't really mean it. But I listened anyway. I didn't have much choice. They always yelled into my ear, because they couldn't hear so well when they were drunk. Sometimes they would launch themselves at me, hold onto me, say I was a good man, a rock, that I shouldn't stand for it when people called me a killjoy, even though no one did, because

I'm not one. I'm just different. But Grandfather had once told me that in a sense everyone was different, and so I was completely normal. The drunk partygoers said I could always count on them if someone was making fun of me, but I knew that they would have forgotten about it by the next morning, because when a person is drunk, they're not the person they really are. They said they'd much rather have someone like me up here than some Mussulman who'll blow himself up. That you only had to turn on the TV to understand the connection.

"Paris! Loads of Muslims! Boom! Get it? Raufarhöfn! No Muslims! No boom!"

And that was true, so the drunks were surely right about that. But from Nói I knew that there were Muslims in Reykjavík too, and that was clearly going smoothly, because so far no one there had blown anyone sky-high or driven a vehicle into a crowd or stabbed people with a knife. And yet I'm sure the Muslims in Reykjavík would have had reason to. Because they wanted to build a Muslim church, but then a few Icelanders threw pigs' heads into the meadow where the Muslim church was supposed to be built. Perhaps Muslims are vegetarian, and that could be why they're not very popular in the north-east of Iceland, because nobody up here is vegetarian. At least, I don't know anyone who is. No, wait, that's not true. I do: Dagbjört is vegetarian. I know that because a few years ago she arranged for a vegetarian dish to be put on the menu in her father's hotel restaurant: mushroom risotto. And one day when she was helping out, as she often did, she served me the risotto, on the house, and asked me to try it and tell her what it was like, and I did as I was told but grated a lot of cheese onto it. The risotto was actually really delicious, I even cleared my plate, and

Dagbjört was so happy that she raised her fist in victory and cried "Yes!" And that's why I've never told her that I still prefer hamburgers – this is why I'd waited behind the filling station by the rubbish containers until Magga had finished filling up her tin can and driven away. Only then did I go in and order a hamburger with fries and Thousand Island dressing from Sölvi for 1,845 krona, even though it was only eleven o'clock, but that didn't matter, because at the care home they didn't have lunch until twelve thirty, and I didn't tend to like the food there very much. The mashed potato was fine, and the sauce usually was too, but not so much the carrots, the broccoli and the cauliflower. I'm not a rabbit, after all!

But I was out of luck. The only occupied table was mine. This was the table I always sat at. Because it was right by the wall beneath the map of Iceland. That's why I had never eaten at another table. Sölvi had noticed too, but he just gave me a tired look and cleaned his hands on his apron. Perhaps he was wondering how he could help me, but then he shrugged and disappeared into the kitchen. He was probably in a bad mood. So I simply stood there and looked over at my table. They were tourists. A young couple. A man with a sparse beard and a slender woman with a headscarf and pigtails, but they weren't Muslims. Even I could see that. Their backpacks were on the floor, leaning against the wall. They were wearing heavy hiking boots and talking in Foreign. French perhaps. Or Turkish. I took a few steps towards them, turned my back on them and stood there. Waiting. They paused their conversation. I could feel their gazes on my back. Then I went over to the table next to them, leaned against it on my fists and looked over at them. They still didn't notice that they were at *my* table. That's exactly why I preferred it in Raufarhöfn! That was a wonderful example! In Raufarhöfn, everyone knew who I was and which chair I had to sit on. In Raufarhöfn, there was no reason to worry.

The couple exchanged glances, then the young man gave me a questioning look. I sighed loudly, but they stayed sitting there in utter confusion. I walked closely past them to the next table and then did the same thing, leaning on my fists and looking at the shameless tourists once again. They spoke to one another, the woman looked nervous. Was it really so difficult to understand?

"Kalmann!" Sölvi was holding a packet of frozen fries beneath his arm and waved me over with his free hand. "Can you not sit at a different table today, just this once? Look, they're all free. All of them!"

How stupid can a person be? Sölvi knew me, admittedly, but he wasn't my friend. And he was probably a bit slow on the uptake, because I could see that all the other tables were free. I had eyes, after all. I didn't move from the spot.

"But they're sitting at *my* table!" I explained, loud and slow, so that he understood what this was actually about.

"It's not *your* table," said Sölvi. "It's *my* table. All the tables are mine. And today you may sit at another table. Please!"

I rubbed my face. Some days you're better off not even getting out of bed! What Sölvi had said was unfortunately true, but that wasn't what this was about. The customer is king! That's what it was about! *He* of all people should know that. So I pointed my index finger at the tourist couple.

"But the table doesn't belong to them either! I always sit at that table! It's *my* table. I sit at the table with the map of Iceland! You know that! Everybody knows that! It's just the way it is!"

"You really are unbearable!" cried Sölvi, tossing the packet of fries on the counter and throwing his hands in the air. "What do you expect me to do, ask them to switch tables?"

"Yes!" I cried, and Sölvi groaned up at the ceiling.

"Sorry, can you please sit at another table? My buddy here is special, you know…" he said, in English so the foreigners would understand.

"Why?" asked the man.

"That's my table!" I said loudly in Icelandic.

"It's not his…" Sölvi clutched at his hair in exasperation. "Just sit at another table, yes? Please! Sorry."

"Sure, whatever," said the stubborn tourist in irritation. His wife was already standing up. She said something, after which he stood up too. Women usually wear the trousers. That's how it is. The couple gathered up their stuff and switched tables, choosing the one furthest away from mine. I stared after them angrily.

"This is my table," I muttered, sitting down at my table. Something like that can really spoil your day. It's a simple rule, you might think, but people are impossible! I was hopping mad, so I craned my neck and called in English after the tourist couple: "This is my table!"

"Kalmann!" bellowed Sölvi. "Hold your tongue! You've got your table now! You're not the only person who can make demands around here. Your goddamn shark is stinking up the place!"

I wanted to defend myself, but Sölvi seemed to have got out of the wrong side of bed today, and I did want a hamburger with fries from him after all. So I held my tongue. But I was so angry that I slammed my fists on the table a few times, and the young tourist wife let out a few squeaks.

Women.

By the time Sölvi finally served me the hamburger, I had calmed down a little and almost thanked him, even, and with the first few bites the rage dissipated, because perhaps I'd just been hungry, but it was still *my* table. And it would stay that way in future.

I usually ate alone. Apart from Sölvi I didn't know anybody here, but he was busy or at least acting as though he was, and he still had an annoyed look on his face and probably didn't feel like talking to me. The tourists studied their guidebook, and I wondered whether they had even ordered something or were just sitting in the filling station to kill time. And so I lost myself in my thoughts.

I thought about a lot of things. I thought about the dance in Kópasker, when I had driven the drunks, a whole carful, back to Raufarhöfn. During the first few kilometres they bellowed and blustered, but then they suddenly calmed down and fell asleep, and all of a sudden it became quiet in the car and the driving very pleasant. For at least a moment I felt surrounded by snoring, stinking men, as though I were a normal young man like everyone else. No one noticed that I scraped the car when I dropped off the bachelors in front of their houses, not noticing a hydrant, and so there was no reason to worry.

I would have liked a car. It would be a Toyota Land Cruiser. With that I could speed across the Melrakkaslétta to hunt snow grouse and Arctic foxes. And in winter I would be able to drive the snowy streets to Húsavík without any problem, even when they weren't yet ploughed, to visit Grandfather. Then I would no longer be dependent on Magga and wouldn't have to hide away behind the filling station building any more. That would be great.

9

GRANDFATHER

I cleaned my plate and left the filling station cafe without saying goodbye to Sölvi, who in any case had disappeared into the kitchen. The two tourists watched me go, and even smiled at me, but I ignored them.

Outside, the sun was shining. It was a really pleasant day. Springlike. Here in Húsavík, the snow still lay in the shadow of the buildings, heavy and dirty. I wanted to go up to the care home, but I spotted Magga's car in front of the store and so made a detour.

They knew me in the care home, I didn't have to call ahead or anything, so I simply wandered into the building like I always did. I knew where Grandfather's room was. But he wasn't there, nor was he in the toilet.

"Ah, Kalmann. Hello, young man!" Kolbeinn called over to me as I stepped back out of the room. "Are you here to see your grandfather? How nice of you!" Kolbeinn shuffled towards me with his hand outstretched. "You're lucky you caught me, I'm just off to the construction firm. I saw your grandfather in the Chapel Corridor."

I nodded and shook his hand. Kolbeinn was no longer all there; he probably still believed he was in charge of something. But he actually lived in the room next to my grandfather. I didn't know what he used to be in charge of. Perhaps he had been a carpenter. Sometimes he greeted the residents over lunch and enquired as to everyone's well-being, checking the chairs as he did so, shaking them a little and promising to repair this or that chair as soon as he had a moment – which he never did.

"Great," I said. I left Kolbeinn standing there and headed into the Chapel Corridor. All the corridors and sections of the building here had names. For example, there was the Main Corridor, which led away from the main entrance, the Harbour Corridor and the Garðar Hall. My grandfather lived in the Náttfari Corridor. But he really was sitting on a chair in the Chapel Corridor, as Kolbeinn had claimed – so perhaps he hadn't yet lost all his marbles after all. Grandfather was smartly dressed, in a white shirt, black trousers and red, fluffy slippers, just sitting there and looking out of the window. His chin jutted out a little, and he was grimacing as though he had something stuck in his throat. He had become even greyer since I'd last visited him, exactly a week ago.

Grandfather looked at me in confusion as I pulled up a chair and sat down next to him.

"Hello, Grandfather," I said. "How are you?" No answer. "Are you thirsty?" Grandfather muttered something. "Do you perhaps want a cola?"

"No," he said.

I stood up and went to the drinks machine in the Main Corridor, bought a can of cola and took it back to Grandfather. But he still wasn't thirsty, so I drank the whole can myself.

"Róbert is probably dead," I told him. Grandfather looked at me, furrowing his brow. "You know, Róbert McKenzie, our king. But it turns out his name isn't McKenzie after all, that's what Óttar said. Did you know that? Róbert gave himself the name. I showed the police the spot where the blood was in the snow, up by the Arctic Henge. It was his. And there was lots of it too."

"McKenzie!" cried Grandfather suddenly. "It's only what he deserved!" He looked at me with such fury that no one would have been able to hold his gaze.

"Well," I said, then looked away and said in a voice that somehow wasn't even mine: "They haven't found him. They don't know what happened to him. They're still looking for him, now the snow's almost gone, but there are no traces. All they know is that they won't find him alive. That's a certainty. So no reason to worry."

"It's what he deserved, the bastard! Fuck off!"

Grandfather was still staring at me. His gaze was angry and fixed. I was familiar with this. Sometimes he wasn't at all the Grandfather he had once been. "That devil, that damn dog! Go to hell, you bastard!" Grandfather went all red in the face. He was shaking, and his eyes began to well up. Did he mean me? He was scaring me quite a lot, so I looked down at my hands in my lap. They were completely white.

A nurse came past and must have noticed that something wasn't okay, because she asked me whether everything was okay. I could have cried. Because everything really wasn't okay. Grandfather was no longer Grandfather! He was so angry he was scaring me.

"Come on, Kalmann," said the woman, who I didn't know well but had seen here a few times. "Your grandfather doesn't mean it. People in his situation are sometimes very angry for reasons that are unclear. But he doesn't mean it. I'm sure of that!"

I nodded sadly and followed her, even letting her take me by the hand, because with women I sometimes make an exception. Besides, I almost couldn't see a thing; everything was blurry.

The nurse led me into the staff break room. "Do you want a piece of cake?"

I nodded and wiped the tears from my eyes.

"Come on, we still have some left from yesterday. But" – and now she held her index finger to her lips and said "Shhh!" – "don't tell anyone. Lunch is in half an hour."

The woman sat down with me for a little while and drank a coffee, asking me what the weather was like in Raufarhöfn and whether the missing hotel owner had been found, but she kept looking at her watch. Clearly she hadn't watched the daily news, and that's why she didn't know I was actually famous today. Before long she had finished her coffee. It probably hadn't been very hot. She excused herself and left me alone in the break room.

I thought about Magga. About the other things she'd said during the long car journey. Something about quota speculations. I knew what she meant by that. Grandfather had once explained it to me, back when he was still him. He was annoyed about the quota speculations, probably because he was a commie, and when I asked him to explain it all to me, he thought for a while and then explained it to me with a good example.

"In the store they sell sweets, right?"

I nodded. I loved sweets. That's why I had to go to the dentist every year to have holes drilled. I didn't love that at all.

"Now, Kalli, imagine that everyone can help themselves to the sweets. For free. What do you think would happen then?"

My eyes gleamed. "I would take an entire sack full home with me!" I said.

"Correct," said Grandfather. "And all your friends?"

"Them too!" I said, even though I didn't have any proper friends.

Grandfather was content. "Correct. And what then?" I didn't have to think for long before I realized that the sweets would soon all be gone. "Correct. The sweets would soon be used up. That's exactly what happened with the fish in the ocean. All the fishermen caught as many fish as they could, until there were no more fish left. But then the state imposed a catch quota, which means that everyone can only catch a certain quantity of fish, kind of like if every child can only take three sweets."

"Every day?"

"Hm. Let's say every week."

"For free?"

"Yes, for free."

"Okay," I said. That sounded fair.

"Yes, it's actually okay," said Grandfather. "Not at all stupid. But now everyone who wants to can sell their quota. Let's say you prefer potato chips to sweets, so you sell your quota to Heidar's boy —"

"Gulli!"

"...Gulli, who loves sweets, and you get ten thousand krona from him. For that he can take six sweets from the store from then on."

"Ten thousand krona?"

"It's quite a lot, isn't it? With that you can buy an awful lot of potato chips or a new bike."

"A new bike?"

"It doesn't matter what. But Gulli has a plan. He buys up all the quotas until no one apart from him is allowed to take sweets. So now he owns all the quotas. And anyone who wants sweets has to buy them from him, and for a great deal of money."

"Then it's lucky that everyone has ten thousand krona."

"Hmm," said Grandfather. "But now something really bad happens. Gulli moves to Reykjavík. And he takes all the sweet quotas with him. Because they belong to him, after all. The sweets stay in Raufarhöfn regardless, it's just that no one can help themselves to them any more. And then you idiots up in Raufarhöfn have no sweets left. Nothing but new bicycles, which you can't use in winter anyway!"

I was offended. I was angry. I wondered what the police would say about it. They should just get rid of the quota! Now I understood that it worked similarly with the fish and that the quota speculations were unfair. And what's more: the fish actually belonged to all Icelanders, as Grandfather had once explained to me, but only a few people were making a fortune from them.

Grandfather was always able to explain everything to me in a way I understood. Back then. Not any more. And yet I would have been really interested to know what Grandfather would have said about the whole missing person case, and I was struggling to imagine what he might have said.

Grandfather wasn't where he was before, but I didn't have to search for him long, because he was in the bathroom, where he was peeing into the sink. Catching sight of me, he grunted with irritation and slammed the door behind him.

After a while he came shuffling out of the bathroom, his trousers open. His belt was almost slipping out of the loops and dangled between his legs. I helped him close his trousers. He let me. But I didn't dare look him in the eye. I was still a little insulted because he had been so angry with me, even if he hadn't meant it. He smelled funny.

"Are you going to Keflavík again today?" he asked me.

"Do you mean Raufarhöfn?" I asked him.

"No, Keflavík!" he insisted, but then didn't even want to hear the answer.

Then the lunch gong rang, and we went to eat, but Grandfather wasn't hungry and silently pushed his plate away. I ate only the mashed potatoes, the sauce and the pork, but when it came to the vegetables my stomach was full to bursting.

Lísa was sitting at our table, as she often did. I don't know why she always sat with Grandfather. And she usually asked whether the fourth place at the table was still free, because her friend was coming to visit her, but to this day her friend had never come. So the fourth place always remained free. Lísa was always dressed as though she were about to go out, with her handbag, hat and everything. Sometimes she stood outside the entrance and waited for the bus, as she explained, and yet there wasn't even a bus stop in front of the care home. The people here really had lost their marbles. At least Grandfather was in good company.

For dessert there was carrot cake. It was delicious. I ate Grandfather's piece too, until I started to feel sick and couldn't force down another bite.

"My daughter fell out of the window yesterday," said Lísa, smiling at me expectantly. She always said strange things like that, so you didn't even need to react.

"She's crazy," said Grandfather, and then Lísa looked really sad.

Once we were back in the room, I pulled out my little plastic container of hákarl. I always had a little folding knife with me. It had a good edge to it. I cut the hákarl into little pieces, and Grandfather watched me impatiently. Once I was done, he helped himself and hummed contentedly.

"It's enough to bring tears to your eyes," he sighed.

I was so proud.

There was a knock, the door opened, a nurse stepped into the room but immediately came to a halt, as though she had run into an invisible wall, said "No thank you!", turned on her heel and hurried out again. But before she closed the door behind her, she cried out: "Open the window, for God's sake!"

"Are they biting?" asked Grandfather. And suddenly he was there! I didn't hesitate. When Grandfather was suddenly there, you had to seize the moment.

"I got new bait," I said quickly. "But I'm leaving the pieces in the barrels a little longer, and then they'll bite for sure, you'll see! Perhaps I'll go out tomorrow, or the day after tomorrow, let's see."

Grandfather nodded and chewed. "And *Petra*'s running well?"

I nodded. "I changed the oil. Sæmundur helped me."

Grandfather studied me. "You're really good at it," he said. "I always knew you would be." I nodded and tried to suppress a grin. Grandfather grabbed my hand and squeezed it tightly, so much so that it almost hurt. "Your shark is really delicious. The best shark in the whole of Iceland!"

"You're pulling my leg!" I cried with a snort.

"No, I'm not! The shark catchers in the Westfjords might as well throw in the towel!"

I was so proud! But I didn't have time to be proud for long, because Grandfather was tired and asked me to fetch him a coffee. I wasn't quick enough though, because when I came back, he had already gone to sleep and couldn't be woken; he was breathing heavily and snoring slightly. Even when I patted his cheeks he still slept on. I soon got bored, and the coffee got cold, but it wasn't long anyway until Magga would pick me up, so I quietly said goodbye, kissed Grandfather on both stubbly cheeks and his forehead, gave him a long hug and left.

Outside, I sat down on a bench and waited until Magga arrived. I wasn't happy at all, it was as though I had a hole inside me. Half an hour later she came speeding around the corner, and she must have underestimated it, because her tin can was leaning precariously. If she'd had her foot on the accelerator any more, the thing would have over-turned and rolled, taking Magga with it, into the nearest garden. But she came to an abrupt halt pretty close to the bench. I pulled in my feet. I saw immediately that Magga was in a good mood. The back seats were piled high with shopping bags, up to the windows, and one of them was for me, I knew that, that was understood, we always did it like that. Magga had a new hairdo, and to make sure I noticed, she carefully touched her palms to her hair, prompting me to comment that she had a new hairdo, which made her even happier. Magga often went to the hairdresser when we drove to Húsavík, but you couldn't always see the differ-ence. The very first time, when I of course hadn't noticed a thing, even though she had a completely new hairstyle, she explained to me that you always have to be very attentive in the presence of women and give them compliments, that women like that. This was a good piece of advice, because I really wanted a wife but hadn't yet found one, and so good advice was like gold. It was important that I did everything right, and that's why I practised with her, always being very attentive and trying to notice when she had a new hairdo. We even made a kind of game out of it, and sometimes, if I didn't notice, I would lose points, even though we didn't actually have a points list. But if we had had a points list, I would have been many points ahead. So Magga smiled this time too, flattered, and said I'd gained ten points, and already she was stepping vigorously on the accelerator pedal, racing over a speed bump which was actually intended to slow down the traffic, so that we almost became airborne, but we were instantly brought back down to the ground, the front bumper taking the brunt, yet once we had left Húsavík behind us, Magga didn't drive at seventy kilometres per hour any more, because a few vehicles passed us on the other side of the road. She talked the entire way to Raufarhöfn, and at times I wasn't even listening properly, but I pricked up my ears when she started to tell the story of a fight which seemed to have occurred in Húsavík at the weekend. A drunken Romanian had been putting the moves on women in the Gamli Baukur restaurant, and even felt one of them up, prompting her to give him a clip round the ear, which made the Romanian, who the Húsavíkings called Troll, angry. He gave the woman such a hard shove that she fell across the table, knocking all the beer and wine glasses down to the floor. She got really bad cuts on her hands, which resulted in a fist fight between the Icelanders and Romanians. Magga shook her head in disgust. She had encountered this Troll once in the store, she said, and had immediately had a bad feeling. The Romanians, she said, were a problem, because the ones we ended up with weren't the best specimens. Not like the Poles, most of whom, despite barely knowing any Icelandic even after ten years, were at least hard-working, both the women and the men. And if all this immigration continued, we would end up the same as the Europeans, plagued with bands of robbers from eastern Europe.

I knew from Nói that Romanians and Lithuanians in particular stole things, but that the majority of house burglaries were committed by drug addicts, and they were Icelanders, because drug addiction has nothing to do with nationality. And I told Magga that, even though I usually didn't say much.

Magga looked at me, and was either surprised because I'd said something or because she'd believed it was only ever Romanians who made trouble. In any case, she looked at me, and this meant she wasn't looking where we were going, until the wheels ended up at the side of the road and began to spray up slush. Magga let out a startled cry and wrenched the steering wheel around, but accelerated at the same time, and the thought came to me, as I gripped my seat and gritted my teeth, that I might perhaps have seen my grandfather for the last time.

"Lithuanians?" she said. "But the ones in our village are Lithuanians, aren't they? In the hotel, they're Lithuanians!"

That was true. And that's why I nodded emphatically. I was sweating.

"Aren't they?" asked Magga, looking at me again.

"Yes, Lithuanians!" I cried and pointed at the road, because I wanted Magga to look at the road too, which she then did.

"Poor Róbert," she said. "Perhaps the Lithuanians murdered him." She paused, went quiet for a moment, then added: "Organized crime," and sighed and continued: "In our Raufarhöfn. Nowhere's safe any more. We'd have to go to the North Pole to be safe."

"There are polar bears there," I reminded her, and Magga laughed and said to give it a rest with my polar bears, otherwise they really would come! Then she told me some things about Róbert, who apparently used to be a handsome man, a proper heartthrob who numerous women had been in love with, a young, successful bachelor who had even lived in exotic foreign lands for seven or eight years, and had made a fortune with fish farming in Brazil.

"Aquaculture," said Magga. "Farming fish, that's genius. You don't even have to catch the fish. They're already in the net!"

"But you have to feed them," I said.

"Still, it's much easier," said Magga.

"Big fish eat little fish," I said. I knew that from Grandfather. "That's why you have to go fishing regardless." But Magga shook her head and looked kind of sad, she said that poor Róbert had worked far too hard, and then there was the whole stress with the quota, the hotel and the financial disaster of the Arctic Henge. The financial crisis had hit him hard, she said. And the strain could be seen on him. He had changed so much in recent years, had started drinking too much again, but she didn't even want to know, couldn't even imagine what he looked like now, in other words dead. But Magga shook away the thought and asked me how Grandfather was, and I told her that I had brought him some hákarl, and that he'd then chatted with me for a while and —

"How wonderful! Well done you!" cried Magga. She explained to me that we connect memories with our sense of smell and so on, I wasn't listening properly any more, because I was thinking about Grandfather and what he'd said, trying to remember precisely, because I really didn't know whether I would survive this car journey. "Your hákarl is the best in all of Iceland!" Magga seemed in high spirits, where just a minute ago she'd been sad. Now she was in a really good mood, as though she'd won the lottery. She alternated between crawling along at sixty, then speeding along at a hundred, whatever she was thinking about seemed to transfer to her right foot, and that's why she had to ask me twice whether I still had some on me.

"What?"

"Hákarl!"

Yes, I did. And when she dropped me off in front of my house, I gave her the entire plastic container with the remaining hákarl, that's how happy I was that I'd survived the trip, and Magga was really appreciative, saying that she would go home right away and have a decent piece, along with some Brennivín aquavit to wash it down, and she sped off contentedly. I saw Elínborg opening her curtains, first staring after Magga and then fixing her gaze on me.

I went into the house and lay down on the sofa, feeling completely exhausted, turned on the TV and had a nap.

Nói woke me, or rather my laptop woke me, tooting as Nói tried to reach me on Messenger.

"Mr N!" I yawned.

"Forget the Pressure Cooker," said Nói as he picked up a can of Red Bull which was in the picture, lifted it out of the picture, downed it, crushed the can with some effort and threw it into the waste-paper basket that presumably stood beside him. It sounded as though there were already other cans in it.

I of course had known for a while that the Pressure Cooker hadn't killed Róbert. You sense that kind of thing, but I didn't want to spoil Nói's fun.

"How come?" I asked, playing the innocent.

"It can't have been him," said Nói.

"But why not?"

"His alibi's watertight."

"Alibi?"

"One hundred per cent! At first, I thought I was on the right track. Did you know the guy isn't allowed to go out to sea any more because he has psychological problems?"

"Really?" I hadn't known that.

"He's a sick bastard. On his last trip out, he almost beat the engineer to death."

"Oh, *that* story," I said, because I knew the story, but I hadn't known that Óttar wasn't allowed to work on a boat any more because of it. And he hadn't actually beaten up the engineer, who was his brother-in-law, he'd just shoved him around a bit. But then the brother-in-law had got a divorce and moved away, so there was no need to worry.

"The engineer probably complained about the soup," said Nói, laughing loudly and holding his belly, and I imagined, but couldn't see, him throwing back his head. Then Nói began to cough, and he coughed and coughed, a dry roar of a cough that really hurt my ears, and I almost saw his face, because Nói bent forwards, but then two things happened almost at the same time: in the background, the door to his room opened, and the connection broke off.

Twenty minutes later, Nói called back.

"He made a few comments on Facebook around the time the hotel owner disappeared. He was all worked up for a good few hours and left thirty-five comments in a feed."

Nói sounded completely different. His voice was kind of monotone, as though his throat were hurting him. His tongue lay heavy in his mouth, like he was drunk.

"Is everything okay?" I asked.

"Of course," said Nói, and then nothing more for a while.

"So what was it about on Facebook?"

"He's right, really," slurred Nói, sitting there motionless. "This whole feminist shit has got out of hand. The Pressure Cooker took on about three women in a forum, and they tried to wipe the floor with him, but he defended himself brilliantly until eventually the women stopped responding. If you ask me, it's true, we men work longer and harder. Have done for centuries. And now the women want to earn as much as we do? Slow down, doll! Pick up a hammer and build a house, then we can talk!"

I laughed but then felt a little ashamed, thinking about my mother, who always worked until she dropped. Óttar only worked part-time in the hotel restaurant, I knew that. That's why he could spend three hours writing Facebook comments. He had also started drinking again. Gin and tonic.

"The Pressure Cooker is an alcoholic too, like Róbert," I said. "He mixed himself a drink recently."

"That makes sense," said Nói. "The way he was expressing himself on Facebook suggests he was drunk. Which leads me to another clue…"

Nói paused, a long pause, and I held my breath. He was wheezing irregularly. Something wasn't right with him. Then the call broke off again. Ten minutes later, he was back.

"Who shot the sheriff?"

"What?"

"Don't you want to hear about the clue I found?"

"Of course!" I said, confused. Nói seemed his old self again.

"So why don't you ask?"

"What's your clue?"

"Money, dinero, cash. Follow the money!"

"Okay. But where to?"

"No!" said Nói.

"No?"

"No."

"So, no."

"Where from?"

"Where from?"

"Where does all the money come *from*."

"I don't know that either, unfortunately," I said.

"We have to follow the flow of cash. The alcohol in the bar. The Pressure Cooker works very little and is an alcoholic. That costs money. It doesn't make sense. Who's paying?"

"Robert," I guessed, because Robert was the only rich man in Raufarhöfn. "The two of them are good friends, they always have been."

"Well then! Róbert's paying. His childhood friend. His employer. The hotel owner is paying. So he has money. But where from? Certainly not from the hotel business. You barely get any guests up there – although I wish you'd get a whole load of them, because we have too many down here."

"No thank you," I said. "I don't like tourists in the slightest. They sit down at my table!"

"Exactly. I know that only too well."

"They should fuck off!"

"Kalmann, keep your eye on the ball! Remember that the hotel owner built this heap of stones, the Arctic Henge or whatever."

138

"But only half of it."

"So he ran out of money."

"That's true."

"But!" Nói raised his index finger. "Where does the money come from?"

"People gave donations. And he made his fortune farming fish in Brazil."

"Oh, that was him?"

"And he also has a catch quota."

"Interesting. Very interesting. It all makes sense. The quota kings are the richest bandits in the country. But why couldn't he complete the Arctic Henge? Did he really run out of money?"

"Good question."

"Or better, *why* did he run out? There are several possibilities. One. The Arctic Henge made him go bust. Two. The hotel made him go bust. But perhaps that was the plan; a debt scheme in order to pay less tax. Three. Women. Four. Alcohol..."

"Women?" I felt dizzy.

"Correctamundo. But now I ask you..." Nói paused again, leaned forwards and said: "What came first? The money or the alcohol?"

"What?"

"The chicken or the egg?"

"The chicken," I guessed, because an egg can't lay itself.

"It's possible, after all, that the hotel owner is distilling alcohol. Or the Pressure Cooker! Or the Lithuanian drug mafia! And the hotel owner got wind of it, wanted to blow the whistle on them and was bumped off."

"The Lithuanians are really nice," I said without hesitating, "especially Nadja."

"Who's Nadja?"

"She works in the hotel and she's reeeeally hot!"

Nói straightened up and started tapping away on his keyboard. "Do you know her surname?"

"No."

"Nadja…" Nói clicked the mouse a few times. "…Nadja Staiva! Wait… Wow. She's really hot! Ay caramba!" Nói jiggled around on the chair. "And the broad's nice too, you say? Why didn't you tell me that earlier!"

A few mouse clicks later, I had pictures of her on my screen which Nói had found on Facebook. Selfies in sunglasses or with friends, her lips pursed into a pout, at Gullfoss Falls, at Geysir Falls, at a lighthouse, at a party and in a city, but certainly not Reykjavík, probably in Lithuania. I had never seen her with so much make-up on, and she was even more beautiful in the pictures. But now I realized that she hadn't grown up on a farm.

Nói was pissed off. "And you're always complaining to me that there aren't any babes in Raufarhöfn!"

"What I meant by that," I said, defending myself, "is that there aren't any women here for me, I mean, ones I would have a chance with. Either they're too old or, like Nadja, too hot. And already taken."

"Fuck me!" said Nói. "That sucks balls, bro!"

I nodded. Nói opened a can of Red Bull while I told him about the Lithuanians: "There's another Lithuanian woman, but she has her boyfriend with her too. They're all friends."

"They're probably all doing it with each other!" speculated Nói, taking a drink.

I nodded sadly and thought about Nadja. When she first came to Raufarhöfn, she had ignored me. That was two or three years ago now. But ever since I had run into the Lithuanians while they were out on a boat trip, Nadja had been really nice to me. She asked me for advice now and then too. She wanted to know where on the internet you could find the weather forecast for sailors. High and low tide, wind maps, ocean currents and so on. I also told her about the website that shows you exactly where all the ships in the world are, which made her very interested and happy. I didn't even know Lithuanians liked making boat trips so much. But then there was so much I didn't know about her. For example, that all Lithuanians can speak Russian. I thought that was badass. If you look at the map of the world, you can see how big Russia is. And Nadja could speak to everyone there! But on the map you can also see that Lithuania is on the Baltic Sea, which explains the fondness for boat trips. And I learned that Lithuanians like to make soup. You can tell by the menu at the hotel. Recently there were also potato patties. They were delicious, even though I preferred fries with Thousand Island dressing.

"Her boyfriend is called Darius," Nói established. "Darius… Ziol… Ziol… Ziolkowski. Terrible name. I don't like the look of him. He looks suspicious! An army guy." Nói was still tapping around on Facebook. He sent me a picture of Darius sitting on a tank in camouflage gear, a gun resting on his thigh, making a victory sign with his fingers. "A professional killer," said Nói.

I shuddered. All this information was overwhelming. It was unpleasant to find out that a professional killer was working in the hotel and had a woman who was probably far too sweet for him and who could have been my ideal woman. This Darius had never even said hello to me. That was suspicious in itself. Nói agreed.

"What do you know about the other two?" he asked, and I had to admit that I didn't know a thing about them. I'd heard their names, sure, though I couldn't remember them because they weren't Icelandic, but Nói wanted to try and get to the bottom of the matter using the internet. At least I was able to describe what the Lithuanians looked like. Nadja's girlfriend was a little heavier than her, but had great lips and a kind of dot on her cheek, a fleck. And long brown hair…

"Sexy!" groaned Nói. He had found her.

Her boyfriend had short black hair, a broad head, broad shoulders and a tattoo on his upper arm that you could see half of, because he usually went around in a T-shirt even though it was cold. I knew that they all smoked, that they did all the work in the hotel: cleaning, laundry, doing the dishes, waiting on guests, serving food, painting, mending things, changing light bulbs and taking out the rubbish. They did everything. I knew that once a week they clambered into their rusty Subaru and drove to Húsavík to buy groceries. I knew that they sent money back home – Nadja had told me once. I knew that Nadja was saving money and wanted to buy a house in Lithuania.

I told Nói all of this, and for him it confirmed his theory that there was something off about the Lithuanians, that they needed money, that they didn't intend to stay in Iceland, and that they knew how to kill somebody. Nói instructed me to keep on the alert and see how the Lithuanians behaved now. Were they shaken up? Were they cheerful? Downbeat? Relieved? What did Nadja have to say about the whole thing? Nói told me to engage her in conversation, which made me really nervous, because it was usually Nadja who spoke to me first. And that's why that evening I couldn't fall asleep for a long while. I lay awake in bed for ages, looking at the clock, until it was one o'clock, half past one, two. Then half past two. I was so worked up inside, yet at that point I didn't even know that Magga was lying dead in her kitchen and, like me, staring up at the ceiling.

10

CORPSE

I wondered where the strange light on my bedroom ceiling was coming from. I had just woken up, and I don't always know where I am, who I am or what's happening. I stare up at the ceiling and study the strange, dancing light, as though the sea level has risen overnight and lifted the house from its foundations. As though I'm adrift on the ocean. It's the sunlight, reflected off the waves and flickering through the window. Then I have these silly thoughts. About climate change. Melting glaciers. I thought about Grandfather, who had sometimes said that Iceland is swimming on the sea, it's just that no one's noticed. There's this movie in which all the glaciers have melted and the water's so high that there's no land left. Nothing but sea. The hero is half-man, half-fish. He can breathe underwater, but he's good-looking, not like a fish. That's called evolution. And anyone who doesn't believe in evolution is mentally disabled. That's what Nói said. You only have to switch on the TV to start wondering whether it's right to bring any more children into this world. I do like children, though. And there was a time when I knew who the mother of my children would be: Dagbjört. But life doesn't always work out the way we want. My mother says that too.

In those half seconds when I'm waking up but still asleep, I sometimes think about sex too. Even though I wasn't in love with Dagbjört any more, I wouldn't have said no if she'd climbed into bed with me to make babies. Those are the embers of love. They burn a whole life long. Even if the fire has long since gone out, the embers smoulder, deep within the ashes. Magga said that.

Anyway, these were the thoughts I was caught up in as the flashing blue light danced on my ceiling, as I lay there in bed with a rock-hard penis, and it dawned on me only gradually that there was a police car in front of my house. The knock on the door propelled me out of bed, I stumbled in just my underpants down the steep staircase and flung open the door. Only then did I properly wake up.

Police Commissioner Birna looked me up and down, said: "Get dressed!" and I closed the door, and in the same moment it occurred to me that I should have left it open, because Birna knocked on it once more. So I immediately opened it again and hurried upstairs, where I got dressed. Then I came down the stairs as quickly as I could, wanting Birna to know that I was taking things seriously, even though I didn't know what she wanted from me, and wondered whether perhaps I shouldn't have opened the door at all but instead pretended I wasn't home. In the meantime, Birna had come inside and was looking around. Today she was uniformed and armed, she even had pepper spray and a truncheon on her belt. From her shoulder hung a small police walkie-talkie. Birna was scowling, and she looked tired. Older.

"Sit down!" she said, pointing towards a chair at the table.

I sat down and now really regretted having opened the door. My head started to feel hot, and that meant it would also be red. Birna towered over me, her hands resting on her truncheon belt. She gave me a long, hard stare.

"Why are you smiling?" she asked, and I shrugged, trying not to smile but failing. "Is this just a game to you? Police cars, flashing lights – there's finally something happening in Raufarhöfn? Is that it?"

I shrugged again. Birna sighed, looked down at the floor, exhaled in a strained manner and shook her head.

"I need coffee," she said, but not as if she was asking me for a coffee. She was just talking to herself.

"Magga is dead," she said then, out of the blue. My eyes widened. Magga was dead? *The* Magga? The one who had dropped me off in front of my house only yesterday? Birna studied me again and leaned forwards. "Dead. In the kitchen. On the floor. Blue face. Dead."

Perhaps my question wasn't well timed, but I was struggling to think clearly. I had only just woken up, after all, and the police commissioner was staring right into my face, which was unpleasant, but I heard myself say:

"So who's going to drive me to Húsavík now? It's just that Magga drives me there every Saturday…" I fell silent. But Birna's expression softened.

"Do you like Magga?"

I shrugged. "Mostly. Not always. She's nice to me. But she talks so much that your ears practically fall off!"

"So what did you two talk about?"

I looked at Birna in horror. The journey from Raufarhöfn to Húsavík takes two hours. So that's four hours there and back. And Magga had talked almost without pause. Was I supposed to summarize all four hours of the conversation? I mean, most the time I hadn't even been listening!

"Take your time," said Birna. She didn't sound so abrupt now, and even sat down opposite me at the table. I looked at her out of the corner of my eye and completely forgot to think back to yesterday. "Did you talk about the weather?"

"No… Yes! Perhaps."

"Did you talk about your grandfather?"

I was genuinely grateful for her suggestions. Because now I remembered what we'd talked about.

"Yes!" I said in relief. "About Grandfather and about the whole thing with Róbert."

"There we go," said Birna with a tired smile. "What exactly?"

I shrugged. My head wasn't fully awake yet.

"Was Magga sad about Róbert's disappearance?"

"A bit," I said. "Perhaps a little. She said that Róbert used to be a really handsome and nice man. A heartthrob. So maybe she was sad."

"But she didn't like him any more?"

"Magga always complains about everyone and everything," I said. And then I remembered something else: "Magga had just had her hair done. And she was pleased with my hákarl."

Birna frowned. "You gave her hákarl?"

I nodded. "I always take some with me when I visit Grandfather."

"You can smell it," said Birna. "Her house smells like yours." Birna wrinkled her nose and looked lost in thought. "Why didn't she like Róbert any more?"

"Róbert? I think she did like him. She was just sad. But she didn't like his workers, the Lithuanians."

Birna sighed and mumbled: "No speaka íslenska."

"That's what she said too. She doesn't like the Lithuanians nor the Romanians nor the blacks nor the youths nor the politicians nor the tourists nor the weather nor the traffic."

I felt as though I was being helpful.

"What did she say when she dropped you off here, last night?"

"She said thanks for the hákarl. She likes my hákarl. I make probably the second-best hákarl in the whole of Iceland."

"I believe you," said Birna. The walkie-talkie fastened to her shoulder suddenly started making noises, and then a crackly voice asked for her. Birna turned her head towards the walkie-talkie, pressed a button and said that she was done here and would be right over. Then she looked at me again, for quite a long while. And I returned her gaze, because I thought she was about to say something, but she didn't, she just looked at me. She was tired, I could tell that by looking at her, and she was kind of staring right through me. Then she sighed, clapped her palms down on the table, got up and, without a word of goodbye, walked out as though I was no longer even there. She slammed the front door behind her, fired up the car engine, and soon the blue lights on the ceiling had disappeared. And I sat there at the kitchen table, and only then did I fully realize that Magga no longer existed. And I wondered again who would drive me to Húsavík to see Grandfather now. And so I called my mother.

11
MOTHER

Three hours later, she was there. And I had fallen asleep on the couch again. Perhaps she'd been there a while already, because I hadn't even heard her come in, and by the time I woke up she had already cleared up the kitchen and washed the dishes. But when she noticed I was awake, she sat down beside me on the couch, kissed my forehead and stroked my hair.

"Good morning, sleepyhead," she said.

"Mama," I said, rubbing my eyes.

"What kind of mischief have you got yourself into?" she said.

"Mama!"

"Why didn't you call me sooner? You know I can come any time."

I gave a big yawn, making my mother do the same. She looked around and said tiredly: "I should have come sooner."

At that moment, there was another knock at the door.

"Birna," I said in a pained tone.

"Who?"

"The police. Don't open the door!"

"Why ever not? Have you broken the law?" My mother was already on her feet. There was another knock. I hid my face from view under the cushion. "Kalmann!" said my mother accusingly.

"Kalmann?" called Birna from outside. "Are you there?"

My mother went to the door and opened it.

"Stupid bitch!" I cried into the cushion.

And now they were standing opposite one another, my mother and Birna, both looking at one another in surprise. These women were unbearable!

"Kalmann?" said my mother, as I ran up the steps to my room and slammed the door behind me, making the entire house shake.

"Bitch!" I hissed, throwing myself onto my bed. I could hear the two women talking downstairs. I held my breath.

The house I live in was built in 1912. I know this because the year is written outside above the entrance. It's one of the oldest houses in Raufarhöfn, and also one of the smallest. If someone is sitting on the toilet and lets off a loud fart, you can hear it even in the attic room. So I heard every word that was said downstairs. I kept really still, climbed down off the bed, laid down gently on the floor and held my right ear to the floorboards. In this way I was just a few metres away from the two women. The floorboards smelled of wood and sleep.

First, they explained to one another who they were. Birna, after all, had no idea that I had a mother who occasionally checked in to see if I was okay. She was surprised to discover that my mother lived in Akureyri, and even said that I'd never mentioned her, at which point I could imagine the expression of annoyance on my mother's face. She didn't like it when I acted as though she didn't exist, as though only Grandfather had raised me. But my mother didn't say anything, because she wanted to find out from Birna whether I had broken the law, and I held my breath, because I wanted to know that too. No, said Birna, after which my mother promptly moved on to her next question: What business did Birna have being in my house, and didn't she know that she, in other words, my mother, was my legal guardian, and then Birna became flustered and dodged the questions. She swiftly tried to summarize the whole story with the blood and the polar bear and Magga, but I think she shouldn't have said that Magga was lying there dead in her kitchen just a few houses down the street, and that I was the last person who had seen her alive, because that didn't make matters any better for Birna, because now she was subjected to the full extent of my mother's frustration, something I was very familiar with; the frustration of an underpaid nurse who had worked two shifts back to back, and for that reason I almost felt a little sorry for Birna. My mother said that it was completely unprofessional, because Birna wasn't even allowed to converse with me without my legal guardian being present, and for this reason everything I had said to her was null and void, and that she was furious, because law enforcement officials, of all people, were the ones who were supposed to enforce the laws and so on. I could now hear my mother so clearly that I didn't even have to hold my ear to the floorboards any more and could have laid back down on the bed. But I stayed on the floor and smiled with satisfaction.

My mother wanted me to move to a residential community in Akureyri, so she would no longer have to make the three-hour journey to Raufarhöfn to wash my things, clean my apartment and keep an eye on me. But I always told her I could look after myself. After all, I wasn't a kid any more!

When I was a kid, my mother never had time for me and worked almost around the clock. Her problem was that she didn't have a man. There had been attempts. Once, she even introduced one of them to me. A divorced electrician. His hair was nicely parted, and because he was nicely dressed too, he didn't look anything like an electrician. She probably hoped that she'd found a replacement father for me, but you can't just replace something like a father. A person has the same blood in their veins as their father. So there's only one. It's something you feel. That's precisely why, for me, it's completely normal to wear a cowboy hat and a sheriff's badge, it's programmed into me, no matter how much my mother complains.

But the electrician only appeared twice, and because there wasn't any room in our little house, he didn't fit into the picture.

As I lay there on the floorboards in my room, I suddenly heard Birna saying goodbye to my mother. I had stopped listening to what they were saying below me. Birna's tone was friendly, and she even added an apology, saying that she wished she didn't have to work completely alone on this complicated case, that all hell had broken loose in Reykjavík on account of the political summit, as my mother had surely heard, and Magga's sudden death certainly hadn't made things any easier. Róbert's case appeared to be a homicide, she said, and she hadn't got much sleep over the past few days, which was probably evident, but she would be grateful if my mother didn't speak to anyone about the matter, Magga's death, not yet at least, the investigation had barely begun, she needed to knock on a few more doors first, but – and here she laughed wearily – now she had revealed too much again, at which my mother promised not to discuss the matter with anyone, she barely knew anyone here in Raufarhöfn anyway and what's more didn't have the time, because her late shift started at three in the afternoon, she had to be back in Akureyri by then, and as was quite obvious, there was a lot to do here first. Then Birna assured her that I was a good boy, admirable in fact, that I had a place in the community and knew how to stand up for myself, and that I'd cooperated well and been a great help. So she didn't need to worry about me. Then my mother thanked her, and once Birna had closed the front door behind her, I heard my mother immediately begin to tidy up the living room. She put the chair back by the dining table, stuffed the rubbish from the coffee table into a bag and the dirty clothing into an IKEA bag. At one point she paused briefly, listened, said my name, but I wanted to be left alone and called out that she should leave me alone. Half an hour later, though, she came upstairs and knocked on my door, asked whether she could come in, and when I didn't answer she came into the room, sat down next to me on the floor with her back against the bed, and said: "Hello, Kalmann minn."

Although I didn't make a sound and kept my eyes closed, she probably knew I wasn't sleeping, mothers know things like that, and she said she was sorry about what had happened, and asked whether everything was okay, apart from the fact that Magga had died, which must have been a shock for me. But I simply shrugged, and my mother stroked my hair and my arm and my back, kissed me on the back of my head, and I smelled her perfume, her scent, and I was so happy she was there but didn't want her to go again, so I flung my arms around her, pulled her against me, and then I almost started crying, but I didn't want to let that happen, so I bravely swallowed down the tears. My mother asked whether I had noticed anything unusual about Magga, but I shook my head, because I really didn't want to talk about Magga right now, and my mother understood and was content with the answer. Then she just sat there and stroked me, but suddenly she stood abruptly, blew her nose and began to pick up my dirty laundry. She opened all the windows in the house, went out to her car and returned with the IKEA bag full of clean laundry, filled my closet and changed the hand towels in the bathroom.

I went downstairs and made us some tea. My mother liked tea. I actually prefer coffee. But only with milk and lots of sugar. Most people who serve me coffee know that. Mostly I don't even have to tell them any more. But I like tea too. And I know how to prepare it. Once I'd poured the hot water into the cups containing the teabags, I called out: "Mama, the tea's ready!"

I heard my mother sigh with contentment and say that she was just coming. She sat down with me at the table and looked at me in that way only mothers do. And that some-how made me very happy, and being happy is something I like. If I could, I would always be happy. But that's not possible. You can't control your feelings. Only robots can do that. And Dr Phil. Anyway, my mother was completely content too. We slurped our tea, almost burned our lips and told one another that, but otherwise we didn't say any-thing. You don't have to chatter constantly, after all. There was once a woman who talked a lot, and now she was dead. Magga. Now she wouldn't say another word. She'd be silent forever. It's a funny thing.

My mother looked at her watch and sighed. She didn't like it that the hands kept turning relentlessly.

I studied her. I didn't look anything like her, but she'd told me I looked like my father, Quentin Boatwright. He had been stationed on the American military base in Keflavík. That was back when the Americans were still in Iceland, and that was why my mother had been able to make a baby with an American in the first place. She had never told me in detail how it had come about. I only knew that my mother had worked on the military base as a secretary. And after she became pregnant, she worked in the fish-processing plant in Keflavík as best she could with a large belly. Then she moved in with my grandfather in Raufarhöfn, because my grandmother had died unexpectedly.

My father Quentin Boatwright left the military base, where he lived with his wife and two daughters, was suddenly redeployed, and eventually my mother no longer knew where he was, so I didn't reckon on ever meeting him. But then, one wonderful day when I was nine years old, my mother and I drove all the way from Raufarhöfn to Keflavík. After we had been driving for a few hours, she told me that my father was on the island and wanted to meet me. We drove the almost seven hundred kilometres in two days, staying the night with Aunt Guðrún in Reykir in Hrútafjörður, where there used to be another American military base. And the next day we drove straight to Keflavík and picked up my father at the military checkpoint. I had to climb into the back seat, because my father got in the front, I remember that clearly, and that's normal, that's the rule: grown-ups sit in the front. I also remember that he wasn't wearing uniform and was much shorter than I had imagined. He was even a finger-width shorter than my mother, but very strong. He turned around to me and stretched out his hand, but I hid my hands beneath my bottom. My father left his hand hanging in the air for a while, then eventually shook his head and gave my mother a questioning look. But she acted as though she hadn't noticed. He had close-cropped hair, so you could see clearly when he frowned. Mother noticed it too. In that instant, I realized she was on my side. Strange. I can remember that moment so well.

We drove around the area for a while, ate a hamburger in Keflavík and an ice cream in Sandgerdi. I didn't say a single word the whole time, but my parents conversed here and there, exchanging trivial chit-chat. Once my father tried to kiss my mother, and touched her hair too, but she said no and turned away. And so, luckily, I was spared the smooching. Before we drove back to the military base, we passed a warehouse in the middle of a lava field, where my father knocked on the door, lit himself a cigarette and waited until the door was opened. My father disappeared into the dark warehouse, then came back out with a wooden box under his arm, loading it into the back without showing us the contents.

He got back in the car and explained that the box contained a pistol, a Mauser C96, semi-automatic, inherited from his father, who had fought in the Korean War and only just survived. Luckily, I had spent my childhood in front of the TV, accidentally learning English in the process, so I understood practically everything my father said. He talked like MacGyver or like David Hasselhoff on *Baywatch*. As I was his only son, he explained, the gun now belonged to me. That was the tradition where he was from, that's how it was, and that's why he'd wanted to see me, here in Iceland, face to face. But my mother became anxious, and said we didn't need any heirlooms, and especially not any weapons, but my father was really stubborn and insisted on it, and his words echoed in my head the whole journey back, I repeated them in a whisper so my mother wouldn't hear, but I didn't want to forget the words – his last words – and so, even today, I still remember what my father's parting words were: "I want him to fucking have it!"

As it later turned out, as well as an antique Mauser the box also contained whiskey bottles, cigarettes, an entire box of chewing gum, dark chocolate, military clothing including a camouflage suit and military boots, a cowboy hat, a hairdryer, a few American fashion magazines, five hundred dollars and a sheriff's badge.

On the way home, we once again stayed the night with Aunt Gudrún but arrived there very late and rid ourselves of the whiskey bottles; my mother didn't want to bring any alcohol home because back then Grandfather was an alcoholic. But the pistol we had seen for the first time in Reykir stayed in the box, because Gudrún didn't have any use for it and believed that heirlooms had to be accepted, regardless of what they were, that this was the rule.

The next day, as we drove to Raufarhöfn, my mother was so tired that she kept veering close to the side of the road. But because she was so tired and kind of absent-minded, she didn't care how much chewing gum I chewed, and so I crammed one piece after the other into my mouth until the lump was as big as a golf ball and my face muscles ached for days afterwards.

I never saw my father again. And I can't remember his face either. Not in detail. There's a shape in my memory, a precise hair parting, a height, a sound, an "I want him to fucking have it!" But nothing more.

I must have looked sad, because my mother gave my hand a comforting stroke and looked really sad too. Soon she would have to drive back to Akureyri to start her late shift. I had a lump in my throat.

"Who will drive me to Húsavík now?" I asked my mother.

She looked at me for a long while. She was thinking. And while she was thinking, she held her breath. Then she gasped for air and slumped a little, said that she'd need to clarify that, but someone would be able to, and in the worst-case scenario she would come and pick me up, there was no need for me to worry about it, I had only just visited Grandfather yesterday after all, so we still had a few days to organize something, and for now we would drink our tea, and somehow she was right. I asked whether she wanted to stay with me a little longer today. At first she didn't even react to my question, and just stared absent-mindedly into the distance, but then she said: "That's not such a bad idea actually." And then she smiled at me in a way that seemed kind of grateful.

Once my mother had finished her cup of tea, she made a few calls and switched her late shift with somebody who had an early shift, which meant she would have to work two shifts back to back but would be able to spend the afternoon with me and stay until I had fallen asleep. We had all the time in the world! We tidied the house from top to bottom, took a few sacks of rubbish to the dump, made spaghetti and watched an Adam Sandler movie. Then we went shopping, and only then were we reminded, once again, that Magga had just died.

The small village store had outlived the bakery and the police station, the theatre club and the insurance company. And the Landsbankinn, Raufarhöfn's only remaining bank, had been relocated to the community building along with the post office, although the counter was only open for a few hours once a week. Anyone who needed to post a letter could do that here in the store too. Yrsa ran the store, but her sister Gunna helped out occasionally, or her husband Einar, if bad weather stopped him from going out to sea. And yet the store was only open for a few hours each day, and it was much smaller than the stores in Akureyri for example, so there wasn't much to do. Yrsa wasn't all that good at it; there were always some things that were out of stock, and if you bought dairy products, you had to make sure they hadn't already expired. Yrsa was always surprised when that happened. If you found an out-of-date yogurt, you had to speak up, that's logical, because otherwise someone might perhaps buy the yogurt, or it would sit there in the fridge, and then Yrsa wouldn't know she needed to order a new tub of yogurt. That's why I always told her whenever I found something that had expired. Yrsa would then wrinkle her nose in this funny way, like a rabbit, hold the yogurt or whatever up close to her glasses but take a really long time to find the expiry date. Then you would stand there and wait, because she did have to check it, after all. She couldn't just believe me and put the yogurt aside, otherwise anyone could have come and said this or that has expired. Yrsa had grown up in Raufarhöfn too, like me, but she was a few years older and already looked fifty.

As usual, she was standing behind the counter, but anyone thinking this was out of laziness would be wrong. She just didn't want anyone to have to wait at the till for her. That's called customer service, and that kind of thing doesn't exist in Reykjavík.

My mother kind of ducked down once we were in the store, as though she'd suddenly realized she didn't want to be seen. You never know, after all, who you might run into at the store.

"Here goes," she said, grinding her teeth.

"Back again already?" Elínborg looked at us over a shelf. My mother stiffened.

"Yep," she said.

"Not much to do at the hospital?"

My mother glanced down at the floor, but because I was watching closely, I noticed a smile skirting around her lips.

"Thanks to this never-ending winter there's always enough to do, including at the hospital."

Elínborg nodded, as though she'd expected the answer. She turned towards the shelf and placed some canned tomatoes in her shopping basket. Yrsa looked over at us and wrinkled her nose.

"Funny that we're only seeing one another here in the store, even though we're neighbours!" remarked Elínborg, and that was actually a little funny. "You crept into the village very quietly!"

"I came early this morning, and I generally don't beep the horn upon my arrival."

"You wouldn't wake me. I'm already up by six, every day. And I didn't hear you arrive."

"Mm-hm," sighed my mother.

"But the police presence in front of your house was hard to miss. Twice even!"

"Twice?" Yrsa looked amazed.

"Well," said my mother. "Unfortunately, we were unable to help the police any further."

"I see." Elínborg pulled a meaningful expression and disappeared behind the shelf, looking for something.

"So what did they want?" asked Yrsa, curling her upper lip.

"Magga had driven Kalmann to Húsavík the day before. They were probably interested in that," answered my mother.

"Magga won't be driving anybody any more. But who will drive Kalmann to Húsavík now?" Elínborg stretched out her head from behind the shelf and looked at my mother accusingly.

"We'll find a solution, don't you worry."

"Of all the times to go and die, right now, when the entire world is looking for Róbert," said Elínborg conspiratorially.

The door opened, making the little bell tinkle, and Sigfús, the former school principal, came into the store. His ski poles made clicking sounds on the floor. He was already very old and very tall and therefore crooked like a banana, and always propped himself up on ski poles so he didn't fall over.

"Good afternoon, everybody," he said in a hoarse voice, even though he couldn't have seen anybody yet, struggling as he was to free his hands from the loops on the ski poles.

"Good afternoon, Sigfús," said Yrsa, letting out a sigh. "I'm wondering what's going on here in Raufarhöfn! Dead just like that, it's terrible. Hulda said they found Magga on her kitchen floor."

"What was on the kitchen floor?" asked Sigfús, placing the ski poles next to the entrance, picking up a shopping basket from the pile and looking around him.

"Not *what*, but *who*," declared Elínborg loudly.

"Who?" asked Sigfús.

"Magga," Elínborg replied.

"What about her?"

"She's dead."

"Magga? Baldursdóttir? Þórberg's widow?"

"She used to work at the post office," said Yrsa.

Sigfús shot Yrsa an indignant look. "I know she used to work at the post office!"

"Perhaps she was strangled!" I said, and now everybody was looking at me.

"Don't say anything else," said my mother, so quietly that only I could hear, but I had no choice but to explain:

"The police told me."

"Strangled? Now why doesn't that surprise me?" said Elínborg. "It's simply terrible."

Yrsa said she'd seen on TV that there were certain times in the year when lots of people died, and that it wasn't always explainable.

"There's always an explanation for everything," said Sigfús, who was finally catching up with the conversation. "People die around Christmas time and in spring, when a change in the weather is imminent. My mother and my brother died when —"

"Dying isn't the same as being killed," Elínborg interrupted, and she was right.

"What's your experience from the hospital?" Yrsa asked my mother, who promptly swayed her head back and forth. It was a good question. I would have liked to hear an answer from my mother, but she turned to me.

"What would you prefer, popcorn or potato chips?"

"Popcorn and potato chips," I said.

My mother smiled, looking kind of relieved, and put popcorn and potato chips in the shopping basket.

"I think that when the bodies start piling up, we can safely say that the deaths in Raufarhöfn have nothing to do with a change in the weather." That was Elínborg, concealed behind the shelves. My mother sighed and pressed her lips together.

"So is there a connection between Róbert and Magga?" Yrsa asked everybody.

"That's called a conspiracy," Sigfús commented.

Elínborg felt compelled to get to the bottom of the question. "Don't you watch crime shows?" she asked.

"A person can watch too many crime shows," mumbled my mother.

Yrsa looked expectantly at Elínborg.

"Magga and Róbert used to be a couple!" said Elínborg and paused dramatically. "So that makes quite a few theories possible. They even wanted to get married, because Magga was carrying their child. Well, at least her parents wanted them to get married, but whether Magga or Róbert wanted to is anyone's guess."

"Ninety-nine per cent of murder cases are motivated by love and passion," said Sigfús, who had arrived at the meat refrigerator and was putting a frozen half sheep's head in his shopping basket. "Victims and perpetrators usually know each other."

"But here everyone knows everyone!" remarked Yrsa in astonishment.

"But not everyone was a couple," said Elínborg.

"What happened to the baby?" asked my mother, who now seemed a little interested in the conversation after all.

"She lost it," replied Elínborg.

"Oh!" said my mother sadly, but Elínborg just looked at her distrustfully.

I tried to imagine Magga and Róbert as a couple. As hard as I tried, I couldn't. But then I remembered: "Magga told me that Róbert used to be really handsome."

"See?" said Elínborg. "Perhaps she never properly got over it. I mean, she didn't even cry when her Þórberg died."

My mother had now put vanilla ice cream, gherkins, popcorn, tortilla chips, milk and bread in the shopping basket. She placed it on the counter.

"We'd like to pay," she said, as though she were suddenly in a hurry.

Yrsa gave her a funny look but then began to type the prices into the till. I added some chocolate and quickly looked away.

"What else did she say?" Elínborg asked me. She came over to us, evidently having finished her shopping too. But there were still just two cans of tomatoes in her shopping basket.

"You don't need to answer," said my mother, and from that Elínborg concluded:

"If no more questions are allowed, you know something's not right."

"She said a lot of things," I said, and that was true.

"Poor Magga," said Yrsa, then she mistyped and had to start all over again.

"Perhaps she knew too much," said Elínborg, still looking at me.

"No," I said. "She talked too much."

"Same thing," said Elínborg.

"It's not the same thing," I said.

"We have two ears and one tongue in order that we may hear more and speak less," called Sigfús from the freezer section.

"Talk is silver, silence is golden," said Yrsa.

"Empty talk, empty ears," muttered my mother.

12

SÆMUNDUR

I woke up quite early, although it wasn't even eight o'clock yet. There were two possible explanations for this. One: I had slept so deeply that I'd simply overslept. Two: I'd sensed that my mother was no longer there. Now I noticed the silence. The clouds hung motionless too, and the sea lay there in a gloatingly dull way. So I scoffed two bowls of Cocoa Puffs and a few pieces of hákarl, then packed some dried fish, chocolate and a bottle of cola into my waterproof sea bag, pulled on my woollen cap, shouldered Grandfather's shotgun and went down to the harbour. The rescue service vehicles stood in front of the town hall, some of the engines humming away contentedly even though nobody was sat inside the vehicles, perhaps a meeting or briefing was taking place inside, and there was coffee for sure. It almost looked like back when things still happened in the town hall: theatrical performances or even movies. That was when I was a child. Back then the police station was housed in the cellar of the building, which was very practical: if there was a brawl upstairs, the drunkards only had to go downstairs.

At the harbour, I knocked on the window of the office container. Sæmundur opened the window, and I told him that I wanted to go out, which he thought was a good idea. He stepped outside with me, breathed in the cold air and, after sniffing around for a while in a way that exposed his hairy nostrils, gave me the green light. He said the weather would stay calm, maybe there would be a few flakes of snow, but that was no reason to worry, and he promised to keep the forklift and trailer at the ready.

"Sæmundur," I asked then, remembering our conversation from a few days before, "are you a commie?"

Sæmundur looked at me in surprise. "Why do you ask that?"

"Just because." I didn't know why I had asked.

"Do I look like a communist or something? I'm much too old for that, and I don't have a moustache either!"

That made sense to me, even though I hadn't realized communists have moustaches.

I went into the hall, leaving Sæmundur standing there in front of his container, and put on my black and yellow flotation suit, which also functioned as a life jacket. If I fell into the water with it on, I wouldn't sink. And the suit kept me warm. I had never fallen into the water, though.

I fished the fresh pieces of bait out of the brine-rum-vinegar marinade and filled an entire bucket. Without bait you don't catch anything, because no shark's going to voluntarily impale itself on a hook, but sometimes the shark, or even other fish, manage to gnaw off the pieces of bait, and that's why I had to keep putting new pieces on the hooks.

Outside it really had begun to snow again, but only lightly. I lugged the bucket to the pier, where my *Petra* was moored. She was my boat now. I had taken her over from Grandfather. Built in 1959, she was almost twice my age, but still lithe and lissom. Eight metres long, five tons heavy and as strong as forty-five horses. Just imagine! A 1980

Volvo engine. After the oil change, it ran like an absolute charm. *Petra* was content. I checked my electronic devices, the radio direction finder, my satellite compass, my sonar and GPS, untied the ropes and cast off, chugging leisurely out of the harbour, waving at harbour master Sæmundur, who had stepped back outside his container and waved to me too. I laughed. I liked Sæmundur. He was one of the few people who had liked Grandfather.

Soon I was steering around the cape of Höfdi, past the bird colonies and islet, where the fulmars soared and the cormorants posed as though they were doing a photo shoot. I left Raufarhöfn's row of houses behind me and headed out into the middle of the grey, endless sea, which was very gentle today, moving only a little. My shark line was twelve nautical miles to the north-east of the harbour. The journey there would take around one and a half hours. Before, the journey with Grandfather out to the longline had lasted just a few minutes; it was here right by the cape. You could see the buoys from the lighthouse, and some-times, if the weather was calm, you could even make out whether a shark was hanging on it. Back then, there were others shark-hunting too: Jón, who had since moved to Grindavík; Ingvar, who was no longer alive; and harbour master Sæmundur himself, who should be retired. It was a mystery to everyone why there were no longer any sharks in the bay, and I believe that even now no one knows. It's unlikely that we've fished the bay empty, because in the past, around two or three hundred years ago, there was even more shark-hunting, back before electricity existed. Back then people only needed the sharks' liver; the rest was thrown back into the ocean. Oil was extracted from the liver, and the liver oil was shipped to Europe, where it

167

was used to illuminate the city streets. I found this thought crazy. I mean, a Greenland shark, which lives up here in the north at a depth of several hundred metres, in complete darkness, is pulled out of the sea and brings light to the streets of big European cities!

I soon became hungry and scoffed down all the chocolate. Because I'd been lost in thought, I had veered off course a little, and so I corrected it. With Grandfather I'd sometimes skipped school to go out to sea, I was convinced that I belonged more out here at sea than in the classroom. I think Grandfather thought so too. I'm a born hunter, like him. Soldiers are hunters too, in a way, like my American father was. And that's why it's totally logical that I have hunting in the blood.

When I was ten, I fired a full round of ammunition into a shark's head for the first time in my life. Grandfather had warned me about the recoil, but I still landed on my behind. The shark was stunned, though, and that was what mattered. Back then we sometimes used to return to the harbour with three sharks in tow, which meant there was plenty to do, and there was always a certain element of competition between us shark catchers, and anyone returning empty-handed had to put up with the jibes. But Ingvar had us properly fooled once, when he had his boat plough slowly through the water, making us believe that he was hauling back an amazing catch. And as we all stood there on the pier in anticipation, waiting for him, he asked what we were looking at, making us feel like a bunch of idiots, and for ages he went on about the faces we had supposedly made, especially "that one there!" he said, pointing at me. "You should have seen the look on his face!" And then he opened his eyes and mouth wide until spit was dripping from his mouth, even though I don't look that disabled, but it was still funny, and I usually laughed the loudest.

Over time we moved the lines further and further out, and Ingvar, who hadn't caught a single creature all summer long, gave up and found a job working for Róbert McKenzie on the trawler. Sæmundur, who was already old in any case and had no children, stopped then too. He said that the pitiful shark catches might be linked to climate change. The ocean was getting warmer, that could be measured, that was how it was, and the Greenland shark didn't like that in the slightest. That's why we had to go further and further out into cooler waters, he said, and he wouldn't be surprised if before too long I didn't pull even one more shark from the sea. But I didn't want to think about that, because it was my job, and I couldn't imagine doing anything else.

Petra sliced briskly through the smooth water, making little waves. Now it was beginning to snow properly, the flakes fell silently on the water and immediately dissolved, becoming water themselves and therefore part of the sea. Out here, nature is more complete than anywhere else. The snowfall became really dense, and I was suddenly in a completely different world, because everything around me was in motion but I couldn't see even five metres ahead. There was just me and *Petra.* I imagined that the snowflakes were planets and I was flying on *Petra* through space at the speed of light. On the GPS I could see my precise position, even though before long everything around me looked exactly the same. White comes in so many colours. But then the snowfall subsided again. I sailed through the last veil of mist as though it were a curtain, and stood suddenly on the lit stage, but without an audience and without stage fright. The world was now completely still and well-rested, all snowed out, as though it had been freshly created. Grandfather used to love this weather. I could tell by looking at him, even if he didn't admit it. In weather like this he usually didn't say a word, he would stuff his pipe and stare out at the water with an expression of contentment, even though he didn't yet know whether the sharks were biting or not. Sometimes he turned off the engine when we were out by the lines, especially if he had a bottle of schnapps with him, even though it was sometimes a struggle to get the engine going again afterwards. And then, if it really didn't want to fire up again, instead making these farting sounds, Grandfather would laugh, and that meant I was never afraid out at sea, not even the time when we drifted for hours on end towards the North Pole and had to be towed back into the harbour by Ingvar. Grandfather loved this silence, and sometimes said he couldn't understand how people could bear it in a city, where it was never quiet. When it was as quiet as it was out here, the only thing a person could hear was their heart. Sometimes Grandfather took a nap, and then he would snore so loudly that it was no longer silent.

If my *Petra* were to sink, I would bob up and down on the water and wait right where I was until help came. After all, I knew how to send a distress signal. There was no reason to worry. Out here I was completely alone anyway. No one could hear me, no one could see me. But I was never lonely, nor was I ever afraid. My mother was against it at first when I started to go out alone, after Grandfather became too weak for boat trips. But mothers always worry about their sons. That's normal. And that's why I didn't need to concern myself with that. Out at sea I felt much safer than at a dance, or in Magga's car. I didn't need to make an effort out here; I could be who I was and how I was. And somehow, because of this, I was different to when I was at a dance or in Magga's car.

Not everyone likes being alone. Ingvar, for example, never liked being alone. He always took his dog out to sea with him, and after his dog died, he took the cat, until he had a new dog again, because the cat didn't like the sea, even though it could watch the seagulls and snarl at them. Because of the seagulls, you were never properly alone out here. You could even talk to them, although they didn't answer and just looked at you. But they sometimes listened, at least that's what Grandfather said, he always liked talking to the gulls, and in fact to all animals he encountered: gulls and Atlantic puffins, dogs and cats, sheep and horses, even bumblebees, for whom he always had a cheering word.

Soon I saw my buoy, whose location I had marked on my nautical map with the corresponding GPS coordinates. I've never gone out further than to my longline. Why would I? I'm a shark catcher, not a sailor. And further out there's only water, you can see that on the map. And that's what I'd agreed with my mother. That was our deal.

I let my boat come to a halt by the buoy, but left the motor idling so that the same thing didn't happen as back when I had drifted off to the North Pole with Grandfather. I pulled the buoy out of the water with the gaff and laid the dripping wet rope on the motorized winch, set it into motion and rolled it up next to me so there wouldn't be any tangles later. It took almost half an hour until one end of the longline was finally up. Perhaps, if I didn't catch any more sharks here, I would have to let the line down to 250 metres. The trawlers' halibut dragnets went the deepest, and they had sharks as by-catch the most frequently.

Finally the first hook came up, the bait still on it, just as I'd placed it there a few days before. I pulled it off the hook and threw it into the sea. The gulls descended on it, hacking their beaks into the meat, and with that the peace and quiet was over. There was no point trying to converse with them now, because they only had eyes for my marinated bait. But the gulls didn't bother me. It was still quieter than in a city. And I could hear my heart. It was growling at me. And then I realized that it was my stomach growling at me, not my heart. The next hook came up, the next bait, which was a little nibbled by the fish, and the next hook, and the next, ten hooks in total, but no shark. It wasn't so bad. Patience is the hunter's most important virtue. I didn't take it personally. I often went back to the harbour without a catch, that was normal nowadays, and you got used to it. Last year I caught five sharks in total. And that wasn't a bad year. I still had around fifteen kilos from last year's catch. I attached new pieces of bait to the hooks, one after the other, and lowered them down on the line into the depths, said goodbye to the gulls and chugged the one and a half hours back to Raufarhöfn with the incoming tide, and in order not to get bored, I sang, so loudly that I even drowned out the engine. I sometimes did that, even when I didn't have a shark in tow. No one could hear me, after all. No one knew I could sing. Not even Nói, though he'd told me he made electronic music and also sang to it. He had a few songs on YouTube, but not very many views. To ensure there would be new views from time to time, I occasionally clicked on his songs.

It started to snow again. The closer I got to land, the worse the visibility became. All of a sudden everything around me was white, the snowflakes thick and heavy, and

I had to brush the snow off the window with my hand, until my woollen gloves were caked with it, because the wipers had stopped working last autumn. I almost overlooked the islet with the cormorants; because of all the window clearing, I simply hadn't been paying proper attention. I had to quickly correct the course, and as I zoomed into the harbour I was still going too fast, because somehow I wasn't completely with it, and I narrowly missed crashing into the pier. Sæmundur, who was sat on the forklift in the harbour, even though he should have realized I was back far too early and therefore wouldn't have a shark in tow, tore his cap off his head and waved his arms about. But I didn't ram into the pier, I just nudged the car tyres at the edge, which absorbed the impact. But if I hadn't held on, I would have fallen overboard.

"Hey, hey, hey, slow down, young man!" cried Sæmundur, running towards me. I acted as though nothing had happened, and threw the rope to him so that Sæmundur could moor my *Petra*. He grinned. I think he missed the good old times, when there was still lots going on here in the harbour.

"I didn't catch anything," I said, handing him the empty bucket.

"No?" said Sæmundur, even though he of course knew I hadn't caught anything. "At least you didn't get lost out there," he said. It had snowed here too, he told me, but it surely wouldn't settle, because soon the wind would turn to the south-east and bring rain with it, and then the snow would disappear in next to no time, and perhaps then Róbert might be found.

I'm forgetful. That's one of my weaknesses. I can forget important things just like that. Especially when I go out to sea. As though the sea swallows all memories, or perhaps its immensity makes the brain expand, and then the memories are hidden deep inside like a message in a bottle in the ocean. That's why I only remembered once I was back in the harbour that Róbert was missing.

"Perhaps it'll be easier to see the polar bears then, once the snow's gone. From the air," I said.

"You and your polar bears!" Sæmundur laughed. "Do you still believe a polar bear ate him?"

"No!" I cried. "I was just pulling your leg!"

We laughed, and Sæmundur shook his head. Then he gazed out to sea, absorbed in his thoughts, and asked what had become of Raufarhöfn, but I didn't know and wasn't even sure he expected an answer, so I packed my stuff together and clambered onto dry land.

"Did you know that Róbert was planning to sell his quota to Dalvík?" asked Sæmundur, looking at me. "As though the Dalvíkings hadn't squirrelled together enough catch quotas already. As though it weren't enough that we've lost everything here! Do you know how it's come to this? Oh, forget it, you're much too young to remember. Back then you didn't even exist yet. Some days we had fish coming in twenty-four hours a day and sharks were just by-catch. Look, over there, right under the old smelting plant, there was a landing stage where we piled up so much salt for the herring vats that eventually it collapsed and all the salt fell into the sea. At first, we were hopping mad, then we laughed because we finally knew why the sea is so salty! And today? Look around you! Along with Siggi, Einar and Jú-Jú, you'll soon be the last Mohican to have a boat here and actually use it."

"What's a Mohican?" I wanted to know.

"An Indian. The Americans killed them all."

"But there are still Indians."

"But no Mohicans. And soon we won't exist either. It's the saddest thing. And then in Reykjavík they'll give us an official stamp as an endangered community, big words on white paper, but hooking up a patient to a machine doesn't mean he'll get better. He just doesn't die. And that stubborn mule McKenzie wants to go and flog the quota too so he can complete his idiotic tourist project. Hasn't he grasped it yet? We're simply too far out in the sticks! That's how it is. And even if he manages to lure a few tourists in with that heap of stones, he'll still be the only one to profit from it. And he won't create any jobs for the locals if only Poles and Romanians want to live up here."

"And Lithuanians," I said.

"And Lithuanians," grumbled Sæmundur. "At least someone still likes it here."

That evening, my mother called me.

"Kalli minn," she said, "don't be alarmed!" And so of course I was alarmed. My first thought was: Grandfather has died. But before I could ask my mother, she told me that Birna, the police commissioner, had just informed her Magga had choked to death, and to be precise – and I really wasn't to get alarmed – on a piece of hákarl.

My mother said a few more things after that, but I was no longer listening. Because I didn't know what I was supposed to think or how I was supposed to feel; it actually didn't matter to me what had happened to Magga. Because when somebody's dead, it doesn't matter how they died, because by then they no longer exist. First and foremost, I was happy that Grandfather wasn't dead. But I understood that the whole thing was now kind of connected with me, because I had given Magga the hákarl, though I hadn't stuffed it into her mouth myself, so it really wasn't my fault, and I told my mother that and she agreed with me, but I could tell she was close to tears, which I found a bit much. Women are always a bit much! And that's why I didn't feel like discussing it any longer, so I said "Bless" and ended the call. And then I immediately began to stew over it, because something like that could happen to me too; choking on a piece of hákarl, I mean. Mostly I was home completely alone, nobody would be able to help me, and I would choke to death like Magga, silently, because when you've got something stuck in your throat, you can't tell anyone. First it would become quiet, and then dark. But who would find me?

Suddenly I knew what I would do if a piece of hákarl got stuck in my windpipe. I would call Nói on Messenger! And he would summon help with just a few mouse clicks. He could probably hack into the coastguard's system and send the chopper himself. And so I clicked on Nói on Messenger. He was of course in the middle of a multiplayer game, but he still chatted with me and managed to calm me down, because he found the whole thing with Magga kind of funny, and he reminded me that I'd once told him I didn't really like Magga, and so I should be happy she'd died.

"Win–win," he said, and I didn't understand that, but Nói still cheered me up. He said I'd committed the perfect murder. A murder that was so perfect that even the murderer didn't know he was the murderer.

Nói could sometimes be really intense. But perhaps he was like that because he had to spend the whole day in his room due to his illness, couldn't go outside, didn't have a proper job, and as a result only ever laid eyes on his parents.

I then told him how I'd imagined choking on a piece of hákarl myself, which was possible after all, and Nói developed the thought further, saying that it wouldn't necessarily have to be hákarl, it could also be a piece of pizza. "Or popcorn," I added, but Nói said that you can't choke on popcorn, that it was scientifically impossible. But he liked my idea of calling him so he would send for help. He even found an internal internet link for the coastguard, where he could see the helicopter's precise location, and because it interested him, he immediately looked: the helicopter was just north of Grímsey, which was about thirty minutes from Raufarhöfn – it would come too late. I would be dead as a doornail by then. Nói realized that too, so he googled a little and then gave me a few tips on how I could survive that kind of thing. Let myself fall onto a chair back, he said. Or squat on all fours and flop down onto my belly, my arms stretched out in front. He wasn't completely content with the search results though, so he scrolled on.

"Run outside, to wherever there are people," he said eventually. "Under no circumstances retreat to a room where no one will notice you." That made sense, he said, surprised that many people who could no longer breathe shut themselves in a bathroom in embarrassment, where they then died, completely alone. "Everyone dies alone," he concluded, and he was right, as the last few days had shown. Magga had died all by herself in her kitchen, and Róbert hadn't even been found. Their loneliness was almost contagious.

"Bitch, motherfucker!" yelled Nói all of a sudden, manipulating his controller. "I'll kill you, dickhead!" But his angry outburst was in vain. He had been gunned down in his multiplayer game, ambushed from behind. There was nothing more he could do, so he flung his hands up, said "See you later, dude!" and ended the Messenger chat.

That happened from time to time. Now it was best not to bother Nói for a while. Now he simply needed peace and quiet. And I gave him that, because I was his best friend.

13
BARREL

The next day was completely crazy, and I probably only survived it because the previous day had been really calm and uneventful and I had recuperated, because out at sea you can empty your head. The events came thick and fast and we weren't used to that here in Raufarhöfn. The day was so crazy that it even led to a hastily convened village meeting.

A mild south-easterly wind blew the snow around, probably it had rained in the night; all around Raufarhöfn everything was brown and wet and only a few expanses of white held on stubbornly. "Typical Icelandic winter," my mother had once explained. "It snows during the day and rains at night. Completely twisted."

Now that the snow had gone, the rescue team began searching for Róbert again. They used drones and also dogs, which sniffed their way across the Arctic Henge and the village, where Róbert's scent was everywhere in any case, but nothing was found apart from his tinted glasses, not far from the pool of blood, and a sock. It wasn't much, and it wasn't Róbert, but they were clues that Róbert was probably no longer alive.

Like Magga too. Dead. I still needed to get used to this fact, because now Magga could no longer drive me to Húsavík, because she had choked to death on a piece of hákarl that I had given her. I was suddenly afraid I would miss Grandfather's death. I wanted to be with him when he died, right by his side. No matter what.

This was how the day began, and I immediately had an uneasy feeling. I thought about Magga a lot, and even though I hadn't seen her lying on her kitchen floor, I still had a clear picture of it in my mind.

From my bedroom window, I could see there were cars in front of Magga's house. Relatives, probably. Towards ten that morning, there was a commotion down at the harbour, because the coastguard helicopter was hovering next to the islet, just a few metres above the water. I saw that from the living room window. The cormorants had flown off. A man had been lowered down on a rope like a spider on a thread, with Siggi's boat a few metres away. I got dressed in my full outfit, cowboy hat, sheriff's badge, Mauser and everything, and hurried down to the harbour.

"A sea mine," guessed Sigfús, who was leaning against his ski poles and knew a great deal about the Second World War. A crowd had gathered down in the harbour. Óttar was there, harbour master Sæmundur of course, the car mechanic Steinarr, my neighbour Elínborg and a good dozen other people, including some from the rescue service. There were no children there, they were probably in school, but most certainly watching from the classroom window. People greeted one another, conversed, and agreed with Sigfús. A sea mine couldn't be ruled out. It would explain the helicopter. Sæmundur had a pair of binoculars with him, which he eventually passed around. I had binoculars too. They were in my cutter, so I quickly went to fetch them, looked through them and was suddenly really close to the helicopter. I told the people what I was seeing. Óttar asked whether he could borrow the binoculars, but I ignored him, because I had to tell the people what I was seeing. In addition, I didn't think the Pressure Cooker knew how to operate a pair of binoculars. After all, he'd only been a cook back then on the ship. Steinarr was amused that I didn't want to part with my binoculars, and informed Óttar that I was the binoculars expert, which was kind of true.

The man on the rope didn't do anything for a long while, merely dangled just above the water, and Siggi kept at a safe distance in his cutter, floating on the spot. He held his arm protectively in front of his face, because the helicopter was churning up the water. So Siggi had something to do with it, and Sæmundur was able to confirm that Siggi had returned from his lumpfish catch having found something in the water, that he'd also stayed on the spot for a long time. At first, he'd thought that Siggi had engine damage, but that wasn't the case, because Siggi told him over the radio that he'd spotted a black container in the water, and Sæmundur had cautioned him not to get too close, because it could be a sea mine. Sigfús nodded vigorously, took a few very small steps, clicked his ski poles on the tarmac and remarked that Sæmundur had reacted correctly.

But not everyone agreed. Elínborg doubted that some-body would recognize a sea mine when they saw it, and she was promptly asked whether she'd ever seen a sea mine bobbing around in the water, which she sulkily had to admit she hadn't, and so the possibility of a sea mine continued to stand.

"It's almost definitely a sea mine," repeated Sigfús for the tenth time already, even lifting one of his ski poles and pointing it out to sea. And then he reminded us that a few years ago in Hólsvík, where Róbert's golf course was, a sea mine from the Second World War had been washed up onshore.

"Two hundred and twenty-five kilos of TNT in a spherical container. With knobs." Sigfús sketched the size of the mine in the air using the ski pole. Magnús's sister-in-law Ragna had discovered the bomb on a walk, he continued, even though we were all familiar with the story, which had been in the paper after all. The mine had probably been left behind by the Brits, who, during the war in north-east Iceland, had laid a carpet of sea mines which had then become their own downfall. "A convoy of English–American warships was on its way westwards," narrated Sigfús, and everyone listened, because it was a really good story. I knew it too. "Nineteen ships, in bad weather, bad visibility, fog and rain and a strong north-easterly wind." We gathered closely around Sigfús, because the helicopter was making a hell of a racket. "A misunderstanding, an incorrect coordinate, an iceberg that was mistaken for a headland, and boom! It rained metal, fire and water. The first ship was almost torn in half, capsized and was surrounded by burning oil. It sank quickly, and took half the crew with it. Boom! A second explosion. A second warship was in danger of sinking, the crew saved themselves on a lifeboat, and boom! Fire and smoke and fog, to the front and behind and all around."

"It was their own fault," said Elínborg.

"Well, that's war for you," explained Sigfús, getting excited: "The convoy didn't know about the sea mines and thought they'd been attacked by German submarines, so they shot their heavy artillery at shadows in the fog and scattered the water bombs, creating gushing columns of water, flashes in the fog, burning water. When a sea mine explodes, the pressure makes other sea mines in the area explode too."

"A chain reaction," said someone from the rescue service. "Like dominoes."

"How many lives were lost?" asked another, who wasn't from around here.

"Many," said Sigfús darkly.

"At least the sharks had something to feed on!" said Elínborg, which made some people shake their heads and turn away from her. "What?" she said. "It's true, isn't it, Kalmann?"

I couldn't help but laugh, because it was true. Sharks will eat pretty much anything.

But it turned out not to be a sea mine in our bay after all, because the man on the rope was pulled up, and Siggi laboriously fished the black container out of the sea and then chugged into the harbour. The helicopter flew off, soon disappearing over the horizon, and calm was restored to Raufarhöfn after that. I thought about Nói, who could probably have told me exactly where the helicopter had gone.

We waited impatiently until Siggi had finally arrived in the harbour. Sæmundur fetched a pitcher of coffee and fried *kleinur* doughnuts, so the atmosphere was great. A few more people came and joined us, for example the poet Bragi.

"Comrades!" he said by way of greeting.

"Watch out, things are about to get poetic!" warned Steinarr, but Bragi didn't say anything more.

Nadja and her boyfriend Darius appeared in the harbour too, but they remained a little to the side, as though they didn't belong. Nadja spotted me and waved me over, but because I stayed where I was, she eventually came over and asked to borrow my binoculars. I showed her how to hold them against her eyes and sharpen the image. Unfortunately, she didn't stay standing next to me, but instead took my binoculars back to her boyfriend, who then used them too, even though I hadn't given him my permission. He stared through them for a long while, talking to Nadja, but I could neither hear what they were saying nor would I have been able to understand it. Eventually Nadja came back over to me, probably to return the binoculars. She was smiling at me even from a distance, and Óttar commented that my beloved was coming, making me blush, which kind of annoyed me.

"Kalli, you've gone completely red!" he said teasingly. Why was he picking on me? Normally he was really nice to me, especially when I ate dinner at the hotel. "Are you not feeling well?"

"Leave him alone," said Bragi, who had suddenly appeared next to me.

I almost wished Nadja weren't coming over, because now I was so embarrassed that everyone was looking at me and grinning, but I didn't want to send her away either, because she was holding my binoculars in her hands, which were always nicely manicured despite her hard work at the hotel. I almost wished I'd never lent them to her. Women can really make problems for you!

The people around me eavesdropped in amusement.

"Thank you, Kalmann," said Nadja as she handed me the binoculars. "I have to go. Lots to do at hotel. So much!" She looked at me apologetically, as though she would have liked to stick around for a while to chat with me, which made me kind of proud. Now Óttar was sure to be jealous, but I presumed Nadja's boyfriend Darius would be even more jealous, and he called out Nadja's name, so I shot him a look, but he'd already turned round and was heading towards the hotel.

"But don't you want to know what's in the container?" I asked Nadja.

She brought her face close to mine, her lips almost touching my left ear.

"You'll have to tell me what's inside," she whispered, so no one else could hear. I gave her a conspiratorial nod. "Promise?" She smiled at me again, kind of sadly, like how you look at somebody you're never going to see again, and so I didn't know what to say next. I probably just stared at her dumbly. Then she turned around and ran after her boyfriend, who was already a good stone's throw away from us and not even waiting for his girlfriend.

If Nadja had been my girlfriend, I would always have waited for her. Even in the wind and rain or if I were hungry. Because it would be worth it. I stared after her until she had disappeared into the hotel. Perhaps, despite everything, I had a chance with her. I felt all worked up, and so that Óttar couldn't make any more comments, I turned my back to him. I was pleased I would see Nadja again, that I even had a proper reason, even though I had no idea what was in the mysterious container. But I was already imagining how the conversation would go: I would go to her in the hotel, and she would be working on something and suggest that I follow her outside because she wanted a cigarette, and I would follow her, and outside she would light a cigarette, and I would say: "You won't believe what's in the container!" and then I would pause and Nadja would say, "What? Tell me!" "Nothing!" I would say, because right now I didn't yet know what was in the container, and anyway, it would have been really funny if nothing at all were in the container and the helicopter had been sent to Raufarhöfn unnecessarily and all the people down at the harbour had been waiting in vain for some big event. Nadja would laugh and blow smoke up into the sky and offer me a cigarette too, and I would push my cowboy hat back a little and smoke one with her, and our free hands would accidentally touch, but she wouldn't pull her hand away but instead clasp her little finger gently around my little finger, and then all of our fingers would touch and become intertwined, and Nadja would look at me, with those eyes, and I would lean towards her, and we would kiss, and she would put her hand into my trousers and say "Wow" and I would be a little embarrassed, but she would tell me: "You can touch me if you like" and I would touch her breasts, and —

"Kalmann!"

I almost dropped my binoculars. Sheep farmer Magnús Magnússon was giving me a strange look. He must've only just joined the group, because he hadn't been there before. He wasn't the kind of person you could easily overlook; he was tall and bulky and always wore the same knitted pullover. Magnús asked me whether I needed any bait, because he had an old nag he had to get rid of. But I didn't need any bait, I had enough at the moment, and wasn't catching anything anyway, so I shook my head, and because it took another few minutes for Siggi to finally arrive with his cutter, we tried to chat, but somehow it didn't work, because I was still really worked up and, in my thoughts, already on my way to Nadja, so we ended up standing next to one another in silence, watching Siggi slowly chug into the harbour.

By now half the village was waiting on the pier like a reception committee and staring into the open boat. Siggi had once again caught two entire bulk cargo containers full of lumpfish, and people congratulated him, but the really interesting thing was the black barrel standing there on the planks. Steinarr said, sounding disappointed, that it was no sea mine, and we all laughed, but Sigfús interjected that you could never be too sure, that we should still be cautious, because if there were explosives in the barrel then half of Raufarhöfn would be blown sky high, and people found that funny too, I even found it so funny that I almost fell into the water, but sheep farmer Magnús Magnússon managed to grab me by the sleeve just in time and said: "Careful, boy!" He smelled of sheep. Most of the people hadn't noticed my mishap, because all attention was on the barrel. Sæmundur joked that it would be good fortune for Iceland if half of Raufarhöfn were to be blown up. The latte slurpers in Reykjavík would certainly be relieved! And people found that funny too, even Bragi smiled, but the laughter wasn't so loud any more, because now the priority was to inspect the slightly battered barrel. But first it was heaved onto the pier, then there was a discussion about whether it should be opened or whether we should wait until the police arrived, because Birna had already been informed and was on her way from Kópasker. A few more people from the rescue service, who had clearly given up the search for Róbert, came over to join us. I knew their faces, but not their names. One said that we could probably count on finding Róbert in the barrel, though not necessarily in one piece, and the reactions were a mixture of horror and laughter, which was really funny, because now the mood was a completely different one, kind of subdued, and suddenly people were no longer keen on opening the barrel. Birna was sure to be here any moment, Sæmundur assured us, but Siggi grumbled impatiently, announcing that he was going to open the barrel now, that he had found it after all, and what a person fishes out of the sea belongs to that person, this was the law, and if the thing with Róbert hadn't happened then people wouldn't be making such a fuss, because not a blessed soul would be interested in what was in the barrel, given all kinds of things float around out there, and he was now regretting not having opened the barrel on the boat, because if he'd known that the inhabitants of Raufarhöfn were such a bunch of drama queens who would call the police over flotsam and jetsam, he wouldn't have said anything in the first place! And that he didn't have the time anyway, because he'd caught two entire cargo containers full of lumpfish, and so there was work to be done.

No one raised any objections. His words even met with agreement, and people now decided it was logical that the finder inspect his discovery himself, so Siggi set to loosening the clasp of the barrel, which was easy, because the barrel didn't seem to have spent that long in the sea, it was almost like new, just a bit battered.

No one said a word. Three dozen people and not a peep. You had to hear it to believe it! I was so excited that I almost laughed out loud. I went up really close to the barrel, and even had to push a few people out of my way, because I didn't want to miss such a strange surprise. I mean, usually hardly anything happens in Raufarhöfn! Siggi took off the lid, laid it gently on the floor and peered into the barrel. I saw transparent plastic, and something which smelled odd was wrapped in the plastic. And now the people made strange sounds, some took a few steps backwards, others forwards; movement came into the crowd. I was even shoved around a little. Siggi pulled out a fisherman's knife and deftly cut open the plastic. My first presumption was: broccoli. Vegetables for Yrsa's store. But my presumption was wrong, because Bragi, who had clearly seen something like this before, declared:

"Marijuana! Sweet Mary Jane! An entire barrel of it!"

"I've got nothing to do with it!" cried Siggi. He raised his hands defensively, climbed back onto his cutter and busied himself doing the things he needed to do. But now the hubbub on the pier kicked up a notch, everyone talking over one another, everyone jostling around the barrel, but Sæmundur closed the lid and said:

"Make room!"

Someone from the rescue service suggested that perhaps a photo should be taken so the police knew no one had tampered with it or removed any, to document the status quo, and so Sæmundur took off the lid again, and some people pulled out their phones and eagerly took photos, immediately sharing them with their friends on the internet. And that's how many in Iceland were informed about the discovery before Birna had arrived in Raufarhöfn.

Sæmundur closed the lid again and said no one should touch the barrel, because otherwise the police would find all kinds of fingerprints, and Óttar said that Siggi's fingerprints were all over the barrel anyway, at which Siggi called up to us from his cutter that he had only found the barrel by accident, Sæmundur could confirm that, and he'd reported it immediately, and anyway it had looked like a sea mine, because it had been floating upended in the water. But someone said that Siggi shouldn't get worked up, that he now owned fifty kilograms of marijuana, so he should roll himself a joint and relax! And with that comment the mood in the harbour improved again, there were jokes and laughter, the shock dissipated. Perhaps people were just happy not to have found Róbert hacked into pieces in the barrel. But the estimate that there were fifty kilograms of marijuana in the barrel was immediately disputed, because it was a sixty-litre barrel, as Óttar knew. Sæmundur also said that the barrel couldn't weigh forty kilograms, given that it had only taken two of them to heave it up onto the pier. So Sæmundur and Óttar grabbed the barrel and put it on the scale in front of Sæmundur's container, which was usually used to weigh and register the fishing catches. They kind of ignored the fact that they weren't supposed to touch the barrel, because of the fingerprints. But I stayed out of it and watched, because I really didn't want to bring suspicion on myself for a third time.

As it turned out, the gross weight was thirty-four kilos, which prompted people to guess the weight of the barrel, until Siggi reminded them that the tare weight was punched into the base, but then Sæmundur interjected and said to leave the damn barrel alone once and for all, and I didn't hear anything more, because it struck me that I had seen a barrel like that before, one exactly like it, actually, but I could no longer remember where. Then I remembered I had to tell Nadja what was in the barrel, and so I left half the inhabitants of Raufarhöfn behind me and hurried over to the hotel, feeling a tingling in my stomach. It was the anticipation. Nadja would be wide-eyed. I quickened my pace, and Bragi called after me: "Where are you off to in such a hurry, young man?" But I had no time for explanations. I had to keep my promise. And this wasn't even close to being the end of the crazy day.

14

ARCTICA

I went into the hotel through the main entrance. The building had been constructed during the herring boom as worker accommodation, and once the herrings were gone, it was made into a hotel for tourists. On the walls hung numerous black-and-white photographs from the herring boom era. They showed all the ships crammed together side by side in the harbour, so that you could have walked across the entire bay without getting your feet wet. The hotel building was also visible in the background on some of the pictures. A few old wooden barrels, which had been used to ship the salted herring all over the world, still stood in the hotel lobby. There was a fishing net stretched across the reception counter, with starfish entangled in it. Here and there, buoys had been used as decoration, and some even had bulbs screwed into them, so that they gave out light.

Nobody was in the lobby. Nobody was in the restaurant either. Not a single soul. I looked through a window down to the harbour. The people were still standing around the mysterious barrel, chatting, laughing and shaking their heads. They had put the canister of coffee and empty plastic cups on it, as though it were a table in a bar.

"Nadja!" I called, but nobody answered. Thinking she might be in the kitchen, I went into the kitchen; Óttar was still down at the harbour, after all. The kitchen was deserted too. I went down the stairs into the cellar and to the laundry room. I knew my way around the hotel really well, like I did most of the buildings in Raufarhöfn, for that matter. There aren't many. The doors here are always open. Nobody locks them, apart from the old factory halls, where the children could fall down rusty staircases. The cars are never locked either. Some even have the ignition keys left in them.

There wasn't anybody down in the cellar. As I climbed back up the stairs, I heard the whirring of the rescue helicopter, a sound I was now familiar with. Had it already come back? In the hotel restaurant I looked out of the window and saw that a police car was just driving into the harbour. So Birna was now back in the village and could tend to the barrel of drugs. I was happy she was back. I took the stairs up to the bedrooms. Nadja was sure to be busy cleaning.

"Nadja!" I called. The noise was pretty loud now, the helicopter must be landing directly in front of the hotel. The entire building began to shake.

"Nadja!" I yelled.

A door opened and a head poked out into the corridor: dark hair, slender face, a questioning glance. I recognized it. It belonged to the tourist who had sat at *my* table in Húsavík! Whether he recognized me, I didn't know. I did have my cowboy hat on, after all, and it was really dark in the corridor.

"What's happening?" he asked in English, but I had more important things to do than inform him about the situation in Raufarhöfn.

"Have you seen Nadja?"

"What?"

"Nadja. Beautiful woman. Where?" The man was clearly slow on the uptake, so I tried again. This time louder, and all in English. "Nadja. Lady! Where, where, where!" I presumed that he had finally recognized me, because he looked at me with an expression of complete disbelief.

The windows shook. The young man closed his mouth again, turned and disappeared into the room. I heard him talking with a woman. I glanced into the room to make sure Nadja wasn't with him. But she wasn't in the room, only the girlfriend I had already seen in Húsavík, but this time she was only partly dressed, in her walking trousers and a red bra. She had really small breasts, kind of like apples. Her hair was curly and fell almost to her breasts. Her boyfriend had pulled on a sweater and now pushed me back into the corridor, closing the door in my face, meaning that I couldn't see his girlfriend any more.

"What the fuck is going on?" he asked, this time sounding rather unfriendly.

Tourists can really get on your nerves. But perhaps he could help me in my search.

"Come with me!" I said, gesturing with my hand to indicate that he should follow me. And he did. We went down the steps, the young tourist right behind me.

"Hellooooooooo!" I yelled, as loudly as I could. The sound of the helicopter was deafening. The building was almost taking off. Nadja was perhaps in the lobby now, because she must have noticed the helicopter racket too, so I signalled to the tourist to follow me. We hurried through the lobby and pushed open the door by the main entrance. Not a good idea. The wind from the rotor blades almost swept us off our feet. Too late, I raised my hand to hold my cowboy hat against my head. But it had already departed, and went spinning back into the lobby. Dust whirled into my face, burning my eyes, and I couldn't help but close them, but just beforehand I noticed that there were men in black clothing standing in front of the hotel entrance. That seemed strange to me. I held my hand protectively in front of my eyes and blinked into the dust. The men were masked and carrying the kind of guns you usually only see in movies, because no one has them in real life. They're called semi-automatic machine guns.

With hindsight, of course, you always know better. These men were from the national police task force and therefore actually the good guys. But I was so scared that I reacted instinctively and fled back into the hotel, after my cowboy hat, and accidentally barged so forcefully into the tourist that he fell into the lobby with me.

"Close the door!" I roared, but the useless guy did nothing of the kind, he simply stayed there on the floor with his hands behind his head, ready to be arrested. Perhaps he hadn't even heard me. Wind and dust were still blowing against us, so it was difficult to form a clear thought. A few of the framed black-and-white photographs fell to the floor, the decorative buoys swung back and forth. I struggled to my feet to close the door. My hip hurt, because I had fallen sideways onto my Mauser. The belt had slipped a little, and I was afraid I'd damaged the pistol in the fall. Leaning against the wall, I pulled it out of its holster. I hadn't noticed that some of the masked policemen, with their machine guns at the ready, had stormed into the lobby.

"Drop the gun! Drop the gun!" they yelled, and I wish I'd dropped my pistol at once, but I was so startled, because out of the corner of my eye I spotted more masked figures, who had got into the hotel through the back door and were now coming through the restaurant, their guns cocked, kind of like in a movie, and now the tourist and I were completely surrounded. I was so bewildered that I became rooted to the spot and couldn't do what the masked men had asked me to. The tourist stretched out his limbs, and for a moment I thought they'd shot him, so I got really frightened. This was some serious shit.

"Drop the gun! Drop the gun!" they were yelling still, and Bang! A hand grenade exploded in front of me, or at least that's what I thought, because of course it wasn't a hand grenade but a smoke flare, yet it still kind of robbed me of my senses. The smoke wrapped around us, biting into my face, and because the flare had exploded next to the tourist, he now began to scream at the top of his lungs, and in Foreign too, which meant no one could understand him, which in this situation didn't help anyone, and suddenly a strong man from the task force rammed me from behind and dragged me skilfully to the floor. He had probably done that kind of thing before. So there I lay, coughing, my eyes streaming, and the Mauser was no longer in my hand, but I saw it slide across the floor and beneath a bureau where coffee and tea always stood at the ready. Today was no exception. The task force guy pulled my arms behind my back and pinned me down with his knee. That hurt quite a lot, and when I tried to move it hurt even more, so I too began to scream. I lay next to the tourist, we looked at one another and screamed simultaneously as loud as we could. But not for very long, because soon we couldn't catch our breath any more due to the stupid smoke, and so our yelling turned into coughing.

But after that it wasn't so bad. The smoke flare was thrown outside, and someone turned off the fire alarm, which up until then I hadn't even noticed. Windows were opened, and thanks to the wind generated by the helicopter, the smoke dissipated. The task force guy loosened his grip and sat me up on my behind, because Birna had appeared and told the men they'd arrested the wrong guys. But they wouldn't let us go that easily, me and the tourist, because we had resisted arrest after all, but Birna managed to put in a word for me, and she explained who I was, how I was and that neither I nor my toy gun posed any danger. I think the people from the task force then realized they'd taken things a little too far. Even the tourist managed to prove that he really was just a tourist. He was escorted to his room, and I never saw him or his girlfriend ever again. The ones they'd wanted to arrest, namely the Lithuanians, Nadja, Darius and everyone, had long since fled, so the masked men hurriedly clambered back into the helicopter and, amid much clattering, disappeared. Birna and a few police officers from Akureyri and Húsavík stayed behind. All of this only took a few minutes, but I was as exhausted as if I'd spent the entire day sawing up bait. I was completely drained.

It calmed down in the lobby. Birna sat me down at a table in the restaurant, close by the window, served me a bottle of cola and took a seat opposite me. Only once I held the bottle in my hands did I notice how much I was shaking and sweating, and yet I felt as cold as ice. My eyes were burning and my hip hurt. What the hell had happened? Down in the harbour, most of the villagers had disappeared, because the police had arrived on the scene; four officers in two police cars. They barricaded off the harbour with yellow plastic tape and sent even Sigfús away. Only Sæmundur and Siggi stayed nearby.

"I'm really sorry you got caught up in that, Kalmann," said Birna. "Always in the wrong place at the wrong time!

How do you do it?" She attempted a smile but wasn't very convincing. "What are you doing here in the hotel anyway?"

I knew I didn't have to answer her, because my mother wasn't here, and without my legal guardian I didn't have to say anything at all, that was the law.

"I was looking for Nadja," I said.

"Why?"

"I promised to tell her what we found in the barrel."

"Why did you promise her that?"

"She didn't have time to wait until the barrel was opened. She had to work. She's always very busy."

Birna nodded, as though she believed me. "And? Did you find Nadja?"

"No!" I said, and now I felt close to tears, because somehow everything was going wrong today. "It's like the ground has swallowed her up, she wasn't in the kitchen or in the laundry room. I looked everywhere! Do *you* know where she is?"

Birna shook her head tiredly. "She can't be far, right? We'll find her soon, I'm sure. Didn't she tell you where she was going?"

I thought hard. I really wanted to help Birna, but I couldn't. "Back to the hotel," I said eventually, but it gradually dawned on me that she had lied.

Birna nodded, looked at me for a while, then said that I should stay where I was, that she would be back soon, she just had to make a call, and then she went.

The police officers in the harbour were studying the barrel closely now, then they took photographs and loaded it into a delivery van. Birna sat back down with me and put her phone away.

"Listen, Kalmann, you can't just wander armed through the streets, scaring people."

"I'm not scaring anybody," I said, defending myself.

"That could have ended badly today, do you understand? If I hadn't been there…"

I thought about my mother. "I don't care," I said.

Birna looked at me with a crooked smile. "There are people from the TV out there. I suggest you don't do any more interviews, is that understood?" I nodded, but Birna still wasn't content. "Go out through the back door, okay?"

"No reason to worry," I said.

"Good. Go home and call your mother. She's sure to be worried."

I nodded, but I indicated to Birna that I wanted to stay sitting down for a moment longer, as my hands were still shaking. Birna let me, and once I was finally alone in the hotel, I laid down flat on the floor in front of the bureau and fished out my Mauser from under it. Luckily it was still intact. Of course it was still intact. It had survived a couple of wars, after all. Imagining how I would have engaged the task force guys in a wild shoot-out, I ducked behind a herring barrel, aimed at the door and said Bang! Bang! Bang! But then the door suddenly opened, because the reporters had pushed their way into the hotel, not caring whether they had permission from the police or not. So I hurried through the lobby, ducking low, and found cover under the buffet table in the restaurant. There were only two reporters, and I recognized them at once: the bald man with a bow tie and the tall cameraman. They hadn't spotted me. I peered out from beneath the table and aimed my gun first at the reporter, then the cameraman. Bang, bang! I could have shot them one after the other.

"Kalmann?" called the reporter from national TV. Caught in the act, I crawled out from under the table and ran away as quickly as I could, fleeing through the kitchen and the pantry to the back exit, and dashed out into the open air. Then I crept around the hotel, so I could give them the slip.

My escape was successful. They didn't catch me, they just watched me go, shaking their heads. Man, that was exciting! I whooped loudly, ran through the village and felt really good, like a proper movie hero. "Yeah, bitches!" But then I started to feel dizzy. My limbs became heavier with every step, and I was suddenly exhausted. My legs could barely carry me. Once I arrived at my little house, I felt sick, and threw up next to the front door. Quickly and violently. Then, with the last of my strength, I made it inside. In my opinion even movie heroes would end up looking foolish if they were taken unawares by a task force unit and pushed down to the floor, with a cocked semi-automatic machine gun at the back of their neck and everything. Those guys in Hollywood have no idea what real life is like. In other words: it makes you sick.

15
HALLDÓR

All the residents of Raufarhöfn had gathered in the town
hall. This usually only happened for the Þorrablót festival,
for the national holiday, and for now-rare theatrical events.
Halldór was busy lining up additional chairs, clearly not
having believed that all one hundred and seventy-three
residents would turn up – minus the schoolchildren and
babies, of course, so around one hundred and fifty-five
people in total.

"Kalli, help me with the chairs!" he cried, and I helped
him with the chairs, because he was already sweating. My
hands were no longer shaking and I was fully functional
again after the shock in the hotel. I'd watched *The Biggest
Loser* at home and was feeling calmer. On the stage, Halldór
had set up a long table, and behind it sat everyone who
had something to say: Birna from the police, in uniform,
Arnór from the rescue service, in full gear, and between
them Hafdís from the town council, elegantly dressed and
made-up, looking professional and not at all nervous. The
media people hadn't been invited, which I was pleased
about. Hafdís didn't look as serious as Birna or Arnór; she
was smiling. And yet the tension in the hall was tangible. I
was excited too. I didn't want to miss anything, which is why
I quickly sat down on a vacant chair in the second row, even
though there were still people streaming into the hall who

didn't yet have a chair, but I ignored Halldór, who shot me an indignant look and flung up his hands in frustration. The coloured lights from the last Þorrablót festival still hung over our heads, putting everybody in a festive mood, even though there wasn't really anything to celebrate. People greeted one another, chatted and laughed.

Hafdís clapped her hands and declared the information event open, because it was eight o'clock, and she had informed everybody by text message that the event would start at eight o'clock, and that anyone arriving late – and there were some who always arrived late, like the sheep farmer Magnús Magnússon, for example, or the poet Bragi – would simply be too late. She introduced herself and then Birna and Arnór, who were sitting to her left and right on the stage, and said that we, the people in the hall, would get the opportunity to ask questions, but that she wanted to try to keep the event as short as possible, and that's why she immediately wanted to hand over to Birna, who would inform us about the day's events.

Silence fell in the hall, everyone who wanted to be there was there, and Birna became really nervous. I could tell by looking at her, because I knew what she was like when she wasn't nervous. She fidgeted around on her chair, bunched together the papers in front of her on the table, fiddled with her uniform, then finally opened her mouth to speak, but we could barely hear her until someone further back yelled "Louder, please!" That threw her off a bit, so she started from the beginning again, louder this time and with a very red face.

"As everyone knows, Róbert McKenzie has been missing since the morning of the nineteenth of March. He was last seen in the Hotel Arctica, where he left the building at nine o'clock in the morning, intoxicated and dressed only in light clothing. At around three o'clock in the afternoon, Kalmann Óðinsson, who was up on the Melrakkaslétta hunting a fox, discovered a pool of blood in the snow and immediately informed Hafdís, er, Helgadóttir, but at that point Róbert McKenzie wasn't yet officially missing, so the police weren't involved. The —"

"Who was the last person to see Róbert alive?" asked Elínborg, who was sat in the front row, a few seats diagonally from me. She had a loud voice. Startled, Birna looked out at the audience and was about to reply, but Hafdís got in first:

"Please save questions until the end!"

"It's okay," said Birna, looking down at her papers and searching for words. "Er … Nadja Staiva, who worked in the hotel, saw him leave the hotel. She was clearing the breakfast away at the time."

"The Lithuanian!" commented Elínborg, crossing her arms. She had no further questions.

"Birna, please," said Hafdís, signalling to her to continue.

"Yes, that's her… Now. The police were informed on the early afternoon of the twentieth of March, and by late afternoon the pool of blood, which unfortunately had been covered by snowfall, was forensically secured and inspected, and by dusk the first search party set out, working together with the rescue service." Birna looked at Arnór. He nodded and raised his hand in greeting.

"We left no stone unturned," he said.

"Even Róbert's Arctic stones?" called someone, at which a suppressed giggle went through the crowd. Arnór didn't smile.

Birna continued: "A DNA test revealed that it was in fact Róbert McKenzie's blood, and we also found fibres of

202

material from his clothing, a sock as well as his glasses, but the search for clues was difficult because the site had been snowed over and completely trampled."

A few people looked at me, but I didn't know why, and so I probably blushed.

"That, unfortunately, is all we've found of him, but considering the estimated quantity of blood in the snow and on the ground it's very unlikely, although not impossible, that Róbert McKenzie is still alive. We are currently working on the assumption that it was a homicide."

Now a few people stared at Dagbjört, who was sat quite far back in the hall, as still as stone; her husband was next to her, wearing a tie, holding her hand. He glanced at me while I was looking over at her, even though by now everyone else had turned back around. Dagbjört stared straight ahead, ignoring everybody. Birna continued:

"Arnór will tell us how comprehensive the search was, but there are two more things I'd like to mention first. The death of Margrét Baldursdóttir has nothing to do with this." Birna looked around to make sure everyone had been listening. "Magga unfortunately choked to death on a mouthful of food, and because she was alone in her house, nobody was able to help her. I think that all rumours concerning a possible connection with Róbert McKenzie's disappearance are therefore rendered invalid. I… er… would like to thank you all for the numerous phone calls we've received. But we are only able to pursue the leads which are concrete or substantiated."

At this a murmur rippled through the hall, and Birna waited a few seconds until it quietened down. A few people looked at me again, and not in a particularly friendly way.

"Quiet please!" called Hafdís. She was really good at that.

Birna took a deep breath. "What happened today, however, the discovery of the drugs and the subsequent task force mission, is very likely to be connected with Róbert McKenzie's disappearance, but we can't yet confirm that. To be completely clear" – and now the hall was once again totally silent – "it's not yet confirmed. Sigurður Dagsson, also known as Siggi, found a barrel in the bay today, and did the only right thing, namely notifying the police."

"Sæmundur notified you, not me," called Siggi. "I just notified Sæmundur."

"That's right!" cried Sæmundur.

Birna acted as though she hadn't heard. "Unfortunately, the barrel was opened before the police arrived, and at this point I would like to emphasize that all potential evidence and discoveries of any kind must be secured until the police arrive!"

A few people in the hall shook their heads. Somebody said that bar tables didn't count as evidence, which provoked laughter.

"Quiet!" Hafdís really didn't have much of a sense of humour today.

Birna continued: "It transpired that the barrel contained just under twenty kilograms of marijuana and about five kilograms of amphetamines. As I said, a connection with Róbert McKenzie's disappearance hasn't yet been established, but given that a similar barrel was confiscated around six months ago in Reykjavík, in connection with a Lithuanian drug dealer, we've been able to —"

Birna's words were drowned out by muttering. This time Hafdís didn't succeed in quieting people down, which I found funny and so couldn't help but laugh out loud.

"People!" she cried. "People!" She waved her hands. Birna looked tired.

"Are the Lithuanians from the mafia? Here, in Raufarhöfn?" cried Elínborg in utter indignation, drowning out the whole of Raufarhöfn.

Now things quietened down again in the hall, because it was a good question.

"We can't confirm that at the moment, but —"

"Have you arrested the Lithuanians?"

Arnór grinned all of a sudden, covering his mouth with his hand. Hafdís tried once more: "Settle down now! Let Birna finish, then you can ask questions!"

Birna gave her a grateful nod. "Yes, the four hotel employees were apprehended and taken into police custody by the task force, up on Route 85, by the craters."

"Those aren't craters," said Sigfús.

"Are they suspected of having killed Róbert?" asked someone.

"At this moment in time no one is under suspicion, as we don't know where Róbert is or whether he really has been murdered, but anyone who was connected to him is under suspicion. That's why —"

"Do the four Lithuanians belong to the mafia?"

"We're not able to confirm that based on our current knowledge."

"Have the Lithuanians been interrogated?"

"We are in the process of interrogating the Lithuanians, but I can't give you any further information on that."

People weren't at all satisfied with Birna's answers. An animated discussion followed, and no one wanted to hear from Arnór about all the places the rescue service had searched, because they hadn't found Róbert anyway. People were much more interested in whether Róbert had been in cahoots with the Lithuanian mafia, and why the presence of these Lithuanians had been tolerated among us for so long. Elínborg said that Róbert should never have been dragged into the whole thing and that the Lithuanians should be forced into a confession, because then the case would be solved.

"There are ways and means!" she cried.

Hafdís managed to get the hall under control a few more times, but no more information could be extracted from Birna. The most important thing, as she said in conclusion, was that Róbert be found as soon as possible.

The event lasted a whole hour. It got really warm in the hall and the windows steamed up, even though Halldór had opened all the windows it was possible to open. There was a moment when things became unpleasant again, because Yrsa from the store asked whether it could be ruled out that a polar bear was roaming around up here, at which Birna finally smiled and said that she could rule it out in good conscience. Then lots of people looked at me again, and I heard my name being murmured. I didn't like that, and so I said that polar bears could swim from Greenland to Iceland, but only the people who were sitting near me heard. No one wanted to back me up, and everyone looked towards the front again.

Once the event was over, I helped Halldór clear away the chairs. Not because I wanted to, but because Dagbjört was helping too. As a teacher, she probably felt obligated. She rewarded me with a smile, said that it was sweet of me to help, and I was so proud that I immediately piled up four chairs in one go and lugged them behind the stage. Normally you only carry three at once, but a strong person can carry four.

I was surprised that Dagbjört had even come to the event; after all, it was about her father. And she didn't seem sad in the slightest.

"Have you caught a shark yet?" she asked me.

"No, not yet," I said, feeling a little aggrieved. "I mean, I've only just started up again."

"Oh, okay," said Dagbjört with a smile.

"Aren't you sad?" I asked.

"What makes you ask that?"

"Because your father is dead."

She gasped for air.

"Kalli! Help me with these!" Halldór was standing on the stage and waiting by the tables for me.

Before I could clamber up onto the stage to help him, Dagbjört said: "Perhaps he's still alive."

"I don't think so," I said.

"Kalmann!" shouted Halldór. "Come here now!"

I don't like it when people shout at me. I mean, I was only having a completely normal conversation with Dagbjört. Was he jealous or something?

"Why don't you think so?" asked Dagbjört, looking kind of pale.

I was confused. Hadn't she been listening? "The blood!" I said. "That amount of blood loss... Birna said it herself! And Birna is from the police."

Dagbjört put the chair she was holding back on the floor. "He hasn't been found yet," she said tonelessly.

"Kalli! Leave poor Dagbjört in peace!"

I glanced over at Halldór. "Who does the hotel belong to, if Róbert's dead?" I asked Dagbjört. I hadn't intended to ask that, but somehow a fuse had blown in my head when Halldór had yelled at me like that.

"It's okay!" said Dagbjört in Halldór's direction. "Kalmann is just curious." And to me: "I don't even want to think about that."

"Then you'll be rich," I informed her.

Dagbjört looked at me, turned around and left. I watched her go.

"Idiot!" said Halldór.

Once Dagbjört had left the room, I grabbed a chair and flung it across the hall at Halldór. The chair crashed against the stage with a clatter, and I saw Halldór jump back, then I stormed out of the hall, barely paying attention to his cursing. Only once I was outside did I come to a halt, because there were still some people gathered in front of the town hall, talking away, and I saw Dagbjört too, standing with them and being hugged by Óttar's wife, Ling.

"Kalmann," said Marteinn, the sports teacher, "what were you doing in the hotel, you know, when the task force unit wanted to arrest the Lithuanians?"

I looked at him. Everyone who was standing near him looked at me. It became clear to me that the event had been continued out here by a few people. It was probably better if I said nothing, because until now I had only been laughed at whenever I'd said something.

"No comment," I said, and just stood there. I had been planning to leave, but it was as though I were rooted to the spot. The people exchanged glances.

"What do you mean by that?" asked Marteinn, crossing his arms. "Do you have something to hide?"

"No comment!" I repeated, and I realized that I must have said it rather loudly, because Marteinn took a step back and dropped his arms again.

"Calm down, I was only asking a question!" he said.

"It has nothing to do with you!" I yelled.

"Kalmann!"

Was the entire village suddenly against me? What had I done wrong?

"Kalmann, come on!" Dagbjört was calling my name; I hadn't even heard her at first. I stared pointedly at the sports teacher, who sometimes went on a bender in the Hotel Arctica, and so I could just as easily have asked him what he was always doing in the hotel, because sports teachers weren't supposed to drink alcohol, everyone knew that, that's how it is. And I was almost about to ask him that, but then Dagbjört grabbed my hand and pulled me away, not giving me a choice in the matter, over to the road, away from everyone. She said quietly that she was sorry she'd reacted like that before, but that she herself didn't know what to believe. She hoped her father was still alive, because if there was no proof, you had to presume a person was still alive. And she said all of this quietly to me as she led me away. And I simply calmed down, because I had never held hands with Dagbjört, and she'd never whispered words into my ear, and so I began to feel really warm, and I wondered what I should say, because actually I didn't agree. I mean, she might as well forget it right now, her father wasn't still alive. I knew that. And I wanted to tell her that. But then I remembered I had to protect her, shield her from everything bad, that I'd promised to. And all of a sudden she left me standing there on the street, said she had to go home now and that I should go home too.

"Bless, Kalmann." She kissed me on the cheek, and then she was gone. And I stood there, completely alone, staring after her as she walked home, then I looked back at the town hall, but I was too far away to be accosted by the people, and so eventually I shook my head, looked up at the starry sky and noticed the Northern Lights. Rather beautiful ones at that. And so I yelled as loudly as I could:

"Northern Lights!"

Now the people in front of the town hall looked up at the sky too. But I went home then, because I wasn't in a Northern Lights mood in the slightest. I opened my laptop and called Nói, wanting to tell him about the meeting. But Nói was kind of moody, he didn't even comment on what I told him, even though he wasn't in the middle of a multi-player game but just sitting there, kind of hunched over, and I still didn't see his head. His sweater seemed a size too big. Soon his mother came into the room and said that Nói had to lie down and that was enough of the computer. The fact that Nói simply obeyed her order surprised me. He didn't even say goodbye, simply broke off the Messenger conversation, disappearing from my screen, and then I sat there and felt empty, because I could have done with a friend, and that's why I don't know how long I stayed sitting in front of my laptop. I only pulled myself together when blood started to drip onto my trousers, and as I felt the wet blood on my skin, I noticed that I'd scratched the back of my hand raw.

16
HUNT

After I had patched myself up, I lay down to sleep. It was actually rare for me not to watch TV before going to bed. But I wasn't a child any more, and grown-ups can skip watching TV from time to time. That's why I felt pretty well rested the next morning, but I still decided to spend the day in such a way that I wouldn't be constantly running into people. I wanted some peace and quiet. The weather was amazing, even a little springlike, with a few clouds in the sky. Like little sheep in rank and file. The fog that had clung to the bay at dawn evaporated. The grass was damp and matt between the rocks, and apart from in a few shady spots, the snow was now gone. The pool of blood at the Arctic Henge had probably trickled into the earth. So I packed chocolate and dried fish into my backpack, put on my cowboy hat and fastened on my holster. Behind the town hall I clambered up the slope, turned around again and gazed out over Raufarhöfn, which after all the turmoil lay there with astonishing calm. There was no sign of recent events in the village, because helicopters and task force guys don't leave any traces. I set off, heading to the north-west, clambered across the foundations of the old British military site, veered off northwards at the radio mast, marched at a safe distance past the Arctic Henge and on across the tundra of the Melrakkaslétta, kind of aimlessly, but I was following my instinct, my gut, and was convinced my inner compass would lead me to Schwarzkopf. I would see snow grouse for sure, because at this time of year the cocks were still in their white winter plumage and easy to spot against the brown terrain. The females already had brown flecks in their feathering, camouflaging them against the falcons. The men sacrificed themselves for the women, so that at least their offspring would be protected. That's the balance of nature. You can't change it. That's just how it is. Women and children first. The falcons' favourite dish was snow grouse, and when there are only a few, there are fewer falcons, because then they have nothing to feed on. And if there are fewer falcons, there are more snow grouse. And when there are more snow grouse, there are more falcons. This example can most likely be applied to humans too, but at this moment I can't think how.

True enough, a pair of snow grouse flapped away in agitation, and I wondered once again about their limited flying skills and belch-like coo, which betrayed their presence across wide distances. Nature makes it very easy for the falcons and Arctic foxes. I didn't see any falcons, though, and Schwarzkopf didn't show any sign of himself either, but there were quite a few short-billed geese and whooper swans, which had probably only just arrived in Iceland.

I went up to the lakes, which until recently had been frozen over and covered with a layer of snow. Now a pair of whooper swans were gliding through the water – it's always the same couples, every year. That's why swans are such romantic creatures. They are loyal to one another and their little lake. Sometimes I wished I were a swan.

I sat down on a rock with the warm sun on my face, ate chocolate and thought. I would have liked to lie down on the grass, but the ground was still damp and cold. From here, I could no longer see Raufarhöfn. Just moss, brown grass and rocks, decorated with lichen, as far as the eye could see. If I hadn't been able to see the Arctic Henge in the distance, I could easily have been on another planet. Sitting alone in this landscape was like being out at sea, but completely different. The Melrakkaslétta rose and fell, swaying like shallow waves, even though it was of course completely still. One of the green lakes lay at my feet. There were fish in these lakes. I often used to go angling with Grandfather, and we would stand in our waders in the water, which shimmered golden in the midnight sun, for hours on end without speaking, standing there and angling, and sometimes we came back after midnight with half a dozen Arctic char. That's pure bliss.

I once suggested to Nói that he visit me in Raufarhöfn in summer, and then I would take him angling, but he refused, saying angling was boring. And yet I'm sure he would have liked it; after all, he'd once told me his dream of living in a hut somewhere in Canada or Alaska and living off nature alone, completely independent from his mother. But with an internet connection and modern guns and lots of whiskey.

As I sat there and looked out across the water, I noticed movement on the other side of the lake. I held my breath. It was Schwarzkopf, roaming around, crouched low. It really was. He must have noticed me a while before that, because he was looking over at me in a distrustful way, moving a few metres along the shore, pausing, looking over at me again and then repeating the whole thing. I didn't move, remained completely still, and eventually Schwarzkopf also came to a standstill, his head lowered, his legs taut and

213

slightly spread, ready to flee, as though he were expecting me to do something. So I did something.

The distance across the lake was just fifty metres, and I might have been able to get him with the shotgun, but it wouldn't have killed him, because the bullets would have been too scattered. But I didn't have the shotgun with me anyway, so I reached for my holster in super slow motion, so that the fox wouldn't be able to make out any threatening movement. And he really did turn a little away from me and snuffle at a crowberry bush, then trot further along the shore, entirely relaxed, as though he no longer believed I would do something, but then he paused again and looked over, as though he didn't entirely trust me after all. By now I had the Mauser in my hand, the safety off. My right index finger on the trigger, my arm outstretched, I aimed at him over the front sight, one eye shut, breathing shallowly, inhaling, exhaling. Schwarzkopf looked at me, completely unsuspecting. He wasn't afraid of me. He looked at me as though he tolerated me up here, as though he knew exactly who I was. And that's why it was so hard for me to kill him. No, it would have been wrong to pull the trigger. My gut feeling told me that.

Grandfather had taught me how to listen to and trust my gut. He believed my gut would usually know what was right and what was wrong. I simply had to learn to understand my gut reactions. He asked me where I felt sadness in my body, and told me to point my finger at the spot. It's not as simple as you might think! First, I pointed at my head, because I was stupid and thought that everything plays out in the head. I mean, you would think everything happens where your brain is! Because the head is like a wheelhouse, where the driver sits and steers. If no one turns on the engine, nothing happens. Not even the most powerful engine would be of any use. And that's why, without your head, you can't shovel snow, for example, or be sad. I tried to explain that to Grandfather, but he wasn't satisfied with my explanation, he said that a driver couldn't do anything if the engine was damaged. Then it wouldn't even help if you changed drivers. He said not to point to where I thought the feeling of sadness would be, but to where I felt it, and that we would try again, which made me a little nervous, but Grandfather said I didn't need to be nervous and should close my eyes. And he waited until I almost opened my eyes again, because I wanted to know whether he was still there. At the same moment, I was trying to find out where the damn sadness was, if not in my brain. But I didn't find it, and so I got even more nervous and didn't want to play any more, but Grandfather insisted that I not open my eyes under any circumstances, and then he reminded me that it was almost Christmas, and so I completely forgot I was supposed to be looking for the sadness, but Grandfather asked me whether I was looking forward to Christmas – stupid question! And that I should now show him where the happiness was located, and without even thinking I pointed at my stomach, because that's where the butterflies were, and Grandfather laughed and clapped his hands.

"That's excitement, happiness!" he confirmed.

I was so relieved! It was such a weight off my mind. And now I was ready to track down other emotions. Sadness, as it turned out, was located in my chest, love was in my stomach too, and rage in my arms. I didn't find longing, because I didn't exactly know what longing was, but Grandfather was satisfied with the results and explained that not everything was upstairs in the head, that not everything was as easy as you might think. The Greenland shark, he explained to me, has practically no brain, merely connections from the eyes to the vertebrae, but that certainly doesn't mean the Greenland shark is stupid or doesn't have emotions.

I found that incredible. A Greenland shark had feelings too? Is he sad, down there on the seabed in the darkness? Is he lonely? Or is he happy? Does he have friends? Can he fall in love? Is he afraid when we pull him up to the surface?

"Do fish feel fear?" I asked my grandfather, and he thought for a while and then said that he'd never heard of a fish swimming voluntarily into the jaws of a Greenland shark or into a fishing net, and in his opinion that would never happen. And I must have looked at him in confusion, because he said he wasn't really sure, but that was what he believed. His gut told him, not his head, and it was important to listen to the gut, because the head had very little to do with feelings, and feelings are essential for survival, otherwise we would stick our heads into the jaws of a lion through sheer curiosity. And that made sense.

If Grandfather had been up here with me now, he wouldn't have said a word. He would simply have sat motionless beside me and watched Schwarzkopf through squinted eyes. He wouldn't have told me that I should hurry up or shoot. No way. He would have left me to it because he would have known I'd do it right, even if I wasn't as clever as him. We both had good gut instincts.

Perhaps the fox was looking at me so calmly because he too sensed I didn't mean him any harm. Perhaps he really did recognize me. Perhaps he had also given me a name, like I had him. After all, he had surely seen me wandering across the Melrakkaslétta and heard me singing numerous times. So we just looked at one another, certainly for a few seconds or even more, and I aimed my Mauser at him, thought about Grandfather and said: "Bang."

On my way home, I passed by Bragi's house. And because I looked over at his living room window, expecting to see the poet standing by the window, I didn't even notice that he was standing outside the front door, smoking a pipe.

"Kalmann!"

I jumped and came to a halt, looking around for Bragi. He chuckled, sucked at his pipe and puffed contentedly, as though he had intended to scare me. His lips were painted red.

"Hello," I said, and thought of my grandfather, who used to smoke pipes too but who had never worn lipstick. Perhaps I would smoke pipes as well, once I was as old as Bragi, but I would never wear lipstick.

Bragi pointed the pipe at me. His fingernails were painted black today, and he was clearly in a chatty mood.

"Didn't shoot anything today?"

"No."

"That's what they call an armed stroll."

"I think so."

"Just a harmless stroll. And that's good," said Bragi. "Today is no day for... that kind of thing..." He paused mid-sentence and frowned, as though he was searching for words, but then he simply put the pipe back between his teeth.

He was dressed very elegantly, really old-fashioned: a striped shirt, brown waistcoat, beautiful dark green trousers. All that was missing was a hat. It could have concealed his messy hair.

Bragi was studying me too.

"Yesterday was crazy, wasn't it? Like being in a movie."

"Yes," I said, feeling the weight of the task force guy's knees on my back.

"You liked the girl, didn't you? Nadja?"

I shrugged and looked down at the ground.

"Come in. I'll make you some coffee," said Bragi, turning around and going into the house.

Now I could no longer say no, and walking away would have been impolite, so I took off my shoes by the front door and followed him inside the house. It wasn't the first time in my life that I'd been in there, because I used to accompany my mother when she took books out from Bragi's library. They always used to have conversations, although back then I didn't understand what they were talking about. But I hadn't been into his library in years, and so in a way it was kind of like the first time again, because I had changed and was no longer the same person. His house was built in the 1960s, and it was low, one storey, with large windows and carpeted floors. There wasn't much empty space on the carpet, though. Boxes filled with books were piled up on the floor, the walls were covered in bookshelves, and there were also books on most of the chairs and armchairs, and not only books, but also newspapers and videocassettes, lamps and kitchen utensils. On the windowsills and between the chairs there were plants. A great many plants. It was really warm in the house too. And damp. The windows were steamed up around the edges, and a few spots between the window panes shimmered green. Next to the living room door was a writing desk, laden down with an old computer and more books.

Bragi had disappeared into the kitchen, and that was filled with junk too. I was even able to glance into his bedroom, because the door stood wide open, and it was the messiest room I've ever seen in my life.

"I have to go now," I said. "Bless!"

"Stay right where you are!" called Bragi. He came back into the living room, cleared a few books off the chair and said: "Sit down! Relax!"

I sat down, but relaxing was out of the question. Bragi remained standing and looked down at me, as though he were contemplating what to do with me. Then he went back into the kitchen, leaving me sitting there. After a while he returned with a piece of cake on a plate, gave me the plate and sat down at his desk. He took a book from the pile, turned it over in his hands and leaned forwards, close to the computer screen.

"So many boxes," he sighed. "They just get sent to me, as though I had a use for all this junk, and I haven't even asked for it. Or do you want to read this?" He looked back at the title page of *Kan du høre mosset viske*? "A tear-jerker, and in Danish to boot. Can you speak Danish?"

I shook my head.

"Nor can I, *for helvede*!" thundered Bragi. Evidently he could swear in Danish. "Now I have to input all this nonsense into the system, assign the books numbers and laminate them. It's not like we have anything better to do up here, right?"

I was glad I didn't have to work in a library. It sounded really demanding.

Bragi pointed the black nail of his index finger at the book rack next to me. "You see this whole row of books here? *The Saga of the Ice People*. These volumes are still being read. They'd actually be sufficient for a village library."

I had never read a book, but I didn't want Bragi to realize that, so I said nothing at all and bit into the cake. It was chocolate, and as dry as stone. Bragi turned back to his computer. Hearing the hiss of the espresso pot from the kitchen, I pricked up my ears, but Bragi was so immersed in his work that he probably hadn't heard it, and so I said: "The coffee's ready."

"*For helvede!*" said Bragi once again, then he shuffled into the kitchen.

I exhaled, feeling tense, wondering how I could escape. My gut instinct was giving me signals.

"I saw you, Kalmann!" Bragi called to me from the kitchen. "On that day. In the snow. What a stressful thing!"

I held my breath, waiting for him to continue, but Bragi paused, so I bit into the cake again; the sooner I had eaten it, the quicker I could get out of here.

"Didn't you see me?" Bragi came back into the living room with two cups of coffee. "Surely you must have noticed me? You ran straight past me."

In order to take the coffee, I put the cake on a pile of books. Bragi grinned.

"These books are useful for that at least." He sat back down at his computer. "We're very similar, Kalmann, even if it's not obvious at first glance." It was as though Bragi were talking with his computer. "You're young. I'm getting old. You're strong, a hunter. I'm not. But we're both different to the others, you and I. Two people who don't belong here, who scare the tourists. Two people who didn't fit into *his* picture. Such horseshit. And yet we're guardian spirits, you and I, do you know what those are?" All of a sudden Bragi looked directly at me.

I felt hot. It was hot in here. And I wanted to go.

"Spirits are dead people," I said.

"Not necessarily. Sometimes they are. Guardian spirits can also be dragons or giants, but sometimes in human form, disguised, do you see?"

I nodded, because I didn't want him to trot out any more explanations.

"Don't worry. You don't have to puzzle your head over it," murmured Bragi, picking up the next book. "*Frihedens kirsebær*. Now that's a good book."

I sipped the coffee, even though Bragi hadn't offered me milk or sugar. "I want to go now," I said.

Bragi leaned back in his chair and looked at me. "There's no need to be afraid of me. We're accomplices. We're in cahoots, you understand?"

"I'm not afraid of you," I said.

Bragi chuckled. "No, because you're a guardian spirit. You're the sheriff. And you're not afraid of anybody. Thanks to you, people can sleep peacefully in their beds or read the *Ice People* tear-jerkers. Thanks to you, nobody needs to be afraid of the polar bears or the frost giants."

I put the coffee cup next to the cake and said: "I'm going now." And then I walked across, pulled on my shoes and stumbled out into the open air.

"Don't worry, Kalmann!" Bragi called after me. "If you don't say anything, I won't either. It's a promise!"

I hurried home, suddenly feeling as exhausted as on the day I'd told Hafdís about the pool of blood, when all the stress had begun. I fell onto my couch with a sigh, turned on the TV and was relieved when Dr Phil gave the audience marital tips that I promptly forgot, which wasn't so bad, because I'm not married.

I tried to call Nói, and I wouldn't even have wanted to

speak to him about Bragi or Róbert McKenzie. I just wanted to watch him playing computer games. But Nói was offline. That sometimes happened. No reason to worry. So I tried to reach him on Facebook. But his account was deleted. Or blocked. Either way, he no longer existed there either. And I found that a little strange, but I didn't give it much thought. Not yet.

17

HAND

A few days passed by, around three or four, without Róbert McKenzie being found. I must have caught a chill on the fox hunt, because I felt run-down, and so I didn't go to Magga's funeral, which didn't take place in Raufarhöfn anyway but in Akureyri, where her husband was buried. My mother went though, and she called me later and told me that Magga had been cremated, in other words burned, and I found that only logical, because nobody would have wanted to carry such a heavy coffin to the grave.

I had hidden myself away in my little house and watched the events in the village from my living room window. The rescue service eventually departed, and Birna too only made an appearance from time to time. Calm had been restored to the whole of Iceland. The state leaders had met for their summit, the photos and video recordings of all the handshaking were broadcast everywhere, again and again, and the state leaders wore beaming smiles as though they had won the lottery. They spoke of a significant breakthrough, and everyone was happy that the state leaders no longer wanted to kill one another, and the president of Iceland was shown in one of the photos with the important men, and he was the happiest of them all, beaming as though it was his birthday. Perhaps it was his birthday.

Normality returned to the island. The days were storm-free, and Jú-Jú managed to land several tons of cod on an almost daily basis. I always heard the beeping of the forklift as it reversed, and there was lots of beeping down in the harbour. Dozens of gulls circled excitedly over the cargo containers and helped themselves before the containers could be transported into the cold-storage warehouse. For a while, I even believed the thing with Róbert would now simply be forgotten, because most people only have a short-term memory, as Grandfather often used to say. I tried to reach Nói several times, but he remained offline, which I was now starting to find really strange.

Eventually, it was time for me to go out to my line with new pieces of bait. I had lain on the couch long enough.

On the water, Grandfather and I had spent so many hours with one another that the experiences had kind of become part of the water, leaving traces behind, even though the traces couldn't be seen with the naked eye. I heard Grandfather's words and smelled his pipe smoke.

As always, I listened to my gut before I set off. Weather forecasts are for the head. Standing down at the harbour, looking out to sea, blinking up into the sky and shutting your eyes from time to time is just as important.

Sæmundur and Halldór the janitor were standing in front of the container, talking. They were related, and that's why they did that sometimes; met and conversed wherever they were standing, sometimes in the middle of the street. Sæmundur gave me a travel permit, and said that our gut instincts were in agreement. "Just head out, Kalli minn," he said, adding that he would be here when I got back. "I'm always here anyway, where else would I be?"

I didn't know. And so I didn't say anything, even though Halldór gave me a surly look. Clearly I had interrupted the two of them in a conversation about the state leaders' summit, because Halldór continued: "And I ask you: who's paying for all of it?"

Had he asked me?

"The taxpayers, as always!" Halldór said, answering his own question. So he hadn't asked me.

"That's always the way," said Sæmundur, giving me a wink. "Nothing's free in this world."

Halldór didn't comment on this, saying that the preparations had been very expensive. The security services, the snipers on the rooftops, bulletproof vehicles that had to be flown into Iceland especially, road cordons, traffic obstructions, all of Iceland's security forces, the coastguard, as well as a four-hundred-strong entourage for the state leaders, a few hundred journalists from all over the world, and just for one photo opportunity, a handshake and nothing more.

Halldór shook his head, disgruntled. Sæmundur turned back to me. "Kalmann," he said, "we can count ourselves lucky to live in Raufarhöfn. There would never be that kind of theatre up here. Well, apart from the special forces unit storming the hotel like that."

"Did they really point semi-automatic machine guns at you?" Halldór asked me. "I mean, that's completely over the top!"

"I want to go now," I said, and went. Now I had lost a few minutes standing there with the two of them, I had the unpleasant feeling that I was running late, which was nonsense, because time is irrelevant out on the water. Nonetheless, the journey out to the line felt longer than usual. The impatience tingled in my legs.

In retrospect, I realized that I must have sensed the shark that was hanging on my hook, and that I had to free him from his unfortunate position. Letting *Petra* chug away, I headed out to sea, staring eagerly in the direction of travel and trying to spot my buoy early. A mild wind ruffled the surface of the water, and *Petra* had to crest countless little waves, but she enjoyed that. It was better than being bored in the harbour.

Finally we arrived, the Melrakkaslétta in the far distance, the Arctic Henge a pebble stone monument on the horizon. Finally I pulled up the line, hook by hook. The gulls were delighted with the pieces of bait.

Nine hooks and no shark. I was already starting to believe my gut instinct had been giving me the runaround, but then I saw the great grey shimmering through the water, a bright shadow emerging from the blackness of the sea. It definitely wasn't the first Greenland shark I'd caught, nor was it the biggest, even though it had an impressive length of around fifteen or sixteen feet and probably weighed an entire ton, but as usual I got this rush of happiness I really like. I feel it in my entire body. I let out whoops of joy and am happy there's no one around to hear me.

I pulled the shark out of the water as far as I could with the winch, until my boat was at a sharp angle, meaning I had to be careful not to fall overboard. The shark moved around in the water lethargically. A strange, slow fight for survival, like a yoga dancer in slow motion.

I removed the cartridge from my grandfather's shotgun – you have to check it like that – and put the cartridge back into the chamber. Then I hooked the gaff into the creature's jaw, using all my strength to pull the head a few centimetres out of the water so I could hold the opening of the shotgun between the shark's eyes – and pressed the trigger. Bang. I sent a load of ammunition from my hip into its head, and with that a 512-year-old life came to a premature end.

When you have a ton hanging from the cutter, the journey back to the harbour takes longer. Instead of the usual one and a half hours, it takes two to three. It also depends upon the weather a little. But the wind was good, the tide came in, *Petra* rode the waves briskly, and I managed it in just over two hours.

Sæmundur was waiting for me in the harbour, as though he'd been standing there the whole time; he had seen on his computer where I was. He knew I'd made a catch, because he didn't just have the forklift ready, with which we would lift the shark out of the water, but also a small wooden trailer, onto which we would load the pieces of meat. He began waving to me even from a distance, and seemed as delighted about the catch as I was.

"Congratulations, the first catch of the year! A prime specimen!" he cried contentedly, and then again: "A prime specimen!" And yet he hadn't even taken a proper look at the shark yet.

We put on aprons and pulled on rubber gloves, tied a rope around the shark's fin and heaved it out of the water with the forklift. On the dock we let it hang just over the floor, spat into our gloves and, without wasting any words, got to work. Sæmundur didn't have to help me, because he was the harbour master after all, but there wasn't much going on in Raufarhöfn harbour right now: Jú-Jú were still a good two hours away out on the water, Einar had only just sailed out, and Siggi was packaging up his caviar.

Some other people joined us, a few kids on their bikes, and pensioners, including the car mechanic Steinarr, who since his retirement had been making scrap-iron sculptures which looked like trolls. Sigfús was there too, clacking his ski poles in excitement and even congratulating me. The children cried "Woooow!" and were wide-eyed. They came a little too close to us, until Sæmundur ordered them to keep their distance; after all, we were both handling sharp knives that were as big as small machetes. A little later, Bragi, who must've got wind of the catch, joined us too. He was pale and had dark bags under his eyes, but he winked at me pointedly. He was wearing leather gloves, so you couldn't see what colour his fingernails were painted. I was so proud that I didn't even have time to remember my strange visit to Bragi's. I couldn't stop myself from shouting with joy, that's how proud I was, but I didn't want people to notice, so I buried my face in my hands. I was so relieved! My first shark of the year!

"Don't stab your eye out!" cried Sæmundur. But I was careful, because I knew very well that the knife he'd brought me had a sharp edge.

First, we cut off the big grey's head. We put it aside and let the children take a closer look. Really carefully, they touched the rows of teeth with their fingertips and screamed. Óli squatted down on the floor and looked the shark right in the eye.

"Hey, baby!" he cried. The children laughed and the grown-ups chuckled.

We cut off the spinal and ventral fins and threw them onto the trailer. These I sold to Eysteinn, who also caught shark but in Vopnafjördur, and he sold the fins to Japan or China. They made soup out of it, as expensive as I don't know what. Then we positioned a plastic basin beneath the shark, and I climbed onto the rim of the basin and slit open the shark's stomach. I put my gloved hands into the stomach and let the innards slosh down into the basin. The liver was superb, I would sell it to Reykjavík, where it would be made into liver oil capsules. I was excited to see what would be in the stomach of a shark like this. The onlookers were curious too, and stepped closer. I pulled the basin out from under the shark, squatted down and cut open the stomach. There were all kinds of unrecognizable things, digested, half digested, but among them, grey-white and yellowish, completely bloated and puffy, lay a human hand.

With the knife in my hand, I took a step back and looked down at my glove, because for a moment I thought I had accidentally sawn off my own hand. Shock rippled through the people. The children let out shrill cries.

Then silence.

Then Sæmundur: "I'll be damned! That's Róbert's hand. Róbert's right hand!"

And now the peace in Raufarhöfn was gone again, I knew that right away, and the whole spiel began all over again, but I thought the only logical and proper course of action was to take a closer look at the hand, to at least free it from the inside of the stomach, and because it was my shark, it was kind of my hand too. But as soon as I touched it, the yelling began, as though I was doing the stupidest thing ever.

"Let the hand go, you idiot!" cried somebody, and I'm no longer sure who it was, it could have been Sigfús. It didn't matter. I was so insulted that I didn't let the hand drop but instead lifted it up a little, held it in front of my face and studied it more closely.

It was swollen and multicoloured, from yellow to violet, and kind of black under the fingernails. There were clear bite marks on it, but beneath the wrist it was a clean cut.

"Don't touch it, you idiot!"

"Man! Are you completely stupid?"

"Put the hand back! Don't you remember what Birna said?"

Numerous people were yelling at me. I kept my head lowered and didn't move. I just looked down at the ground. But my insides were twisting, and my brain swelled up so that there was barely enough room inside my head. It didn't help that they were shouting even louder. I stood there like that, with the hand in one of mine and the machete in the other hand, and wondered, although only for a second, whether I should cut a few throats, because then I would have some peace and quiet. I'm actually a peace-loving person, at least I've heard my mother say that a few times, and others too, but I believe it wouldn't have taken much to push me over the edge. Luckily someone intervened, namely Bragi, the poet. He positioned himself in front of me and shielded me, saying in a quiet, even friendly tone but still rather firmly that I should put Róbert's hand back in the basin, because the police had to take a look at it, that was how it was done, preservation of evidence, he said, and then something clicked inside my head, because he was completely right. When part of a corpse gets discovered like this, the site has to be secured until the police arrive, that's the law, and sometimes it even happens that the police secure the evidence until the detective arrives, who then gets really mad, because even the police have done a lousy job. I knew that from the TV, and that's why I also immediately knew what Bragi was talking about. Bragi was probably well informed about such things, because in his life he had read all the books from his library. Perhaps it was also the smell of his pipe smoke that calmed me down, no idea. In any case I threw the hand back into the plastic basin, in such a way that it splashed and people cried out in horror. Then there was lots of chatter, but I wasn't even listening, instead I got to work on the shark. The kids were loud now, because they had called 112 in the meantime, asking to be connected to the police and explaining loudly what and who they had found and where they were, which took a while, because two boys and a girl were yelling simultaneously into the phone, and they also said that I'd touched the hand, and evidently they were asked who *I* was, because they said I was the retarded shark catcher, at which Sæmundur grabbed the phone from the children's hands and took over the conversation with the emergency services, but the damage had been done, I was furious again, feeling it in all of my limbs, and everything went kind of flat and quiet, apart from my pulse, which was pounding in my ears, and I began to dissect the shark, cutting big pieces, also cutting a slit in the skin so that the pieces could be grabbed more easily, and throwing them on the trailer, and because Sæmundur was now speaking with the police, no one interrupted me, so that by the time the police arrived I had dissected almost the entire shark. Birna wasn't there, it was two police officers who I didn't know. Men. And they glanced at one another. But because Sæmundur put in a good word for me and talked insistently with the police officers, I was able to finish my work. Then I stood there again, covered in sweat, breathing quickly and holding a small machete in my hands. Unfortunately I wasn't able to transport the pieces of shark meat into the cold-storage space, because of the securing of evidence, as they said, and Sæmundur asked how long the meat would have to stand there like that, because it couldn't stay there forever, and the police officers promised to let us know as soon as the meat could be taken into the cold-storage space.

"Kalli minn, your knife," said Sæmundur, stretching out his hand. Then he sent me home.

But as it turned out, I was the only one sent home. All the others stayed down at the harbour, albeit at a slightly greater distance from the basin containing the shark innards. That's why I felt like I used to long ago when I was sent to bed while Mother and Grandfather stayed in the kitchen and talked over a glass of wine about things that weren't allowed to reach my ears. I could have gone somewhere else, of course, but I was still quite angry, and so I went home and broke a few things: crockery, an empty flowerpot and a chair. With the broken chair leg, I hit my shin a few times, but I felt nothing. I ripped my shirt, making the buttons hail down to the floor, and also ripped my T-shirt in half. And I made a hole in the wall with my fist. That kind of hurt, even though the wall was only plasterboard, but I got angry at the wall, and before long it had four holes and my hand was bleeding. That felt good. When the blood came, the rage ebbed away, because it was in my arms and hands.

Suddenly I heard a humming, which I immediately knew was the coastguard's helicopter. I limped over to the window. The helicopter flew low across Raufarhöfn and landed down at the harbour. Right out by the pier. So it was easy to see who was getting out of the helicopter and hurrying along the pier to the plastic basin. Birna and some men. Hallelujah! The whole circus was starting all over again!

232

I stood by the window, my eyes burning, and yelled at the top of my lungs. No one heard me. The people were talking, something was put in a bag and taken to the helicopter. Two further men, dressed in diving suits, climbed out of the helicopter and jumped into the water. The police officers climbed into my boat and nosed around.

Birna looked up at my house. I knew right away that she would come here. So I patched up my bleeding wound, doing a really good job of it, but it looked awful because the adhesive plasters were crisscrossed over my knuckles.

When Birna knocked on my door, my courage vanished. I needed backup. My grandfather or at least my mother. And that's why I then remembered that my mother had to be there when I was interrogated, which Birna had confirmed, after all. My mother was my legal guardian. That was the law.

I stayed in the bathroom, watching the plasters saturate with blood. My shirt and T-shirt were hanging off me in strips. My shin was pounding. I held my breath. The small bathroom window was right next to the front door, and as always it was open, and so I couldn't see Birna, but I could hear her wheezing, because she was out of breath having hurried so much. She was just a few centimetres away from me, but my house protected me.

She knocked on the door once again.

"I'm not here!" I muttered.

"Kalmann!" called Birna. "May I speak with you briefly?"

"No way!" I said.

"Why not?"

"I don't want to!"

"But surely you can tell me where you found the hand?"

"In the shark's stomach!"

"No, oh, yes, of course. I mean where you found the shark."

"Out there, at my line."

"And where is your line?"

"That's secret."

"Kalmann… It's important, because we might find more body parts out there."

"You're not allowed to talk to me," I said.

"I know," sighed Birna. "But this is really important, and I'm from the police after all, and you're also not allowed to obstruct police work."

For a long while I said nothing. I almost hit out at my reflection in the mirror. But I controlled myself.

"You know what?" said Birna. "I have an idea. We'll make a deal. You just have to say yes or no. And for that you don't even have to come out, okay?"

I sighed so loudly that she heard it.

"Now then, Kalmann. Are the coordinates marked on your map in the boat?"

"Yes," I said.

"Is it at Point L1?"

I was silent.

"Is that where your line is? Kalmann?"

"Yes! Yes!"

"Have you checked all the hooks? I mean, could there possibly be more sharks on the hooks?"

Never in my life had I heard such an idiotic question. "No way!"

"I'm only asking."

"I always check all the hooks! I'm not stupid!"

"Okay, Kalmann. I know that. I'm just asking."

"You won't find anything there," I said.

"Why not?"

"The sea is 332 metres deep at that location. The sharks would have eaten him ages ago."

"I'm sure you're right. We'll send the helicopter. Perhaps it will spot something floating on the water. We have to try, do you understand? Protocol is protocol."

"Is that like the law?"

"Something like that, yes."

I said nothing, but when something is the law, there's nothing you can do.

"Well, thank you, Kalmann. And see you later," said Birna, and then she left. A few moments later, from the living room window, I saw her walking back to the harbour. A short while afterwards, the helicopter lifted off, carrying the divers, and left Raufarhöfn heading north-east.

I felt completely exhausted and lousy, totally alone, as though someone had dropped me on a rock in the middle of the North Sea. My body probably wanted to become sick again, I had muscle ache, a headache, possibly I had a fever, definitely I had a fever, and so I called my mother, which I generally tried to avoid, because mothers can sometimes be overbearing and they always make such a fuss, but she is a nurse after all. I told her what had happened, and she said she would drive up to see me this evening and be here before midnight, which comforted me. I mean, it comforted me enormously. But I still had the rest of the afternoon and the entire evening to get through, even though I was so tired that I could have already gone to sleep at six o'clock, but I didn't want to sleep yet.

There was quite a lot to watch. Soon an entire convoy arrived, the three dozen people from the rescue service traipsing along the entire length of the beach, where they once again hoped to find body parts between the rocks. They crested hills and scanned the shoreline with binoculars, using drones too. Their attention was clearly directed at the sea, the bay and the beach. The Melrakkaslétta behind the Arctic Henge no longer interested them. After two hours, the helicopter returned, probably having gone to fill up in Húsavík, and then flew along the coastline. Only once darkness fell did things calm down. The fleet of cars belonging to the rescue service and the police, which had been lined up by the hotel, had significantly reduced; some left Raufarhöfn, others probably intended to spend the night in Hotel Arctica, even though it was closed, but Óttar must have opened up and at least put some beds at their disposal. Perhaps he was also operating the beer pump.

Once it became properly dark, I tried for the hundredth time to call Nói. He would definitely have fallen about with laughter over all this. But he was still offline. Had something happened to him? Had he had another operation? Or did he no longer want anything to do with me? Had he been banned from the computer? I realized I didn't even know Nói's full name. So I had no hope of finding him on the internet or in the telephone book. I was confused and disappointed, a thousand thoughts whirled around my head, and it wasn't a nice feeling. And that's why I was really happy when my mother arrived at a quarter to midnight. I was still awake. She gave me a hug, looking tired, and said that she needed to sleep, so we went to bed as soon as she'd tended to the wounds on the back of my hand. I asked her when we would visit Grandfather, but she simply said Grandfather would have to wait.

In the early hours, we were wrenched out of a deep sleep by a knocking on the front door. My mother groaned and said for me to stay in bed, that she would take care of it.

I heard the reporter from national TV asking for me, but my mother was as hard as nails, telling him in no uncertain terms that she was my legal guardian and wouldn't allow them to speak directly with me. But the reporter was persistent, and so it took a while before my mother eventually slammed the door in his face. And pretty hard too. The entire house shook!

We pulled the curtains shut and had breakfast, ignoring the buzz of my telephone and the noise from the village, the cars, the beeping, the voices and shouted commands, and waited until it was almost ten o'clock. Then we got dressed and drove the car over to the schoolhouse, because my mother had given her consent for me to talk with Birna.

18
DAGBJÖRT

I was sitting on the same chair in front of the teacher's desk, in the same classroom as before, but this time my mother was sitting next to me. I had laid my cowboy hat on the desk behind me, my sheriff's badge gleamed on my chest, but I had left my Mauser at home because Birna didn't want me wandering the streets armed. Somebody had cleaned the blackboard, wiping away the map of Iceland I had chalked on there a few days before.

I was nervous. My mother said I should cooperate thoroughly with Birna, but Birna didn't get anything out of me that she didn't already know. I did, admittedly, tell her where I had found the shark, how often I went out to my line, and how I did it, why I had cut open its belly and so on. But I wanted her to tell me whether I would get the shark meat back, and Birna said curtly that she wouldn't expect anyone to stomach the meat of a shark that had eaten a human being. The shark would be taken to the waste incineration site in Húsavík. Period.

To me that was a total overreaction, because the shark hadn't even digested the hand! I was furious. It was my shark, after all. I had caught it!

"Will Kalmann at least be reimbursed?" asked my mother. I smiled at her. She was on my side.

Birna looked taken aback; she probably hadn't even

realized I was suffering a financial loss here. "Of course," she said eventually. She would refer the matter as soon as normality returned to Raufarhöfn.

"And when might we expect that to be?" enquired my mother.

Birna blew air through her pursed lips, like a broken valve, and simply stared through us, suddenly looking as tired as my mother, and once the air was out, I almost thought she was about to keel over, but then she inhaled again, closed her eyes and shook her head. "I don't know," she admitted. "But we're doing our best."

"Have you questioned the village residents?"

"Questioned them? No, but I've spoken with some of them, and there are as many pointed fingers as there are residents."

"And what about the Lithuanians?"

"That's not my area. We're cooperating with Interpol on that. The four Lithuanians have a watertight alibi, they were in the hotel the entire day Róbert disappeared. There's no way they could have murdered him and then disposed of the body." Birna paused and thought. "There's probably only one thing we can rule out right now. Róbert McKenzie was definitely not eaten by a polar bear."

My mother gave a tired laugh, then shook her head gently back and forth and said: "Róbert certainly had a lot of enemies. And despite their watertight alibi, I would still take a closer look at the Lithuanians —"

"As I said, we're looking into everything," Birna interrupted, her expression extremely cold all of a sudden.

"I'm sure you are," said my mother, standing up. "Raufarhöfn can love you, or it can want you dead, and there's only a very fine line in between."

Birna cocked her head slightly and looked at my mother, frowning. The silence in the classroom was almost unbearable. "What do you mean by that?" asked Birna.

"I mean that you've inconvenienced Kalmann enough now. Come on, Kalli!"

I grabbed my cowboy hat and followed my mother, unable to hold back a triumphant grin. Birna let us go. My mother said nothing, marching briskly along the corridor towards the exit with me in tow. But we didn't get far, because Dagbjört was standing in the middle of the passage, looking at us with an expression of mild shock. My mother slowed down, hesitated for a moment, then went right up and hugged her. Just like that. Dagbjört returned the hug, closing her eyes and squeezing her lips together. My mother was hugging her to express her sympathy. And that's why I was standing at the ready, once my mother was finished, and also hugged Dagbjört. She returned my hug too, but briefly gasped for air and even laughed a little, perhaps because I had pulled her a little too firmly against me. She smelled completely different to how I'd expected. She smelled of woman. So grown up. It was the first time in my life that I was hugging Dagbjört, and I wasn't in the least bit surprised at how good it felt. I should have given her a hug many years ago, back when I had pushed her down the stairs and then had to visit her in the hospital, to bring her flowers and a drawing. Flowers and drawings can't heal broken bones. But perhaps a firm hug can. Grandfather drove me there, and I was so happy that my mother didn't drive me, because Grandfather would have been able to protect me from Róbert if he'd been there and wanting to make shark bait out of me. But luckily, as it turned out, Róbert wasn't there, only Dagbjört's mother, who incidentally I had never seen in the same room with her ex-husband. And she wasn't in the slightest bit angry, she was really nice. She pointed me towards a chair next to Dagbjört's bed. So I sat down and gave Dagbjört the flowers and the drawing. She sniffed at the flowers like a movie actress, closed her eyes for a moment and said the flowers smelled good, and that I should smell them too, and I copied her and closed my eyes. The flowers smelled strange, and I didn't know whether it was a good smell or an odd smell, but I nodded, because I'm not stupid; there was no way I could contradict her at that moment. That's a rule of etiquette. And then she looked at my drawing, which I was embarrassed about, because drawing wasn't my strong point. Nor did I ever know what to draw. Dagbjört could draw much better than me, but my mother had insisted on my bringing her a drawing, and Dagbjört put the drawing aside without saying a word, I mean, it wasn't like she was obligated to, and I agreed after all, and that's why I got in first and said that it wasn't a very good drawing, at which Dagbjört nodded. And then I just sat there, and Grandfather chatted with Dagbjört's mother. It felt to me as though the entire world stood still. It was certainly only a few minutes, but to me those minutes felt like hours.

Eventually Grandfather told me to say goodbye to Dagbjört, and I gave her a wave, because I was afraid of touching her, I didn't want to injure her again. And yet I should have hugged her. And once we were back outside, I realized that I hadn't even apologized, but Grandfather said that sometimes not everything has to be said. But because I felt so guilty, I swore to myself that I would protect Dagbjört to the end of our days, with my fists if necessary. And I kept my word.

And this was precisely what I was remembering when I squeezed Dagbjört against me in the corridor of the school building. I didn't want to let her go. My mother eventually stroked the palm of her hand over my back, and said for me not to crush Dagbjört, and then I let her go and stared at the floor.

"Mothers are cock-blockers," Nói had once said, and he was right. Dagbjört was really moved and even had tears in her eyes, though. She pulled out a tissue and dabbed the tears from her face. I wished my mother would say something, something comforting, because I couldn't think of anything, but she said nothing, just stood there with a motherly look while Dagbjört dried her cheeks. So I felt that it was down to me to say something.

"If you need anything," I said, and gestured with my thumb over my shoulder, "you know where I live."

Now Dagbjört laughed a little and burst into tears, crying and laughing all at the same time, sometimes thanking me in the midst of it, then she smiled and her mouth contorted again. She buried her face in the tissue, and now my mother intervened, spreading her arms wide and pulling Dagbjört against her once more.

I stood there like the village idiot. And I was kind of jealous. Jealousy is located in the gut. I almost ran off, because this women's bawl fest wasn't for me! Eventually Dagbjört composed herself, dried her face with a fresh tissue and said: "I'll miss you, Kalmann."

Now I was surprised. Hugely surprised. "Are you going away?" I asked.

Dagbjört nodded, still fighting back tears.

"But why?"

She shrugged sadly. "There's no future here for me, you know?"

I didn't. She would inherit lots of money now, so it didn't matter where she lived.

"But who will be the teacher?"

"The quota is going to Dalvík. Papa sold it just before his death. It hadn't yet been made official, but all the contracts have been signed. That's how things are sometimes. The cold-storage warehouse is closing down, unfortunately, and quite a few people will move away. So the school is closing in June too. Forever."

"And the hotel?"

Dagbjört shrugged.

My mother joined in the conversation. "I'm so sorry!" she said sincerely, stroking her hand over Dagbjört's back.

"Can you promise me one thing, Kalmann?" Dagbjört asked, looking at me sweetly. I mean, so sweetly that I would have immediately fallen in love with her if I hadn't already been in love with her since our schooldays. But now I had a lump in my throat, so I merely nodded. "Promise me that you'll continue to look after Raufarhöfn, okay? The people here need you." I nodded and regretted not having brought my pistol with me, because it was part of my outfit after all, and I looked kind of unprofessional without the Mauser. "Unfortunately I have to go back to the classroom," said Dagbjört apologetically. "Can you tell I've been crying?"

"Yes," I said, and to my surprise both women laughed, and my mother hugged Dagbjört once more, so for the third time, but Dagbjört must have noticed the unfairness of it, because she hugged me again too, and before she disappeared into the classroom, she said:

"The funeral will be on Friday at two o'clock."

"Here in Raufarhöfn?" asked my mother, which was a good question, and Dagbjört nodded.

"I'll be there!" I promised.

"Thank you," said Dagbjört, then she disappeared into her classroom.

I was confused. Funeral?

"Have they found him then?" I asked my mother.

My mother looked startled and took a gulp of air.

"For heaven's sake, Kalmann," she said. "I think it's pretty clear by now that he's dead."

"But we've only found his hand! So is it just his hand in the coffin?"

"Kalmann!" My mother hurried towards the school exit, with me following behind her.

"So what happens if they find the other hand? Or his feet? Or his head! Will they open the coffin back up and put the pieces in?" I thought these were good questions, but my mother evaded them.

"It's important to draw a line under the whole thing," she said. We stepped outside. "For his family in particular it's important to be able to say goodbye to Róbert, do you understand?"

I think I understood.

"And you?" I asked her. "Are you coming to the funeral too?"

My mother sighed. "I think so."

"And Grandfather?"

"Let's leave him out of all this."

We got into the car and drove off right away, because the reporters might have spotted us and come to bother us. As we left, I noticed movement out of the corner of my eye. At first I thought it was a reporter with a camera sitting up there, but it was Schwarzkopf, standing on the hill behind the town hall and looking down at us. He and I looked at one another for a second. Then he swiftly turned and vanished from my line of sight, disappearing beyond the horizon, before I was able to point him out to my mother. That's why I was no longer sure whether I might have imagined him.

"You'll be okay now, won't you, Kalli?" My mother startled me out of my thoughts. I nodded. "And no more interviews!"

After dropping me off at my house, my mother immediately set off back to Akureyri, and because it was relatively warm and the snow had practically melted even on the Melrakkaslétta, I decided I would go fox hunting – once I had rested a little. But then I lay around on the couch for too long, squandering away the day on YouTube, watching funny fail videos, and that's why it was suddenly too late for a fox hunt. Schwarzkopf would have to wait. But tomorrow, I would mean business.

19

TRACKS

Down at the harbour, there were only a few people left from the rescue service. The national TV had departed again too. There were still three cars that didn't belong to Raufarhöfn in front of the hotel. Everything was almost normal again. Probably it was being assumed that Róbert's other body parts would only be found by chance, like his right hand had been. If at all. If a person gets chopped up and thrown into the sea, you don't find all the pieces again. That's just how it is. I could have easily told the officials that there were still a few hungry sharks lurking out there. For sure they had already taken care of Róbert. Fish food! But they were completely satisfied with this one hand. Why else would they have announced the funeral already? In any case, it could now be said with ninety-nine per cent certainty that Róbert McKenzie was no longer alive. The probability that he would turn up with a bandage around his mutilated arm was rather slim – and rather creepy. The thought of it almost made me chuckle. I knew, of course, that it was completely impossible. I wasn't stupid, after all. It was just a funny thought.

I kept thinking about Schwarzkopf. He wouldn't leave me in peace. That's the thrill of the chase. There's no tea or poultice that can help with that. There's no cure. I simply had to track him down again. Ever since we had locked eyes on the outskirts of the village the day before, even though it was only for a second, I couldn't shake the thought that Schwarzkopf was trying to challenge me, almost as though he were saying: "Well? What are you waiting for?"

This time I took Grandfather's shotgun and a few cartridges, hoping Birna wouldn't see me, and wandered back up to the lakes, to where I thought he was most likely to be. Arctic foxes tend to stick to familiar territory, and that's why I had a good chance of tracking him down at the same spot. But I took a detour; I had time, after all. The weather wasn't a threat. I knew my way around here so well that I could set off without giving it a second thought. I always knew where I was. If a snowstorm were to take me unawares, I could still have found my way home.

Perhaps it was a coincidence, perhaps my instinct led me there, perhaps I found the spot unwittingly – I don't know. But I was a little startled when I found myself standing in front of the rock crevice which, until recently, had been filled with snow and hadn't even been visible on the plain. Kind of dangerous, actually. Perhaps I should have informed the people from the rescue service about it when they were carrying out the search up here. But they probably hadn't even ventured this far back.

Now the crevice was easily detectable. But there was still dirty snow at the bottom, almost three metres in width, right where the sun didn't reach. On the snow lay clothing, and among it all you could clearly make out the barrel of a revolver. But you had to look closely. Once the snow had completely melted, the things would gradually sink down into the darkness of the crevice and disappear.

I stood at the edge for quite a while, looking downwards. I've no idea how long I was standing there and looking down, because sometimes that happens to me. I kind of turn off my brain, and lots of people have made fun of that, especially in the past.

But up there on the tundra there was nobody to catapult me back to reality. There was only me. And when I eventually pulled myself together, to continue the hunt for Schwarzkopf, I had already forgotten what was in the crevice.

I really did track him down again, Schwarzkopf – or at least what was left of him. And it wasn't much. Just his head and his bushy tail. A few innards. Nothing more. It wasn't a pretty sight. He lay there on the moss, as though someone had tucked him into it. He looked at me, and I looked at him. Dead eyes don't actually look, but if you stare into them long enough, you see all kinds of things. Then, from time to time, a dead thing blinks at you.

"Hello, Schwarzkopf," I said. I knew that I was completely alone with him up here, so I could talk to him without being laughed at. "How did this happen to you? Did a snowy owl get you?"

Schwarzkopf shook his head imperceptibly. I knelt alongside him and stroked his head. A hunter isn't supposed to have emotions. You can, it's not forbidden, but it's easier if you don't get sad when animals die. That's just how it is. Because there are always lots of animals dying, every day, especially in the slaughterhouses, but only those who work there see that. The last two weeks had been crazy, though, so I was kind of sensitive. I was very sad when I saw Schwarzkopf lying there so dead. I hadn't been that sad in a long while. I'd set out to shoot him, admittedly, but perhaps I wouldn't have pressed the trigger, perhaps

I wouldn't have been able to bring myself to do it, sparing him once again, merely aiming at him and saying "Bang" without pressing the trigger.

After grief comes anger. That's sometimes the case, but not always. Sometimes you're just sad. But now I became angry. And so I looked around, asking myself who could have made such a mess of Schwarzkopf. I wanted to get revenge, but I didn't know on whom.

Eventually I said goodbye to Schwarzkopf, simply leaving him lying there, because other animals would be able to feed on him. That's nature. You can't be sad about it. We're all food for somebody.

I wiped the tears out of my eyes and tried to find meaning in the whole thing. I tried to find tracks. Schwarzkopf's tracks. Because if I found his tracks and no others, I could assume that a snowy owl had caught him. Or perhaps the ravens. They would eat him up – or what remained of him. They were already waiting hungrily by the cliffs, cawcawing. I aimed the shotgun at them, but I didn't pull the trigger.

In the silt on the shoreline, down by the lake, I found some tracks. They weren't fox tracks, though, they were significantly bigger, yet they were also indistinct. I followed them until they led away from the lake and into the crowberry bushes, where I couldn't track them any further. For that I would have needed a hunting dog or something with the Greenland shark's sense of smell. I went back to the banks of the lake. They weren't hoof prints, nor human footprints, and they certainly weren't mink tracks.

Then I heard a sound, similar to a bull lowing a great distance away, but more mournful, more frightening. A guttural call, carried by the wind across a great expanse. The ravens had heard it too, they were looking in that direction and listening uneasily.

And now I became afraid. Really afraid. It's something you only feel when you believe your life is in danger. The fear grabs you by the neck, it burrows its way in, holds you in its ice-cold grip and sucks the strength from your limbs. Everything becomes heavy, like in a nightmare. I ducked down, checked the cartridge, released the catch on the shotgun and held it in position. Aimed into nothingness. But it was pointless. If there's nothing there, there's nothing to hit. I pulled the trigger regardless, firing a load of ammunition across the Melrakkaslétta. The ravens flew away.

"Get lost!" I roared. "Don't you dare come near me!"

I wondered whether I was going crazy after all, or whether I really was in danger. If only Grandfather had been with me! My backpack felt like it weighed a ton, and the route back to Raufarhöfn suddenly seemed twice as long. But I didn't waste a second, and ran as quickly as I could, falling down twice, getting myself all dirty and cutting my palms. My cowboy hat even slipped off my head. I looked around again, unsure whether I was overreacting, but I felt the fear in the nape of my neck, and when you're out in nature, you have to listen to your instinct and your gut. You can't ignore it, because not everything can be seen with your eyes.

I made it back to the village and ran straight to the school, hoping Birna would still be there, so I could warn her.

In front of the school building I came to a halt, gasping for air and pushing down the nausea rising inside me. The pain in my sides was intense and I spat on the ground, but slowly my body began to recover, the fear ebbed away, and suddenly I was no longer sure whether it was a good idea to warn Birna about something when I didn't know what that something was. I would probably make a fool of myself again. With my hands propped on my thighs, gasping for air, it became clear to me that the police were no help. I was the only one who knew the danger – and the only one who was armed. I was the Sheriff of Raufarhöfn, many people called me that, but now it was my mission, my duty. Even Dagbjört had asked me to fulfil it. "Look after Raufarhöfn," she'd said. So I stood up straight, made sure my shotgun was ready to fire – and set off.

Somebody once told me we all have a purpose in life. No one is here by chance. Nothing happens by chance. Everything has a reason, a meaning, a purpose. And in this moment, I realized everything was okay. Everything that had happened so far, the entire story, was okay as it was. That's the disorder of life. And anyone who thinks that life is sometimes messy, or even unfair, is completely right, because that's simply how it has to be, otherwise it wouldn't be life, it would be a movie. But it was important that I understood my mission and shouldered the responsibility. That's why I decided, right there in front of the school building, to protect the 173 inhabitants of Raufarhöfn – even if I died in the process! That would simply be how it was, and it would be okay. So no reason to worry.

I took a deep breath. The fear ebbed away. I stood with both feet firmly on the ground. The ground was supporting me, and that was good. I pushed back my hat to cool my sweat-soaked brow. And then I patrolled the village, shouldering the shotgun like a soldier, and went up to the Arctic Henge, from where I had a good view of the region. I passed a few residents, the poet Bragi for example, who was standing outside his front door in his dressing gown, without a pipe or a cup of coffee in his hands, as though he had accidentally locked himself out. He was unshaven and looked a few years older. He sometimes had these phases.

"Don't do anything stupid," he mumbled, staring after me.

When I next passed his house, he had disappeared inside, and I couldn't see him through the window either. I noticed the sports teacher Marteinn go into the town hall office, which today was a post office counter for a few hours, and emerge again a short while later with a ten-pack of beer under his arm. As there wasn't any national *Vínbúdin* here in Raufarhöfn where a person could buy beer, wine or schnapps, you could order alcohol by post. Marteinn saw me too, paused briefly as though I had caught him in the act, then immediately walked on. Elínborg came rushing out of her house, wanting me to tell her what the hand had looked like, whether it had been cut or whether the shark could have bitten off the hand so cleanly that it looked like a cut.

"Go back inside!" I retorted gruffly, which promptly silenced her, and because I then marched on, she really did go back inside the house. I also ran into a few pensioners out for a walk. Sigfús waved one of his ski poles from across the street, brandishing it threateningly, and yet he meant well. It's impossible to look friendly with a ski pole. Kata chugged up and down the main street a few times with her little dog on her lap, looking at me with a frown each time she passed. I waved, signalling for her to stop. She wound down the window and looked at me questioningly.

"Don't let Al Capone outside!" I advised her, and then walked on, because I had decided not to reveal any details to people and not to tell them about the tracks I'd seen, because creating panic wouldn't help matters.

Towards the afternoon, though, I became tired and hungry, and so I went home for a while, made myself some food, ate a whole packet of cookies and put my feet up. Nói was still offline. He would get in touch eventually, if he still existed. On TV, Dr Phil was arguing with a young woman who had stalked her internet boyfriend, laying into her until she cried. She probably deserved it, because Dr Phil was always right. But I was so tired that I missed the end of the programme and only woke up once it was getting dark outside. And when you sleep for half the day, you kind of end up in a bad mood, and so I watched TV until late into the night, and when I woke up the next day everything hurt, because I had overexerted myself the day before.

20
FOG

On days like this a person should just stay home and watch movies, with somebody by their side, like a friend or at least a mother, but preferably a girlfriend. I only had one friend, Nói, and for inexplicable reasons he had broken off contact. Perhaps he was dead. As dead as Róbert McKenzie. Perhaps the police had pulled the plug on him because he'd hacked into the coastguard website to see where the helicopter was. Perhaps he would get back in touch soon, as though nothing had happened. I hoped so. Schwarzkopf lay in shreds on the Melrakkaslétta, my mother had to work, and I still didn't have a girlfriend. I had never had sex in my entire life. I hated my life. I hated myself. Perhaps the dead people were bothering me. But sometimes you have to go through hell to get to heaven. With hindsight, that's how it is. I had to die in order to be resurrected. I had to conclude my old life so I could begin a new one. And if you want a girlfriend, it doesn't help matters if you lie around at home on the couch, like I had done for over thirty years. I realized that. I still did nothing, though. Because on that day I really had earned a break. My body was giving me all the signals, and my muscles felt more sore than they ever had before. I was convinced that something dangerous was skulking around on the Melrakkaslétta, and perhaps I should have told someone, but I didn't want to be laughed at again. I had pains in my legs and back that were pressing me down onto the couch with an iron grip. Even if the coastguard helicopter had landed on my roof – I would simply have carried on lying there, because that was my plan. I wanted to spend the whole day eating Cocoa Puffs and watching Adam Sandler movies. That man is funny. And if Nói had got in touch, I would have chatted with him, the entire day, even if only to listen to him play computer games and look at his silly sweater. *You Shall Not Pass!*

Nói. I was so annoyed. I didn't even know who his father was. I had never asked him. But when you meet online, names aren't important. And that's why I couldn't track Nói down. So it turns out names are important after all. I missed him. He was what I wasn't allowed to be. He was my polar opposite, my counterpart, and now that he was suddenly offline, I'd fallen apart and couldn't move from the couch. If I wanted to survive, I would have to take a leaf out of his book.

After the sadness came the rage. All of a sudden I was furious, furious at Nói, furious at our mothers for treating us like children, furious at our fathers for not being in the picture. Furious at the authorities, the police and the Lithuanians. Nadja. She had pulled the wool over my eyes. That was mean.

I stood up, went into the kitchen, took a plate and smashed it against my skull. The shards rained down onto the worktop and floor. It didn't even hurt, but the spot on my head became warm. I touched my fingers against my hair, expecting to find blood, but there was no blood. So I took a drinking glass out of the cupboard and held it poised over my head, but at that moment my phone began to buzz

255

on the coffee table in the living room. With the glass in my hand, I paused, then put it back in the cupboard and walked across. It was Birna. She told me she was being pulled out of Raufarhöfn, that she wanted to say goodbye and thank me, and she would be so delighted if she could see my storage hall before she left, my workplace, because I had told her so much about the sharks, and she would love to see where I processed them.

I simply said yes to everything, even though my limbs hurt at the mere thought of leaving the house. But Birna was really nice, and I felt dizzy, and because she was already on her way, I didn't refuse but instead just said yes, yes and again yes. Before she ended the call, she said for me to wrap up warm, and that she would knock on my door in five minutes' time.

I looked out of the window. Outside there was no wind, but the clouds hung heavy. Fog lay in wait over the sea. Perhaps snow too. The sea was no longer even there. Really nice weather for cooling the mind, then. I pulled the cowboy hat over my bump, affixed the sheriff's badge to my all-weather jacket and fastened the holster around my waist. I pulled out the Mauser, thinking about my American grandfather, who had taken it from a Korean. Had he then shot him with it? I rotated the pistol in my hand, studying it, trying to decipher how much death clung to it, and eventually put it back in the holster. Now that Birna was being redeployed, the village needed me again, and in full attire. Mauser included.

I waited outside the front door and watched Birna as she came up the path. She wasn't in uniform but instead was dressed completely normally, in a beige coat and a black scarf. Her greeting was kind of abrupt, she immediately pointed towards the factory halls in the harbour and said: "Let's go. I have a long day ahead of me."

She didn't say a word as we made our way down, and she seemed moody, even though she'd been so nice to me on the phone. She walked at a swift pace, always two metres ahead of me. I could barely keep up, because my legs weren't exactly thrilled about no longer lying on the couch. But the brisk walk down to the harbour warmed them up, and then the muscles didn't ache as much.

"Do you think it's going to snow again?" Birna asked over her shoulder.

I looked up at the heavy grey sky. "Yes," I said. "I smell snow."

"Fantastic," said Birna, but she didn't mean it like that.

I stumbled on a rock, but didn't fall, just stumbled a little, because Birna was going so damn fast.

"Everything okay?" she asked, without looking around again.

"No reason to worry," I grumbled.

We reached the harbour in no time and passed by the empty halls. No one else was around. Siggi's boat lay moored in the harbour, and Sæmundur's car wasn't in front of his container. I wondered whether it was the weekend again already. I didn't know which day of the week it was, and I didn't like that.

"This one here?" asked Birna, pointing at my hall.

"Yes, this one," I said, surprised she knew precisely which hall was mine.

Only once she had reached the door did she pause and let me go ahead. I unlocked the door, stepped into the darkness and flipped the switch. The light took a little while to come on properly, because the strip lights always put on a little disco first. Birna stood next to me, put her hands on her hips and looked upwards, then to the left and to the right.

"Quite a big hall for just one shark catcher," she said. Her voice echoed.

"I don't use the entire hall, just the part at the back," I said. "The ceiling doesn't leak there."

I led her to my work corner, where my table was, and my knife, my refrigerator, my radio that no longer worked, my USA calendar from 2007, my barrels with the bait and my wooden boxes in which I fermented the shark meat. I began my tour by the wooden boxes, because that's what usually interested people the most, but Birna wasn't in the slightest bit interested. She headed straight for the refrigerator and opened it. She looked at the cola cans, the sliced bread and the liver paste and closed the refrigerator again. Then she looked at the knife on the table, picking it up too.

"Well sharpened," she established.

"I cut the meat into pieces on the table, and here in the fish trough I wash the meat in brine, then I pile it up in these wooden boxes, but only at the end of the summer, to give it time to spoil."

"How long does it stay there?" asked Birna, showing an interest in the wooden boxes after all.

"At least twenty-five days."

"Does the meat not get buried?"

"Not any more. It used to. We used to bury it in the sand down on the beach, so the flies couldn't get at it."

"And why don't you do that any more?"

I shrugged. "This way it doesn't get dirty," I said. "And the flies can't get into the wooden boxes either."

Birna laughed coldly and said: "As though *that* were the biggest problem!"

I didn't understand what she meant by that but didn't dare ask, because something in her manner, in her voice, in her demeanour, was different, or the opposite of friendly. She was impatient. She was angry.

"And where do you hang the pieces?"

"Behind, in the drying hut."

"Where's behind?"

"There." I pointed. "Behind the village. Close to Kata's stables."

"How long does the meat hang out there?"

"Six to eight weeks. But only in winter."

"Because of the flies?"

"Yes, but as soon as the pieces get a brown crust, the flies can't get to the meat any more anyway."

"I see. And then is it" – Birna hesitated – "edible?" She laughed coldly again.

"Yes, then you can eat it. It's no longer poisonous. So you can't get sick from it."

"You don't say! And you hang the meat up on these hooks?" She pointed at the wall, where the hooks from our old lines were hung up on a nail.

"No way," I said. "Those are fishing hooks. The pieces of meat hang on strings in the hut. Not on hooks. I make holes in the meat and hang it from string."

"Those are the fish hooks?" Birna seemed surprised. "You pull a killer whale out of the water with those!" She looked more closely at the hooks, took one down from the nail and rotated it between her fingers. I wanted to contradict her, but she was already bombarding me with a new question: "Why do you have so many hooks?"

"We used to have a few longlines," I explained.

"So, multiple lines with hooks?"

"Yes, a longline between each of the buoys."

"And now?"

"Now I only have one longline with ten hooks. That's enough."

Birna nodded. She pressed the tip of the hook gently into the palm of her hand. "So the pieces of bait are quite big."

I nodded. "About the size of your hand," I said.

Birna looked at me, horrified. "What do you use as bait?" Her voice was no longer harsh but was suddenly kind of guarded. I hesitated, but she didn't avert her gaze.

"That's a family secret," I said.

"I won't tell anyone," she said.

"Each person has their preferences."

"Each shark catcher?"

"Yes."

"And which bait have proven to be the best?"

I groaned in irritation. Birna was wearing me out! "Smoked horsemeat," I said. "But I'm not telling you how I marinate the meat!"

"Excuse me? Marinated horsemeat?"

"The sharks have to be able to smell the meat, because they can't see anything down there."

"I see," said Birna, feigning astonishment. "I'm wondering how we came up with the idea of catching shark, letting it spoil and then eating it." I was about to explain it to her, but clearly she hadn't directed the question at me, because she immediately answered it herself. "We must have been really desperate. And the bait is in this barrel?" She pointed the hook at the blue plastic barrel with the black lid.

I nodded. I was now regretting having brought her into my hall.

"May I?"

"No."

She looked at me. "Kalmann, I would like to take a look in this barrel." She pointed at it.

"No way," I said. My pulse was pounding in my head. Birna stared at me as though she were trying to use telepathy to get me to open the lid of the barrel. That's why I avoided her gaze and began to organize the knives on the table, checking their sharpness. "Family secret. You're not allowed," I said, and even I was startled by my voice. Because I didn't sound anything like myself. Birna took a step backwards and looked over at the exit.

"It's okay, Kalmann," she said, lifting her hands placatingly. "You don't have to show me your bait, okay?"

"You're not allowed to see!" I said firmly.

"No problem." Birna sighed and looked at me for a while. Then she said: "Come on, show me your drying hut, okay? And then I'll leave you in peace."

I hesitated, eventually nodded, put the knife down on the table and took the lead, Birna a good ten metres behind me, light off, door shut. Outside, the fog had crept onto the land from the sea, and you couldn't see much further than the next building. But that didn't matter, because I'd spent my entire life here, so I could find my way around with my eyes shut.

I wondered what Birna had in mind. Had she noticed I was hiding something in my barrel? Would she request a search order or notify my mother? Either way, I was disappointed. I was sad. I was tired. It was as though all my gloominess, all my fears and all my anger were hidden away

261

in my bait barrel, and now Birna wanted to open it. Not a great idea on her part. I had reason to worry. I realized that my life here in Raufarhöfn as I knew it was coming to an end, that the Róbert McKenzie case would be closed today and that, after that, nothing would ever be the same again. I wished I had stayed on my couch, so that the world around me wouldn't have changed. I didn't like change. I didn't do well with it, like back when my mother had moved to Akureyri. Or when Grandfather was put in the care home. Would Birna let me have this last walk to the drying hut before she summoned the task force from Reykjavík? Or was she trying to lure me away from the barrel to win time, to get backup? I didn't know, and I didn't actually care. But I didn't want my life here to end. I hadn't wanted anything to do with the whole thing anyway. From the very start. Why hadn't people just left me in peace! I wished I could have turned back time by two weeks, back to the day I had found Róbert in the snow. I wouldn't have gone on the fox hunt, I wouldn't even have moved from the couch that morning, and then I wouldn't have run into Róbert either.

So I decided to take Birna on a detour. It wouldn't have taken us long to reach the hut, which was a few hundred metres behind the storage hall, standing slightly elevated on a hillside, but I led Birna past it in a wide arc, so that she didn't even notice in the fog. But Birna was from the police. So she had a police intuition that normal people don't have. Because after we'd gone half a kilometre, she came to a halt. The buildings had vanished into the fog. We were just above the village, but we could easily have been in Greenland or on another planet, because you couldn't see a thing.

"Kalmann, stop for a moment! Are you sure we're going the right way?"

I turned around and looked at her. So this is what it looked like when a chapter in your life came to an end; a confused policewoman in the fog.

"I want to show you something," I said. "You'll find it interesting."

"Yes, the hut, right? Is it really this far?"

"It's not much further, we're almost there," I said, already setting off again.

Birna had no option but to follow me. After a while, she stopped again. "Kalmann!" she called out. "Where are you taking me?"

I didn't reply and simply carried on. By now we were near the Arctic Henge, already up on the plain. But here the fog was even thicker.

"Kalmann!" Birna's voice faltered. "Where's the path back to the village?"

"It's not much further!" I assured her. I wanted to show her the rock crevice, the pieces of clothing and the revolver, they were sure to have interested her, but Birna was obstinate.

"Stop right where you are, Kalmann!" she cried. "I want to go back to the village! Immediately!" Now she was running after me angrily, trying to stop me. I went faster, because Birna was catching up. She had almost reached me when the dark silhouettes of the Arctic Henge emerged like giants from the fog. Now Birna too realized where we were. Gasping for breath, she came to a standstill next to me and looked at the rocks.

"Kalmann," she said. "Don't scare me!"

"It's not much further," I said.

"No, stop!" she said firmly. "No more games. Stop it. Stop this nonsense! What do you want to show me, Kalmann?"

Up here in the protection of the fog, I felt safe. There was just Birna and me. She looked at me, and I looked at her. And perhaps it was this intimacy that I had been searching for. Perhaps now I would be able to tell her what I had really found up here.

"Schwarzkopf," I said. "Do you remember? I was hunting him."

"The Arctic fox," said Birna impatiently. "I remember."

"He was roaming around pretty close to the village. And Hafdís told me to teach him a lesson. But I didn't actually want to kill him."

"Who, the fox?"

I shrugged. "It was snowing, I couldn't see much more than we can now, and I didn't find him where I thought he would be. But I walked in a wide arc across the Melrakkaslétta and eventually came past here. And around here I found Róbert."

"You mean, the pool of his blood?"

"There." I pointed into the fog. "Over in the front there."

We stared into the fog for a while and said nothing.

Birna broke the silence. "Was Róbert alive when you found him?"

In my thoughts, I saw Róbert again. I could remember every detail. That's because of being at the scene. When you return to the scene, you can remember the events more clearly. That's just how it is, because everything looks exactly the same, and smells it too, the air and everything.

I saw Róbert, how he had stood there lopsidedly in the snow. He had a red face and was drunk, and was without a winter coat or hat. He wasn't wearing his multifunctional glasses. Probably he had lost them on the way here. He must've fallen over a few times, because his fancy suit had a tear in the sleeve, his trousers were dirty, his fly was open, his tie hung lopsided and loose around his neck. In his right hand he was holding a silver revolver. He let out a rollicking laugh when he saw me, saying I was just what he needed.

"The village idiot!" he bellowed, slapping his left hand against his forehead. "I pray for an angel, and then I get sent the village idiot!" He almost couldn't catch his breath, that's how funny he found the sight of me.

I was so stunned to run into Róbert up here – in this state! Even though he was waving his revolver around in the air, I sensed that he didn't pose any danger. He radiated hatred and contempt. He was a foreign body in this silent idyll. I paused where I was, about twenty metres away from him, and because I was so embarrassed, I let him talk and laugh.

"You know what, Kalmann? Sometimes I wish I were a simpleton like you. Honestly! Just like you. So simple. Everything so easy. An easy life. Everything black-and-white. Everything straight or crooked. A horizon that stretches only just beyond the Melrakkaslétta. Feeling happy here in Raufarhöfn! Ha! Content with the sharks, and I envy you that. The recipe for happiness is contentment, after all. That's abundantly clear! Do you understand what I mean?"

I didn't react. I just looked at him. And I didn't know what he meant.

Róbert could tell: "Contentment is when you're happy with little and therefore have enough of everything. Or is there something you wish you had?"

Several things that I wished for immediately came to mind, even though I didn't want to admit them. So I said nothing.

"Well, what do you wish for, Kalmann? It would really interest me, even if it's the last secret I discover in my life. Tell me what you wish for! Perhaps I can grant your wish. One last wish! Ha!" He bellowed and spat into the snow, rummaged a small bottle of whiskey out of his jacket pocket with his free hand, opened it and took a gulp. He dropped the lid.

I watched him. I was no longer thinking about all the things I wished I had. He wouldn't have been able to give them to me anyway.

"Come on, boy. Strain your brain cells! You'll think of something!"

"A wife," I mumbled.

"What?"

"A wife!" I said more loudly, feeling bitterness rise inside me.

Róbert became still for a moment, pausing with the whiskey bottle halfway to his lips, probably needing to let my wish run through his mind first, perhaps pondering how he could source a wife for me, but then he waved the revolver and laughed contemptuously.

"Women!" he roared. "Believe me, women are nothing but trouble. Just trouble. You'll be better off without them. And the women will be better off too!" He laughed, emptied the bottle and threw it carelessly into the snow. That's not allowed: littering in nature. But I didn't say anything, because I was afraid Róbert would have laughed at me.

It was still snowing heavily. A layer of snow had formed on Róbert's head, and there was doubtless snow on my cowboy hat too. For a while we stood in front of one another wordlessly, almost like in a Western. But my Mauser was still in its holster.

Róbert was having many thoughts, and they all showed on his face. Sometimes he contorted his mouth as though he were in pain, then he smiled again, looking contentedly up at the sky, so that the snowflakes fell on his overheated face and melted away. He laughed, he shook his head, he moaned.

"You have to promise me something. Can you do that, Kalmann? Do you know what a promise is?"

I nodded. Everyone knows what a promise is. But before you can promise something, you have to know what it is you're promising.

"Make me disappear," said Róbert. He was suddenly really serious, really sober. He looked at me so intensely that I felt his coldness. "Kalmann, are you listening to me?" he said, taking a few steps towards me. "You have to promise me! Dagbjört can never see me like this. Never. She can't find me. I don't want to do that to her, do you understand? And I'm sure you don't want to do that to her either, do you? You care about her, after all! Make me disappear. Make fish food out of me! Feed me to the sharks." He came up close and grabbed my upper arm, squeezing tightly.

I looked down at the floor, tried to pull my arm away, but Róbert had an iron grip. And he smelled of alcohol. He lifted the hand that was gripping the revolver and tapped the barrel against my sheriff's badge.

"Sheriff, I'll tell you something. I don't believe our paths have crossed up here by chance. No one but you knows how to make fish food out of someone, do you understand?"

I said nothing. He looked crazy. His eyes were glassy, his tongue heavy and lethargic, his eyelids half closed. But his request was unmistakable.

"You have to promise me! You have to, do you hear? Dagbjört can't find me here, and if it looks like the Lithuanians killed me… then even better. It's because of them I'm in this mess." Now pain and despair appeared on his face again. He let go of me, lost his balance and fell backwards into the snow. He sat there, exhausted, his head hanging down. The hand clasping his revolver was propped against his knees. Snow clung to his blue fingers.

"I lost an entire barrel, goddammit!" He waved the revolver roughly in the direction of the sea. "The anchoring or rope must have come loose, and now it's floating around out there. And yet this damn barrel was only part of my problems. Can you even imagine what it's like to carry the weight of this miserable backwater on your shoulders? As though it were my fault that Raufarhöfn's dying. I've made every resuscitation attempt possible, and now it's time for the death blow. Someone has to do it. Someone just has to do it. Someone has to write *me* off, Róbert McKenzie, this failure."

I was confused. Raufarhöfn was dying? A village can't die! I must have given Róbert a questioning glance, because he said:

"Yes, Kalli minn, we're closing down. The quota is going to the Dalvíkings. The school's closing. And when a village doesn't have a school, it's not a village, you see? And I alone am the scapegoat. Like always. All I ever wanted was to live a good life. Is that asking too much? It seems so! But my daughter can't see me like this. We have to spare her that. You and I. We're in the same boat now. You have to make me disappear. You have to!" Róbert sighed, seeming kind of relieved, as though he were happy to have told me. But I wasn't happy. I hadn't wanted to hear it, because it was really bad news. The thoughts were pounding through my head. And yet I only understood half of what he'd told me, because it was much later that I found out what kind of barrel he'd supposedly lost. But Dagbjört losing her job at the school, I didn't think that was okay. A village without children. That's not a village! And now I understood that a village without children wouldn't survive.

"The school has to stay," I said, but Róbert laughed at me.

"It's too late, boy, it's done! You can quit too. Then at least the sharks will have some peace and quiet."

I became angry. "The school has to stay!" I repeated.

"It can, for all I care. The school can stay, but you can't have a school without children!"

"The children have to stay!"

"Okay, okay!" said Róbert, lifting his hands in a placating gesture, laughing a sickly laugh. "The children stay. I promise. Word of honour. But do you promise to make fish food out of me? Do we have a deal?"

I said nothing, I didn't nod, I didn't shake my head. I just looked at him, not even blinking, because I was angry and wondering how I could save Raufarhöfn.

"You promise, right?"

Then I nodded after all. What other choice did I have? Róbert looked at me thoughtfully, studying me almost lovingly, then he even smiled, as though he was suddenly really happy with me, with himself and everything. He said that he was glad I had found him out here, then he held the revolver to his head, said "Bless" and pulled the trigger.

21
MAUSER

My head exploded. Never before had I watched some-body hold a revolver to their temple and pull the trigger. Suddenly I too was sitting on my behind, because my legs simply took a break, and my head was whistling like a kettle on a glowing hotplate. And that's why it took me a few sec-onds to realize that Róbert was still sitting in front of me in the snow, staring at his revolver in confusion. Because he hadn't been able to entice anything more from it than a metallic click. Róbert shook the revolver, held it up to his forehead once more and pulled the trigger again and again, and then his entire body began to shake, he dropped the revolver and buried his face in his hands. His bitter crying gradually turned into laughter, and then he became properly hysterical, rolling around and pummelling the snow with his fists. I simply sat there and tried to get over the shock, barely able to catch my breath.

Birna had been listening to me in horror, without inter-rupting, and as I told her the story my heart began to race all over again. Now she looked at me with concern, but she still didn't say a word. The memory of that moment with Róbert sloshed over me like a monster wave at sea. And yet up here on the Melrakkaslétta everything was so still, but I was in the middle of a storm, because I had tried to suppress the encounter all these days. I'm pretty good at that. Suppressing things. You learn to, when you're someone like me. The fact that the memories were now appearing so detailed and clear in my head overwhelmed me. And that's why I didn't want to carry on talking. Birna didn't need to know any more than that. But I couldn't hold back the images, they flickered in front of my mind's eye like a crazy movie that's been edited together too quickly. What's more, over the last few days, Róbert's prophecy had come true: the quota had been sold, the school was about to close, and Dagbjört was planning to leave Raufarhöfn. I had tried to delay this moment, the change in my life. Now Birna was standing directly before me, and her expression told me that she wouldn't tolerate any more excuses. She wanted to hear the whole story. To the bitter end. So I took a deep breath and continued. I told how Róbert had lain in the snow for a long while and cried, I mean, really cried, like a child, with tears and everything, and how eventually he had begun to laugh, hysterically, then kind of heartily, as though a great weight had been taken off his mind.

"Probably everything means something," he said after a while, patting his pockets for another whiskey bottle, one that didn't exist. "I'm really beginning to believe that someone's sitting up there making fun of me." He pointed up at the sky. "God puts a broken revolver in my hand and sends me a retarded sheriff with an antique toy gun to help! Ha! The Sheriff of Raufarhöfn! I'm laughing myself silly! The Lithuanians should be afraid of you!"

He laughed heartily again, and somehow even I recovered from my shock and found the whole thing funny, and I was a little proud that he'd called me the Sheriff of Raufarhöfn, he, the King, and that the Lithuanians should be afraid of me, even though I didn't know why. It really was funny. And I felt the opposite of what I had been feeling a moment ago. I had never been so relieved in my entire life! Now Róbert would surely abandon his suicide attempts. He had pulled the trigger, admittedly, but he would leave it at that, even though no bullets had been fired from the barrel. He had pulled the trigger, and that was what mattered. Now he had been given a second chance, he would change direction and start a new life. He would get the quota back, the children would stay, and the school wouldn't close. Dagbjört would keep her job. So no reason to worry.

"Let's have a look," said Róbert, stretching out his hand towards my Mauser.

Sometimes you notice certain things that in hindsight appear obvious too late – or not at all. That happens to me sometimes. But that's just how I am. And when we were sitting up there opposite one another in the snow, Róbert and I, my head was no longer functioning properly. Róbert continued to hold his hand out and insisted:

"Show me your goddamn Nazi pistol!"

I freed the pistol from its holster and handed it to him.

"It's amazing," he said. "And where did you get it from?"

"From my American grandfather," I said.

"And where did your grandfather get it from?"

"He took it from a Korean, in the Korean War."

"Wow." Róbert was impressed. He rotated the pistol in his hands, read the inscription, "Mauser", and said that it didn't sound very Korean.

"It's a German make," I explained.

"So it is a Nazi pistol!" he cried, but now I noticed that Birna's facial expression had changed. That brought me back, and I paused in the middle of my story.

Birna was no longer looking at me. She had turned and was staring intently into the fog. "Be quiet!" she hissed.

I listened into the fog. Had she heard someone coming? Had someone followed us and been listening? But now I noticed it too. Somebody was already here. And we hadn't heard them coming.

It was a snorting, snuffling sound, and I knew immediately what was snuffling around up here, even though I had never heard one snuffling before.

"There," said Birna, turning around even further. She didn't yet know what was making the snuffling she could hear. "Is that a horse?" she asked.

I was about to correct her suspicion, but I didn't need to say a word, because at that moment a piece of the white fog shifted, and that made the polar bear easier to spot.

It was about thirty metres away, its black nose clearly visible. Birna didn't say a word. The polar bear stood there, its head hanging, and sniffed in our direction without really looking at us. It shook its head back and forth, up and down, sniffling and snorting. Birna had gone completely stiff. She took a few steps backwards, away from the polar bear.

"Kalmann, we have to make a run for it." She said it tonelessly, feebly, but didn't run off, it was just a remark, she took only small steps backwards, until I was standing between her and the polar bear.

Birna was right. We had only one chance of surviving: to run. But you can never outrun a polar bear. I knew that. Because polar bears have four legs, and that's why they're twice as quick. There are only a few predators in this world you can outrun. Polar bears are not one of them. What's more, this one must have been very hungry, because it had swum the entire way from Greenland to Iceland after all, and as far as I could tell, it really didn't look well-nourished. It was a slender animal, albeit a big one. Its fleecy fur had a yellowish tone and was now clearly discernible in the white fog. You could even see its paws with the black claws.

So, of the two of us, the one who could run fastest would survive. The case was clear-cut; I was faster than Birna. And I also knew which direction the village was in. Birna didn't. We would run away, the polar bear would follow, Birna would be slower than me, and the bear would pounce and bring her to a halt with a few bites to the head and neck. That's what polar bears do, they sometimes even bite off your head. But not always. Sometimes the prey is still alive while it's being eaten. Compulsory stunning isn't a thing in the animal kingdom. That's nature. Even though in nature there are clear rules. For example: I survive, Birna gets eaten, because I'm quicker, and she's slower. It's actually not in the least bit complicated.

There are moments in life when you don't stop to think. You just act. The body takes over, allowing the brain to take a break, because you don't have time for musings. In moments like these, I'm kind of normal. And that's exactly how it was. I didn't think. I reacted. I simply stayed where I was, because my body knew very well that it had to stay where it was. Because a sheriff doesn't run away.

"Kalmann," hissed Birna frantically. "Come on! We have to run, and as quickly as we can, do you understand?"

"No way," I said, shaking my head imperceptibly. The polar bear looked at me briefly, looked me right in the eyes, then it raised its snout back up to the sky and let out a terrible, guttural sound which I had heard once before, from a great distance. Birna screamed in horror, clapped her hand in front of her mouth and whimpered. I noticed that a gentle wind was stroking the back of my neck, so we were standing right in the wind, and the bear would get a noseful before it filled its belly. I'm sure we smelled good. I was a hunter, like the polar bear. So I knew what it was thinking. I could easily put myself in the animal's mind, and I suddenly thought about Róbert, who had held his revolver so casually up to his temple to drive a bullet through his head, as though that were the only possibility. And that's exactly how it was with me. There was one single possibility, and that's why I didn't even need to think. I stood there motionlessly, facing the polar bear. I knew who I was and what I had to do. And I knew who the bear was. Everything was exactly as it had to be. The world was in perfect balance.

"Kalmann!" Birna grabbed me by the arm and pulled at me, but I was stronger than her and remained where I was.

Perhaps it was something about this place. Why had Róbert come up here to end his life? Had I come here with Birna to end my life too? Why did the polar bear seem to have been waiting for us? Perhaps this damn half-finished Arctic Henge had magic powers. Perhaps the polar bear was Róbert reincarnated.

"Kalmann! Which direction is Raufarhöfn in?"

I turned my head towards her and said: "That direction. Go. Run!" Then I turned back towards the polar bear, snapped open my holster and drew my Mauser.

"Kalmann, no!" screamed Birna in desperation. "Your toy gun won't help you now!"

"I'm the Sheriff of Raufarhöfn," I said, stretching out my arm and aiming the Mauser at the polar bear, which was now trotting in my direction with its head lowered, growling.

Birna bellowed: "Kalmann, your gun isn't loaded!" Then she began to shout, making all kinds of animal sounds, trying to shoo away the polar bear. It was ridiculous. She even threw stones that she gathered from the ground around her, hurling them in the vague direction of the polar bear but missing it by several metres. Her throws were too feeble and despairing. I gripped my Mauser tightly and took aim at the polar bear over the front sight. The bear ducked, as though it knew what I was holding, but it continued to advance towards me.

"Kalmann!" screamed Birna, distraught. I didn't see her face, but I could hear in her voice that she was crying. "You're not a sheriff, you're not a hunter, Kalmann! You're not a hunter! And your gun isn't loaded! Kalmann, please, pleasepleaseplease, run!"

The polar bear was now a few metres away from me, and it slowed its pace, shifting its weight as though it were about to pounce. It looked at me, and I looked at it, and I saw the intelligence in its eyes. And it was a beautiful polar bear. I think this polar bear was the most beautiful animal I had seen in my entire life. And it was massive. I estimated that it weighed at least half a ton, but it moved with the light-footedness of an Arctic fox. And now I also knew what had rattled Schwarzkopf. I noticed that I'd lowered my Mauser a little, that's how awed I was to be seeing this majestic beast close up.

The polar bear paused. Why it paused, I don't know. Perhaps it was bothered by the stones that were now hailing down, even though they bounced off its fur as though they were balls of wool. It paid no attention either to Birna or to the stones. It only gave a deep snarl, a suppressed howl, then snorted loudly and looked at me. That was good. I was its prey. That was what I wanted.

I wasn't afraid. And perhaps people will find it difficult to believe that I wasn't afraid, but I really wasn't afraid. They'll have to believe me, whether they want to or not. Because I knew what I had to do. And my muscles knew it, my body knew it, from my head to the tips of my toes. I didn't need to think about it. I aimed the barrel of my gun at the polar bear's chest, took a deep breath and said: "Bang."

"It's a real shame this thing isn't loaded," said Róbert. "A person could at least depart this life in style with a Nazi shooter like this." He shrugged, held the muzzle of the gun under his chin, grinned at me, said "Bang" and pulled the trigger.

It was an incredibly strange sight. The small layer of snow which had formed on his head hopped a little, like boiling spaghetti water lifting the lid off a pot. Part of the top of his skull lifted a little too, but it stayed attached to the head. The gun immediately fell out of his hand. Blood gushed down over his chest. Róbert was still looking at me, although not for long, half a second at most, then he tipped over backwards into the snow, his eyes rolling back. His knees were bent, pointing up towards the sky.

I closed my eyes and put my hands over my ears. I did it automatically and didn't know why. But now it was pleasantly quiet and dark around me, as though I wasn't even there. But you can't just sit there like that, the world carries on turning regardless. So I blinked at the snow and removed my hands from my ears. Róbert was no longer making a sound. His legs had tilted over to the side. My Mauser lay next to him in the snow. Luckily it wasn't smeared in blood, but it was only just outside the pool of blood. I stood up and stepped towards Róbert, picked up my Mauser and put it in the holster. It was warm.

"Kalmann!" Birna dropped down onto her knees in despair. She flung her hands up into the sky as though she were asking God for help. But that wouldn't help us at all. Up here on the Melrakkaslétta, you don't get any help from God. Here you have to help yourself.

Before the polar bear could begin to move again, I pulled the trigger.

The shot lashed loudly, the pistol jerked furiously in my hand, but the fog immediately swallowed the sound. Birna was speechless, as though *she* had been hit by the bullet, and that's why for a very short moment, just a second, everything was completely silent.

Until I pulled the trigger again. I noticed that the polar bear flinched at the second shot, but it was impossible to tell whether I'd hit it, because the thick fur covered the point of entry. But the polar bear remained standing, ducking its head and throwing it angrily back and forth, as though it were trying to shoo away aggravating wasps.

By the third shot, my gun was getting really warm in my hand. But the polar bear seemed undeterred and began to advance again. The elegance with which this heavy animal set into motion was awe-inspiring, but for me, in this moment, that wasn't ideal. So I fired my Mauser a fourth time. And now, finally, I took the wind out of its sails. I saw it, and I felt its pain. It slumped a little, almost stumbled, then caught itself again, shook its head and came to a halt directly in front of me, just an arm's length. It wheezed pitifully. My fourth shot had hit it badly. Blood seeped out of its fur. It straightened itself up, went up on its hind legs and lifted its paws, towering up before me as though it wanted to show me who the boss was. It stood at least a metre taller than me. I saw every hair on its body, I saw its claws, and I noticed its teats. It was a female.

I had one bullet left in the cartridge. I had kept count. Róbert had laid claim to one bullet. That had been enough to bring him to silence. Róbert wasn't a polar bear. So I knew what was what. There was no hurry. The time passed more slowly somehow, which I found pleasant, because it meant I could really commit this moment to memory. You only experience this kind of thing once, if at all, so you want to be able to remember every detail later. I still had one bullet in my Mauser for this Queen of Creatures, and I sent it straight into her heart, a heart shot, because when you're a hunter, and I am, you know where the heart is located. I held my arm outstretched, the mouth of my Mauser centimetres away from the bear's fleece. I couldn't possibly miss the heart.

With this last shot, I brought down the female polar bear. It fell forwards, and then my body stopped cooperating, because I didn't react, but just stood there, which meant that the beast dragged me to the floor and buried me beneath it.

There's one thing I learned that day up by the Arctic Henge: it's dark underneath a polar bear. And quiet. Probably like in a coffin, but I've never been in a coffin.

I heard Birna calling my name as though from a great distance. It then took a few seconds for me to figure out where I was – under a polar bear, actually – and it immediately felt like that too, because the animal was immensely heavy, and I could barely breathe. Then it became brighter again, because Birna tugged at the bear's front leg, which was covering my head, but the leg slipped out of her hands, and so it got dark again. Birna didn't give up so quickly, though. After all, I had saved her life. She was sure to be happy about that. She cursed like a sailor and tugged angrily at the animal until at least my head was clear and I could get a bit more air. But my ribs felt kind of squashed. A stabbing pain was taking my breath away, and everything was going black before my eyes.

Birna was really relieved when she established that I was still alive. She anxiously stroked my face, said that help was on its way and I didn't need to worry. Then she disappeared from my line of sight, and I was starting to think she had gone to get help, but now she was tugging at the animal again, and this time from the other side. But it's not so easy to roll half a ton of weight across the ground. The polar bear's head lay next to me, its tongue hanging out of its snout a little. I could see it well if I turned my head. And I saw the teeth too. Immediately I knew that a polar bear could win in a fight with a Greenland shark. But now I noticed that the polar bear female was still breathing, although almost imperceptibly. Only a light panting, but it was still alive! And suddenly I felt sorry for it. I felt so unbelievably sorry for it, and I felt so mean for having brought down this animal. Wouldn't it have been logical if it had eaten me? Had I broken the laws of nature? After all, without my Mauser I would most certainly have been defeated by it. I was... Yes, who was I? I wasn't a sheriff. Birna had been clear about that. I wasn't a hunter either. I was a nobody. I was just the village idiot. This polar bear might have cubs. It had swum here the entire way from Greenland, perhaps searching for food for its offspring. It had seen more of the world than I had. It had been places. It was a somebody. I wasn't.

My head could easily have fit into its jaw. In one bite, my head would have been gone. But the female bear was only panting now, I had to hold my breath to hear it – which I was doing anyway, because the animal was pressing down hard on my chest. And then the bear growled, but that too was only quiet, and for sure Birna couldn't hear it. It was a growl that came from deep inside, from cavernous depths, a last stirring, the embers smouldering, the shell already dead, but it was a contented growl, as though the bear was dreaming about something wonderful, perhaps thinking about its cubs, and that comforted me a great deal. I was so relieved, even though that might sound strange now. One last growl, then it was no longer breathing. The polar bear was dead, and that was only logical, because there were five Mauser bullets in its chest, at least one of them in its heart. Perhaps the animal was relieved to put all the hardship behind it, perhaps it had made peace with the fact it would never find its way back to Greenland, perhaps it had been feeling similarly to Róbert, who also hadn't wanted to live any more. Perhaps it had been looking for me, and our paths had had to cross, everything had to be as it was, because the rules of nature aren't something you can avoid. What had Róbert said? *Probably everything means something.*

When you're lying under a polar bear, you have a lot of thoughts. You search for an explanation. That's just how it is. And somehow everything suddenly makes sense, because otherwise you would drive yourself crazy trying to figure out why you're lying under a polar bear. In this world, nothing's wrong. So there's neither good nor bad.

Birna knelt beside me again, asked how I was doing, whether I could breathe, and I nodded. She came even closer, her face really close, closer than it had ever been. She looked surprised, and I was too, because she was a very beautiful woman.

"Oh, Kalmann," she said, stroking my hair. "You saved my life, do you realize that?"

I said nothing, focused on remaining conscious. Birna smiled.

"You did, you nincompoop, you saved my life. I'd be bear food by now if you hadn't been so brave, putting yourself between me and this beast. You're the bravest person I've ever met. And I'm sorry I said all those things. You *are* a proper hunter, I know that now, and you're a guardian too, like a proper sheriff." Birna had tears in her eyes, and she was trembling a little, but I didn't know whether it was from the cold or because she'd come so close to being bear food. "The Sheriff of Raufarhöfn," she said. Then I closed my eyes.

It's warm under a bear. I knew that too now. Even the ground wasn't that cold, because I was bedded down on moss and grass. But the stabbing pain in my chest was becoming unbearable. And trying to catch my breath was difficult, even if I only took really shallow breaths. I regretted not having told Birna that I wasn't doing so well. But what could she have done? Nothing. The polar bear was too heavy for her. Now all I could do was grit my teeth.

"Open your eyes, Kalmann," said Birna, patting my cheeks. "Dear, dear Kalmann. You have to try to stay awake. Help is on its way."

I courageously opened my eyes and looked at her, even nodded. Birna was delighted and smiled. She looked at me lovingly.

"What became of Róbert?" she asked me. Her eyes were so honest, so compassionate. When someone looks at you like that, you don't lie to them.

"Fish food," I whispered. "I had to promise him."

Birna nodded. "Did you kill him?"

I shook my head, or as well as I could, at any rate. I was struggling to stay conscious. If I didn't concentrate on my breathing, I became tired. I would have preferred not to be talking, but I understood that I had to stay awake. And that's why Birna was asking me these questions.

"He did it himself... with the Mauser," I said. "He didn't know it was loaded —" I didn't get any further, because I had to cough, which hurt really badly. I groaned wretchedly, even though I didn't mean to groan. Birna's face was covered in splashes of blood.

"Kalmann!" she exclaimed.

I was startled too, because now I realized that I wasn't doing well. Even the bear began to growl again, but because Birna jumped to her feet with a cry of relief and waved her arms, the growling was probably coming from a quad or numerous quads. Perhaps a helicopter came flying over too, I couldn't see very well, but it was the rescue service in any case, and that's why I now closed my eyes and stopped with the breathing, which hurt in any case, and that's why it didn't hurt so much any more.

Then it really did become dark, a black, starless night, and that's how I know that dying isn't anywhere near as painful as living.

22
COMING HOME

There's nothing in this whole world more wonderful than sleep, especially when you're tired. I felt like I had either slept for ten years or one second, I couldn't say precisely, but when I came around, I was no longer beneath the polar bear but on a stretcher, and lots of people were staring down at me. I even knew some of them, but I don't want to list them, because I'm no longer sure who helped me up there. But I could have sworn that my mother was there, and Nói, whose face I had never even seen, but he was there, with a face, sweater and all. Dagbjört and Sæmundur were there, and Bragi, who was looking at me with his pipe in the corner of his mouth and tears in his eyes. The janitor Halldór was there, with an accusing glare. And Grandfather was there, younger, stronger, telling everyone what to do. Even Róbert was there, standing a little to the side. He was watching listlessly, his gaze empty. I felt sorry for him. Perhaps I didn't know any of my rescuers, and they were simply people, humans, because actually we humans are somehow all the same, not anywhere near as different as you might think. I only know what happened to me through what I was told later, because I closed my eyes again and submerged myself, because sleeping is wonderful.

I was flown by helicopter to the hospital in Akureyri, where, after the operation, my mother looked after me personally. And when I woke up from the anaesthesia, she was by my side, happy and sad and proud and ashamed all at once, everything, the entire palette of emotions, like a rainbow, I could see it on her face, I felt it with her, and then she cried so much that it was embarrassing, because she was a professional nurse after all, and as I lay there in bed, my body black and blue, with five broken ribs which luckily were no longer sticking into my lung, I became aware that I had taken a significant step into my new life. And I was still alive. My mother was there and looking after me, and I would get better, and I found that kind of encouraging.

The peace and quiet in the hospital room didn't last long. My mother told me that lots of people wanted to talk to me, reporters in particular, but Birna wanted to talk to me too, and did I want that, even though where Birna was concerned I didn't necessarily have a choice, and I said I would speak with everyone, as long as she, in other words my mother, stayed nearby, which she promised she would.

Birna brought me a packet of dried fish. And she looked really good in her police uniform. She had lipstick on, and the skin on her face shimmered slightly. She looked very good, in any case, and I was damn proud of having saved her life, even though in that moment, when the polar bear had been standing opposite us, I hadn't even planned to. I just wanted to make sure nobody got eaten. But Birna insisted that I was a hero, and she would know, after all, so that's why I believed her and was very proud of myself. She brought a newspaper with her and read out the article to me, in which everything was described precisely. There was even a photo of the bear. It lay there peacefully on a plastic tarpaulin on the helicopter landing field in Akureyri, its fur smeared in blood, its eyes closed. Six hundred and fifty kilograms heavy. Two hundred and thirty centimetres long. A large, powerful female. But dead. The coastguard helicopter could be seen in the background, and a few people in uniform stood around the animal, grinning proudly into the camera as though they had shot it themselves.

My name was also in the paper, and now I understood why the reporters, who could be heard prattling away outside the hospital room, wanted to interview me. Eventually, after my mother had combed my hair, I gave permission for the door to be opened. Birna sat down on a chair directly next to me; we were almost touching. There were cameras and bright lights, because cameras need bright light. A bouquet of microphones was thrust in front of mine and Birna's faces, and that's the only thing I remember, because I was totally nervous, and I was in pain, even though I was completely high on painkillers. But I remember that the reporters laughed from time to time and were kind of in a good mood, so no reason to worry. The whole thing was a bit much for me, though, and because I probably wasn't entirely with it, Birna answered some questions for me, so she was on my side now, and I was really happy about that.

After the reporters had gone, Birna asked to speak with me briefly, and just one-to-one, without my mother.

I was exhausted. Everything was spinning in my head, and all I wanted to do was watch TV. But a one-to-one conversation would surely be quite easy.

"Kalmann minn," said Birna with a sigh. She was about to say something, but she closed her mouth and then thought for a while, looking at me. Then she found the words: "Kalmann, will Róbert ever be found?"

I shrugged. "No idea."

"Kalmann," said Birna, more firmly now. "Please say no."

And that's why I said no, and Birna smiled with relief and said for me to get in touch with her if I had a problem, and I should stay how I was, because there was a reason that I was how I was, because otherwise she wouldn't be alive any more. And then, as she was leaving, she leaned over towards me and gently gripped my shoulders.

"We'll keep this between us, okay?"

"Okay," I said, because Birna didn't like it when people just nodded or shook their head.

"Róbert took his own life, and there's nothing you can do about that, do you understand?"

"Yes."

"It is *not* your fault."

"I know."

"It would be unfair if we had problems because of him, wouldn't it?"

"Oh yes."

Birna smiled contentedly and kissed me on the forehead. I imagine there must only be a few people in this world who have been kissed by a police officer who knows that they've disposed of a corpse.

Before Birna opened the door, she turned around one more time.

"You have to dump the Mauser out at sea as soon as you can, okay? It's fulfilled its duty now. If someone asks you, say you lost it. Say it fell overboard."

I nodded, but Birna smiled.

"Say yes, Kalmann."

So I said yes.

"It's utterly insane," said Birna, lost in thought. "The Mauser, the Arctic Henge, the bear, I mean – utterly insane."

Shaking her head, Birna left the room, and it surprised me that she hadn't even asked how I had made Róbert disappear, and that's why I hadn't been able to tell her that I'd run into Bragi when I went to fetch the saw and black plastic sacks, and that this meant there was an eyewitness. But I reckon Birna didn't want to give it too much thought, because when somebody drives a bullet into their own head, it's first and foremost their own problem. So I flipped on the TV and watched a repeat of *The Biggest Loser*. The people on it are so fat that it makes you feel slim, even if you're a bit fat yourself. The fat people have to live in a camp where there's no chocolate or sugary drinks, and they have to exercise from morning until night until they sweat and sometimes cry too, because they're so exhausted or suddenly remember that someone from their family who they really liked has died, and that's why they became so fat. And that's why fitness trainers also have to be good listeners, like Dr Phil. Then, after a few days, once the fat people are allowed to go home, they sometimes start stuffing themselves with chocolate and pizza again, drink two litres of cola in front of the camera, and when they go back to the camp, the trainer yells at them because they've gained weight over the weekend, and as punishment they have to run fifty laps in the rain and cold.

When *America's Funniest Home Videos* came on, I was interrupted by a visitor I really hadn't expected: Dagbjört. And she came completely alone. She brought flowers and a drawing by her youngest daughter, so a children's drawing, and that's why in the drawing I didn't look like me, but thanks to the cowboy hat you could still tell it was me. I was holding a gun in my hand and pointing it at a polar bear, but one that looked like a horse, so not at all scary. But then

I didn't know what I should talk to Dagbjört about, because she was kind of sad, and of course I couldn't tell her that her father had killed himself with my gun; after all, I had promised to spare Dagbjört this gruesome image. But she didn't even ask any questions, there probably wasn't anything she wanted to know, so we watched *America's Funniest Home Videos* for a while, and she even laughed a few times, which I hadn't expected her to. I would have liked to laugh with her, but I couldn't, because then I would have lost consciousness because of the pain in my chest. For me the funniest videos are the ones where a father is playing a ball game with his kid, baseball or football, it doesn't actually matter. Usually the mother films the video. And you always know right away what's going to happen: the child returns the ball with surprising precision, either with a baseball bat or the tip of the shoe, and bam!, straight in the balls! The father then falls over howling, and the mother laughs herself silly. "I got it on video!"

When dinner time came, Dagbjört said goodbye. Then my mother sat down beside me on the bed, and we watched the evening news on both channels. I was everywhere, right from the beginning, the "top story", as my mother told me proudly, and I now saw that I hadn't done a bad job. The reporters laughed, because I told them how dark it had been beneath the polar bear, and that, while the bear was advancing towards me, I hadn't even stopped to think, because my head hadn't had time to think, and that's why I simply acted, because sometimes it's better not to think too much. I told them that I'd felt sorry for the bear afterwards, because *he* had been a *she* and really beautiful too, and Grandfather had said, after all, that you're only allowed to shoot animals you're going to eat, to which a reporter responded that my grandfather would definitely have approved of my heroic act, given that the polar bear wanted to eat me, which I agreed with, and then everyone laughed again. Then Birna took over answering the questions, because for a while I was no longer there, probably thinking about Grandfather.

After my interview, an animal expert explained that the female polar bear had in all likelihood come onto land only the day before, so they could almost entirely rule out the possibility of Róbert McKenzie having been eaten by the beast. The search teams had never been in danger, even though the danger should definitely be taken seriously, because in March 1965, close to Raufarhöfn, two polar bears had been sighted, so it was never beyond the realm of possibility.

Then the missing person case was discussed once more, and Birna was even a live guest in the TV studio, so she must have flown to Reykjavík immediately after her visit. And she told the nation that she currently couldn't give any more information, because it was a complex, tragic matter, and probably the only person who *could* explain it was unfortunately Róbert. The TV interviewer also asked whether organized drug rings, possibly from Eastern Europe, were transporting drugs to Iceland. And Birna cocked her head a little to each side and said that she couldn't reveal much information about that either, the investigations were ongoing and in close collaboration with Interpol, but there was definitely a connection, the problem was real, but also not one-sided.

Then Birna hesitated and pursed her lips. And she looked briefly into the camera, even though you're not allowed to do that. Then she said that the drugs in the barrel

290

found in Raufarhöfn had been produced here in Iceland and had therefore possibly been intended for export. I reckon she wasn't supposed to say that officially, because over the next few days the channels talked a lot about it, and there were also raids on hothouses and attics. I think people were a bit confused about Icelanders producing drugs, and simultaneously a bit proud, because the wares were of very good quality.

I suddenly remembered where I had seen a drug barrel like that before: when I had run into the Lithuanians out at sea! Nadja and her boyfriend Darius and the others! And I'd believed that the Lithuanians just went out to sea for fun. I presume they took the barrel out on the boat, and affixed it to an anchored buoy so that Róbert's trawler could pick it up and take it abroad. I almost said something, but my mother said that that was enough now, and so she changed channels and we watched a quiz show in which the town of Akranes was competing against Kópavogur but didn't have a chance, because Kópavogur has frequently been the Icelandic champion. I like Icelandic quiz shows. I always try to answer the questions, and I'm quite good at it too, because I'm good at geography and know a lot about wild animals, and that's why I'm sometimes even better than my mother, but never better than Kópavogur.

Around two weeks after the encounter with the polar bear, I was discharged from hospital. I had missed Róbert's funeral, which I was actually happy about. The doctor praised me. He said I was healing swiftly, that I was a strong lad and he was convinced eating hákarl gave me superpowers. He really said that. A doctor! He would know, after all.

My mother had taken the day off. First, we visited Grandfather, and I told him about the encounter with the polar bear, but he was in a bad mood and got all agitated. Then we drove on to Raufarhöfn, arriving by late afternoon. I was looking forward to a cosy evening in my little house, but I got a big surprise. Because my mother drove directly to the town hall. She said for me to follow her into the hall, and because she was smiling mysteriously, I got suspicious, and that's why I wasn't so completely surprised when I found the entire population of Raufarhöfn in the hall – minus Magga and Róbert, of course. As I stepped inside, the cheering began, and sheep farmer Magnús began to play his accordion, and that made me laugh out loud, which was painful because of my injury, but I couldn't stop until the tears came and I was howling, and I saw that some of the people also had tears in their eyes, though their ribs weren't even broken.

When you're a hero, you have to shake everybody's hand. Everybody's! With children, sometimes even twice! Until your fingers fall off! I didn't even have time to enjoy the dried fish, the rye bread, the smoked lamb, the cake and the coffee. Hafdís made a speech up on the stage, and I had to stand next to her, probably looking like the village idiot because I was so embarrassed. Hafdís pulled me against her – which hurt like hell – and gave me a big kiss on the cheek in front of everybody. Thunderous applause and whistling! Totally embarrassing. Hafdís then pronounced me an honorary citizen of Raufarhöfn! Yes, really! I even got a certificate, so it's in black-and-white. Bragi took a few pictures of us with his old camera, said: "Now laugh, Kalmann!" But I was already grinning as best I could, because I couldn't laugh, but Bragi laughed too, and the following day there I was, laughing in the newspaper, my face contorted with pain, not on the front page, but the very next one.

Being famous is tiring. I was happy when at long last it was time to say goodbye. My mother, who was suddenly also in a hurry to get moving, cleared a path for me. The pain in my chest reminded me that I was far from healed.

But we didn't stay in Raufarhöfn, we drove back to Akureyri, which meant we spent almost the entire day in the car, and we didn't talk at all but simply drove and because my mother was sitting at the wheel, I was really happy. With the certificate in my hands, I stared out of the window and enjoyed being an honorary citizen, and I didn't even notice that I'd fallen asleep, because my mother only woke me once we had arrived in Akureyri. To mark the occasion, we ate a hamburger in a proper restaurant and then went to the cinema, even though it was already late in the evening. We just made the ten o'clock showing, but almost as soon as the movie had begun my mother began to snore in the seat next to me, and I tried to wake her so she wouldn't miss the movie, but she wouldn't be woken, nestling her head against my shoulder instead, and then I had to spend the entire movie sitting still so that she wouldn't fall off her chair. I only woke her again once the movie was over.

I spent the night in my mother's small apartment. She had rearranged her room and cleared away her stand with the owl sculptures, because I was to live with her now, although only temporarily. My mother made herself comfortable, or as best she could, on the sofa bed in the tiny living room.

But I didn't really like staying with her, because an almost-thirty-four-year-old son shouldn't live with his mother. That's an unwritten rule. That's within us. That's adulthood.

The following days were deathly boring. Celebrating my thirty-fourth birthday in my mother's apartment was also not so great. Because of my injury I had to spend most of it sitting still. And I missed my little house. My mother was eventually able to convince me to temporarily move into an assisted-living community in Akureyri, and astonishingly I took to it right away, because the other residents also liked watching quiz shows, eating pizza and weren't as tidy as my mother. So no reason to worry.

Well. That's where I am now. In the middle of my new life. And there, in our assisted-living community, there's a young woman called Perla. At first, I didn't like her at all, because I think a woman shouldn't be heavier than her man. I don't think I would be strong enough to carry Perla in my arms, you see, and you have to be able to do that if you want to get married. But Perla is really nice, cheerful and funny. She has beautiful hair and a learning impediment. She says I'm an old grouch and that she'll teach me how to laugh. And yet I'm not an old grouch, and I actually laugh frequently. I'm just shy, especially when I don't know someone that well, and I can look a bit serious, but I kind of like the role of the grouch, because I've lived through quite a lot after all, and perhaps she's right. Perhaps I've changed. I sometimes correct her anyway: "I'm just thoughtful," I say. "I've seen things, you know?"

Perla is really nice to me, and she puts on make-up for me. She's already made me cookies twice, she packed them into a beautiful little bag and surprised me with them. And she friended me on Facebook and posts a funny saying on my wall every day. I like that, because there's wisdom in the sayings, and that's what Perla is like too. Once it said: *Your face is a gift you're given. Smiling is something you have to do yourself!* And another time: *Your beloved is sometimes closer than you think.* That makes you think, doesn't it? Sometimes we talk on Messenger, even though our rooms are next to one another and we can almost hear each other through the wall. That's fun, and why I don't miss Nói at all. He still hasn't been in touch, because he might have died.

I now spend five days and four nights in Akureyri. Three nights I spend in Raufarhöfn, mostly from Tuesday to Friday. I've put away my cowboy hat and sheriff's badge in the cupboard there. They're just tools I don't need any more. If my father visits me one day, I'll give him the things back. Because they belong to my old life. But I'm still a shark catcher. You don't just set something like that aside. After all, someone has to make the second-best hákarl in the whole of Iceland! That's why different people drive me to Raufarhöfn, and because I'm so famous, it's always easy to find someone. A Facebook group was set up. It's called: *Drive Kalmann to his Sharks!* And I can post there when I want to go, and then someone who's driving to Húsavík or Raufarhöfn comments, and so far it's always been possible to find someone, for example Sæmundur or his wife Sigga. Bragi drove me once, even though he didn't even need to go to Akureyri. Perla asked me whether I would take her with me to Raufarhöfn sometime soon, and I immediately said yes, but first we have to ask her legal guardian for permission. I'm imagining how it will be. I could sleep on the couch and Perla up in my bed. Or perhaps we'll both fall asleep on the couch in front of the TV, next to one another. Body against body. And maybe then we'll have proper sex!!

*

The first time I went back out to sea after the incident, before I met Perla, it was windy yet quite warm, almost summery, but the wind was against me, and that's why it took almost three hours to reach my line.

I was unlucky. There was a shark hanging on one of the hooks, but it was long dead and already kind of decayed. The fish had also nibbled at it, in one spot even down to the bones. It had become bait itself. So I freed it from the hook and let it glide back down into the sea. After 512 years of feeding, it was now its turn. I wound up the rest of the line and threw the few remaining gnawed pieces of bait to the gulls. Then I put my new pieces of bait on the hooks, two, three pieces at once, and let it sink down into the depths. It was a strange sight to see Róbert's left hand disappear down into the darkness of the ocean, as though he were waving at me one last time. Bless, Róbert McKenzie! I was relieved. The last piece of Róbert had now sunk into the sea. I immediately threw in my Mauser after him. I didn't even need to give it much thought. So I had kept all of my promises. You could rely on me. Róbert was fish food, and Birna didn't need to worry that anyone would ever find the King of Raufarhöfn. So there was no reason to worry. I was happy and confident that next week I would have a shark on the hook, because the Greenland sharks seemed to like Róbert.

The whole thing took a little longer than usual because I couldn't make any sudden movements and the wind kept blowing me off course, and so it was afternoon by the time I arrived back in the harbour. Sæmundur was already waiting with the forklift, assuming I had caught something because I'd been out so long. And yet I had caught something! I told him about the putrid shark on the hook, and we laughed, because I could have sold it immediately as hákarl, Sæmundur said. The laughing hurt, and perhaps I had ventured out to sea too soon, because the pains in my chest were almost killing me, and that's why Sæmundur helped me to clamber back onto the pier. And I kind of slipped a little on the wet planks and almost fell back into the boat, but Sæmundur gripped onto me, held me tight and pulled me onto the pier so that I landed in his arms. Sæmundur didn't let go, he wrapped his arms around me, hugged me close and laughed.

23
WHALE

The next day, Hafdís drove me to Húsavík. I had never spent so much time alone with her before, but she was really nice, she told me quite a lot about herself and about Raufarhöfn. I preferred sitting in the car with her to with Magga. Because Hafdís knew how to be quiet from time to time.

In Húsavík, I of course immediately visited Grandfather. I had a few hours to kill, because my mother would come to join us and then drive me back to Akureyri.

It wasn't so windy in Húsavík, but it was fairly sunny. Lísa was standing in front of the care home, waiting for the bus that wouldn't come, and she gave me a brief wave before clutching her handbag again. I wondered whether, if a bus did suddenly come driving up, she would get on it.

I found Grandfather on his little balcony. He was sitting on a chair and was wrapped up snugly even though it was really warm. The summer couldn't be far away, but the staff are careful there. They know that a cold can easily bring down an old person. Grandfather's woollen hat was a little crooked on his head. It had kind of slipped down so that his right eye was almost covered. He looked like an old pirate, but he didn't seem to have noticed. He raised his chin and blinked out from beneath the hat.

I sat down with him and said hello. Grandfather looked

at me briefly and then continued as though we had already been talking for a while.

"Do you see? They've found him now," he said, pointing a crooked finger out at the green-blue sea.

I stared in the direction of his finger and noticed two whale-watching boats on the water, about five nautical miles away. "What do you mean?" I asked.

"Because they're standing still. They have been for a while. They've found him."

"Who?"

Grandfather looked at me as though I was slow on the uptake. "The big one!" he said.

I shrugged. "I was out by the line yesterday, and one had bitten, but it had already gone bad."

"Exactly," said Grandfather, and he nodded as though he had already suspected that, but then he frowned and looked at me a little doubtfully again. Then he turned back towards the "big one", sat silently and motionlessly in his wheelchair and stared out to sea. He had probably already forgotten again who I was or what had recently happened in Raufarhöfn. So I could have told him, but somehow I had the feeling that Grandfather was in the picture even though he didn't know it. Before, he'd always had a good answer ready for everything. And I think there comes a moment in life when you don't have to know anything new, simply because you've heard everything already. You've grasped how life functions, and that's why you've simply heard enough. I believe that Grandfather had reached this point.

That's why I sat quietly next to him, Grandfather, who despite having no idea who I was or what I had experienced, knew everything. Perhaps he didn't know it in his head, but his body was well informed. Family resides everywhere, after all, in the hair, in the fingers, the tip of the nose, in the toes and the heart. You simply feel good. Grandfather knew very well who I was, even if he had forgotten. I was his boy, his blood, carved from the same piece of wood. And that's why I didn't need to say anything.

A nurse asked us whether we were comfortable out here, whether we were perhaps too cold. I shook my head, and Grandfather didn't answer, but he slowly raised his arm and pointed his crooked finger out to sea. "They found him," he said. "The big one."

"How lovely!" said the nurse, straightening Grandfather's woollen hat and giving me a wink. I think she had no idea what he was talking about.

Only once she was gone did Grandfather lower his arm into his lap again. I pulled out my folding knife, took a piece of hákarl out of my plastic container and cut it into little pieces. Grandfather must have smelled it right away, because he was no longer staring out at the whale-watching boats but looking at me as I cut up the hákarl, and as soon as I was done, he stretched out his shaky hand, and I gave him three pieces at once, which he promptly put in his mouth. He chewed and sighed with contentment, nodded and said: "Kalmann minn, your hákarl is even better than mine."

And we sat there on the balcony like that for a long time, even though it did get cold in the end, munching hákarl, waiting for my mother and gazing at the whale-watching boats. From this distance we couldn't see the whale, because whales aren't always as big as you might think. The basking shark can actually grow to almost twice the length of a minke whale. That's diversity. That's nature.

THE END

Acknowledgements

A thousand thanks to the Swiss cultural foundation Pro Helvetia, the thirty-three sponsors of wemakeit crowdfunding, and my godmother Julika. My special thanks go to Dr Matthias Kokorsch, who gave me the idea of setting the story in remote Raufarhöfn. Thanks to shark-catching specialist Elvar Reykjalín and the lovely (and in truth completely normal and amiable) residents of Raufarhöfn; Svava Árnadóttir, Nanna Steina Höskuldsdóttir, Jónas Friðrik Guðnason, Gunnar Páll Baldursson, Magnús Matthiasson and the golden seniors of the Breiðablik gatherings. In Raufarhöfn, there is coffee and cake until you drop! I would also like to mention the initiator of the colossal and inspiring Arctic Henge installation, Erlingur B. Thoroddsen, who unfortunately passed away in 2015. I am grateful to my ever-reliable readers: Stefan, Lukas, Ziad, Riccarda, Juli, Jeje, Camenisch, Mario, Mads, my mother and father, my brothers and my sister. I would also like to thank Edda, who salted herrings in her childhood – in Raufarhöfn, no less – and of course Kristín Elva, who gives me crazy book ideas.

Takk kærlega fyrir mig!